I HATED HEAVEN

Acclaim for Kenny Kemp's

I HATED HEAVEN

". . . An original, comic novel."

— *Booklist*

"A well-written novel with delicious characters and enough truth, satire, romance and mystery to keep any reader turning the pages."

— Linda Thomson, *TPI*

"You hooked me early and kept me guessing until the last page! A wonderful romantic adventure!"

— Jennifer Smith, Los Angeles, CA

"Your book really made me think. Not only was it a great romance, but for the first time, I'm wondering what heaven will really be like. I can't wait for the sequel!"

— Paula Sorenson, San Francisco, CA

"After just three pages, I had to cancel my plans for the evening. I couldn't wait to see what would happen next."

— John Tooey, San Diego, CA

I HATED HEAVEN

To keep a promise
he made on Earth,
he had to break
every rule in Heaven

a novel of love *after* death

KENNY KEMP

ALTA FILMS PRESS • SALT LAKE CITY

I HATED HEAVEN

Copyright ©1998 by Kenny Kemp

Alta Films Press

ALTA FILMS PRESS
10 9 8 7 6 5 4 3

Publisher's Cataloging-in-Publication
(Provided by Quality Books, Inc.)

Kemp, Kenneth.
 I hated heaven : a novel of love after death / Kenny Kemp.
— 1st ed.
 p. cm.
 "To keep a promise he made in Earth, he had to break every rule in Heaven."
 Preassigned LCCN: 98-71894
 ISBN: 1-892442-10-8

 1. Heaven—New Age movement—Fiction. 2. New Age fiction. 3. Religious fiction. I. Title.

PS3561.E42I2 1998   813'.54
          QBI98-729

Cover illustration by Bruce Cheever
Cover design by Rick Thayne Design
©1998 Alta Films, Inc. All Rights Reserved.

Manufactured in the United States of America
by Alta Films Press, a division of Alta Films, Inc.
Box 71395 Salt Lake City, UT 84171 (801) 943-0321

I HATED HEAVEN

For those who believe . . .
. . . and those who would like to.

1

Tom Waring pulled on white gloves, grasped the brass handle, and trudged across the wet grass in cadence with the others. Low black clouds sandwiched the people between earth and sky. Fog sheened his face and he smelled the ocean on a gust of wind.

People stepped back as they set the box down on the canvas strapping stretched across the rectangular hole. Released from their burden, the bearers blended into the crowd. A man draped a purple satin coverlet over the casket. It was quiet except for the steady white noise from tires on the wet freeway beyond the chain link fence.

Tom took off his gloves and walked toward April, who stood stiffly in a gray suit, her auburn hair gathered at her neck, her eyes ringed with grief. She took his hand and rested her other hand on Josh's shoulder as a reminder; the boy could hardly stand still. This was his first funeral.

Reverend Heath, a round, stoop-shouldered man, joined Chuck at the head of the grave. Chuck held a felt hat stiffly in his hands, his lowered head shiny and wet. *That's the first time I've seen him without a hat*, thought Tom. He racked his brain, seeking an image of Chuck hatless. He found one of Chuck taking off his Padre's cap, running a hankie over his head. Tom tried to freeze the image, but couldn't. Instead, Chuck donned the hat and smiled, his teeth showing through his droopy gray moustache, unaware of the tragedy heading his way, which came in the form of a heart attack last Friday night. That smile, so often seen at work, would be hard to find now.

Tom stole a glance at April, who was looking at the hole, her brow furrowed. *Nothing they say will matter.* Josh's face was turned upward, his tongue out, feeling for rain drops. Heath was talking about Carolyn's future. Tom knew she was in heaven, but for April, what once was Carolyn was in that ebony box, suspended over a darkness that knew no future nor light. Tom squeezed her hand, trying to imagine death not as a door, but as a blanket that settled over life, obliterating it. It seemed impossible.

When April handed him the phone Friday night, her face was ashen. When Tom heard the news, he had a safe place to go; his faith was a comfort. But April cried for an hour for a woman she barely knew. Tom cradled her in his arms, feeling helpless.

Tom had known Chuck and Carolyn for five years and he'd grown as close to them as anyone he knew in San Diego, but even though April hardly knew Carolyn, she had unearthed precious insights on the few occasions they spoke.

He remembered the time Chuck and Carolyn came caroling with some members of Tom's congregation. April invited the old couple in because they looked tired. While coffee brewed, Carolyn located cups and saucers. Under April's casual prodding, she told them things that Chuck had never revealed to Tom in three years of working together, including their first date at Belmont Park in 1941. They were both in line to ride the new wooden roller coaster. He noticed her standing alone, hopping from one foot to the other nervously. He asked her if she'd like to ride with him. Her smile was so dazzling that Chuck said he fell for her right then. As they topped the rise and plummeted down, she screamed happily.

They were married a year later. He was seventeen, she was fifteen. That was fifty-five years ago.

Reverend Heath was extolling the Lord's mercy. Tom watched Chuck, whose eyes were closed, his brow furrowed, his head tilted slightly, as if he were listening to some unheard voice.

Heath said, "Through the grace of God, our sister Carolyn, who sleeps the sleep of the just, will rise again on resurrection morning, clothed in glory, her sins forgiven, to dwell with the Lord forever." A few "amens" sounded, buried beneath the hiss of traffic. When Tom shifted his gaze to include April, she was still staring at the grave as tiny rivulets of water trickled down its sides. Tom wondered what kind of backhoe they used to dig such perfectly square holes. He saw a scuffed yellow Hitachi behind an acacia hedge, its arm raised in a rusty salute.

"Without God," Heath said, "man is doomed to everlasting destruction. Our souls exist by His grace, which comes to all who call on His name." Heath looked at April, who met his gaze firmly, as if to say, *It's bad enough losing this dear woman without you laying a guilt trip on us as well.*

Heath lowered his eyes. "Let us pray."

Heath prayed, but Tom wasn't listening. He was picturing Carolyn floating upward against a pale blue sky, gossamer wings moving silently at her back, a smile on her face. White light fell on her, obliterating all detail as angels praised God. Tom felt a tickle in his lower spine and a pleasant lightheadedness that he associated with the Holy Spirit. He knew that Carolyn was safe in God's arms.

"And now," said Heath, "Praise be to the Father, the Son, and the Holy Spirit, forever and ever. Amen."

"Amen," said Tom. Heath looked expectantly at April. Tom and Heath had had many conversations about her, and they all ended with Heath encouraging Tom to be patient and let the love they shared be a bridge upon which faith might someday cross. Tom pondered that hopeful image, but though the bridge was strong, faith had not made the journey. As if in testament, April's eyes were full. Tom put his arm around her shoulder and promised himself to redouble his efforts.

Chuck scattered a handful of dirt into the hole. "Goodbye, Carolyn," he said, his lips barely moving.

The service over, people began talking quietly. April turned away and was immediately engaged in a conversation by an older woman in a black dress. Josh pulled on Tom's coat. He had his mother's expressive face and his father's blonde hair. "Dad?"

"What is it?"

Josh cupped a hand to his mouth and crooked a finger. Tom bent down. Josh whispered, "Is she really in that box?"

Tom nodded.

"And they're gonna cover it up with dirt?"

"That's right."

Josh stared at the box. "Cool." Then he turned to Tom, another question forming. "Dad?"

"Yes?"

"God knows everything, right?"

"Uh huh."

"Will He remember where we put her?"

Tom smiled. "He knows Carolyn, just like He knows you and me. He'll remember where her body is. Besides, even if He did forget, Carolyn could remind Him."

Josh brightened. "Then they'll come and dig her up, right?"

"What in the world?"

Tom turned and saw April. She was composed, but her cheeks were flushed. "We were talking about the resurrection. Josh is concerned about God finding Carolyn's body."

April nodded to Josh. "Honey, go tell Chuck we'll see him at his house."

"Okay." He darted toward Chuck, who was surrounded by people of the age that read the newspaper obituaries first.

April turned to Tom. "Tom, please."

Tom raised his hands. "He was confused."

"Just don't confuse him any more."

"He hears both sides, like we agreed. This is one of your . . . what do you call 'em . . . *formative ritualistic moments*."

"You've been reading my *Psychology Today* again."

"You leave it in the john, what do you expect?" he said, smiling. He took her hand and they walked toward Chuck, who was listening intently to Josh.

"Maybe it will sink in," said April, shaking her head.

"Nope. It just floats there and won't go down when I flush."

"You are horrible," said April, suppressing a smile.

Tom noted how drawn Chuck looked for a man who worked in the sun. He took Chuck's rough hand in his. "You okay, pardner?"

Chuck looked toward the coffin. "I can't feel her."

"Well, she's with the Lord."

"I never figured it like this. I'm a believer. So why do I feel so . . . *alone*?"

April said, "You're tired. You haven't slept."

Chuck looked at Tom expectantly.

Tom said, "You'll see her again, Chuck."

"You think so?"

"I know so."

Chuck nodded doubtfully and turned to April. He put his hands on her shoulders, drawing her close, and whispered, "Thanks for coming, honey. I know it's hard for you and I appreciate it."

April drew back, tears welling.

"See you at home," said Tom.

"God bless you folks," said Chuck.

As Tom and April walked from the grave, the eucalyptus trees dripped. Each granite headstone wore a gray, wet shawl. Chuck stood alone by the grave, his hat in his hands, watching as they lowered the casket. Out over the Pacific, the sky was black. Tom took April's hand. It was cold. Josh skipped ahead, splashing puddles. April looked up at Tom expectantly. As they ascended granite steps to the parking lot, he thought, *I wish you could believe, too.*

2

Morning came, the clouds hovering over the coast, mixing with fog. Tom rolled onto his back. He didn't need to look at the clock; he knew it was five thirty. Headlights moved a tree shadow across the ceiling again and again. Tom heard the *shh* of tires on wet pavement.

He thought about Carolyn's funeral and the open house last night. Chuck sat listlessly, barely acknowledging the guests. Carolyn was loved by the congregation for her easy ways. She was always available to baby sit, to cook for a shut-in, or just to talk. On the other hand, Chuck was more internal and given to strange ideas. His beliefs encompassed almost every unexplained thing. Ayers Rock in Australia, geometric shapes cut into barley fields in England, the pyramids—Chuck somehow found space in his own private Ouija-board brand of religion for them all. But Carolyn's unexpected death put even Chuck's wide-ranging beliefs to the test.

In the kitchen, Mrs. Brooks was telling April about the shroud of Turin and how it was a fake, which proved the papists were all wet. April pleaded with her eyes for Tom to rescue her. She felt uncomfortable with Tom's church friends because even though religion was just a small part of life, they never seemed to talk about anything else.

Tom got up and padded to the bathroom. He reached for the door. It wasn't there. Than he remembered the bath humidity had caused it to swell, so he'd removed it for planing. He reached and closed the bedroom door instead.

In the mirror was a man in his early thirties with light blue eyes and blonde hair. He ran a finger down his nose, pressing in at the bridge, a daily ritual, trying to lessen the bump.

He stepped into the shower and tackled his hair, which required two passes with shampoo. It was so thick he could dive in a pool and surface and his scalp would still be dry. He considered his hair a hassle but April loved it. When they sat together, before long her fingers would be absently pulling through his thick strands. At such times, her thoughts might be far away, but her touches were a reminder that she was close.

Tiptoeing into the bedroom, he dressed quickly: jeans, workboots, a long-sleeved tee shirt. He kissed the crown of April's head. She mumbled something and snuggled deeper in the covers.

Tom walked down the hall, passing Josh's room. Josh lay on his back, dreaming; his left foot moving rhythmically, like he was riding a gas pedal.

In the kitchen, Tom started coffee, knowing the smell would waken April more effectively than any alarm. He pulled an orange from the fridge. From the cupboard he took two fruit pies, which to him represented a balanced diet, if accompanied by a liter of Pepsi. As he peeled the orange, he looked out the window. The palm trees were black against the gray sky. The gutters dripped. Tom grabbed his yellow slicker and headed to work.

April moved into Tom's place in the bed. He slept warmer than she did. Much of the year he would be comfortable under just a sheet, while she lay shivering under the comforter. This wasn't the only example of their polarization. He awoke instantly, showered quickly, ate in huge, throat-bursting gulps, belched, and banged loudly around.

She wakened slowly and with great reluctance, enjoying long, steamy baths, fluffy bathrobes, and cinnamon coffee.

The smell of coffee made her smile. She was domesticating him after all. He still didn't read much and he didn't know who their congressman was, but he was learning to live with a woman, how to shut doors, pick up towels, and make coffee. He would probably never care what Freud thought or what color they should paint the bedroom, but Tom had qualities that April knew she would never take for granted. His skills were strange and wonderful: he could fix *anything*. He could repair a toaster while watching *The New Yankee Workshop*, the only TV show he never missed. He'd watch, shaking his head in wonder at an ingenious homemade dovetail jig that the host Norm invented. Tom sent for the plans, the only time she ever saw him lick a stamp. For a week, he spent his evenings in the garage cutting and filing metal for the jig. The final result was a beautiful mahogany dresser, its drawers fastened with the interlocking dovetail fingers.

April finally got up, going into the bathroom. She hoped Tom would remember to get paint for the door today. She would have to remind him. He used his cell phone like a note pad, and the result was a two-hundred dollar-a-month bill, which could be cut in half if he'd just write things down. Tom had laughed and said, "But I like it when you call and nag me!" April gave up, figuring a note pad would get lost the first day in Tom's truck—its dash filled with empty cups, work orders, invoices and tools. April said, "It's your money," and let it go.

She looked in the mirror. Her hair stuck out and her skin was blotchy. She rubbed her eyes, which Tom called the brownest eyes he'd ever seen, and she knew they worked some magic on him, because whenever they fought, which was rarely, he always avoided looking into them. She learned that when he was upset, if she took his hand, eventually he would look at her and they could solve their differences. He held similar powers over her, but he was largely unaware of them because he always caved in before she did. When he was angry, he would stomp around and find fault with inanimate objects for a while, but soon he would end up behind her, his arms around her waist, nuzzling her neck, and asking her to forgive him.

April didn't mind a good spat; she figured each person in a marriage had edges to be knocked off and disputes were natural. But she liked to win and Tom hated to argue. The result was that their spats always ended sooner rather than later, yet she always felt like *he* won, even if he was dead wrong, because he was such a peacemaker. He reserved his energies for building, not fighting.

Toweling off and throwing on her robe, she went to Josh's room. He was up now, playing with his Legos. "Time to get going, Tiger. I've got to be out the door in twenty minutes!"

Josh pulled off his pajamas. "I got show and tell today."

"Uh huh," said April, searching for a shirt in the dresser.

"I'm gonna tell about Mrs. Blankenship and how they put her in the ground!"

That should get the conversation started.

"And how God will come back someday and dig her up!"

April's jaw tightened as she closed the drawer. She counted to five and turned around. "Which one?" she asked, holding out an orange tee shirt and a red one.

Josh shrugged. "She's coming back."

"Who, dear?"

"Carolyn. You don't think so, but me and Dad do, so that's two to one, and like you always say, maj . . . maj . . . "

"Majority rules," helped April, putting the red tee shirt over his head.

"Right," said Josh. His head popped through victoriously. "So you gotta believe it, too!"

April tossed a pair of jeans to Josh. *He is so much like his father.* When she saw Tom in Josh, it was impossible to disagree with the boy. *That* was her weak spot, but he wasn't old enough yet to know about it. "When Carolyn comes back, I'll believe it. Now scoot."

Josh ran to the kitchen to drown some Fruit Loops.

Tom liked to be the first one on the site. After all, it was *his* job and he had to set an example. He stepped out of the truck and buckled his tool belt.

He looked up at the structure. It was a good house, on one of the last great hillsides overlooking the ocean. All stone and windows, three stories high. A dozen beams jutted out on the second floor, the beginnings of a large balcony. Today they would be installing the railing, getting ready for the redwood deck—if it stopped raining.

They broke ground in September and had been making good progress, but David Balmer felt otherwise. Balmer had an attorney's view of the world: everyone was trying to get away with something but no one was going to pull that on his watch. No one.

Tom scaled the plank to the front door wishing Balmer would spend just one day on the site, then he would see how hard it really was. The lot had to be engineered because of its steepness, a water seep had to be rerouted, and they had to work around a eucalyptus tree because Balmer's wife Angie couldn't bear to lose it.

All this for a tiny profit margin. At this point, Tom just hoped to break even, pay the lumber yard, and get Balmer to recommend him to his pricey lawyer friends.

Tom stood on the second floor looking at the ocean. Bits of blue sky showed through tears in the clouds. Greg Levitt roared up in his Toyota and unfolded himself out of the cab. *Why doesn't he get a real truck?* thought Tom, knowing that Levitt would never be able to swing a loan, the way he went through money.

A white van pulled up and Vince emerged in nothing but shorts. It could be snowing and Vince would show up for work shirtless. He had long black hair and a full beard. They had met on a job site in Escondido and became good friends. It was Vince who introduced Tom to surfing. He knew every break from Huntington to Baja.

Vince looked up at Tom and grinned. "We gotta get these stairs in. Levitt's gonna break his pencil neck."

Levitt raised a middle finger at him.

"We're gonna build the balustrade today," said Tom.

"You think it'll quit raining?" moaned Levitt. "I'm not crawling out on a slippery beam if it's raining." He started up the plank.

"Quit griping, grandma," laughed Vince, kicking the plank, jarring it.

"Knock it off," whined Levitt. "I don't feel so good today."

"Let's get to work," said Tom, waving them up.

Vince and Levitt moved sheets of plywood onto the beams, making a work platform. Tom estimated how much redwood he was going to have to charge on his already overextended credit.

An old green Ford F150 pulled up. Chuck got out, wearing a red and black mackinaw over white painters' overalls. He adjusted his baseball cap and waved. "Hey, guys."

"Hey, Chuck," said Vince. "How's it hanging?"

"In there."

"Hi, Chuck," said Levitt carefully, elbowing Vince. "You okay?"

Chuck nodded.

Tom walked down the plank. "What are you doing here?"

"Would you rather I sat around the house moping?"

Tom shrugged. "Are you sure you're up to it?"

"I'm up to it." His eyes bored into Tom.

Vince and Levitt were finishing putting the plywood in place. Tom turned to Chuck. "Why don't you form up the stairway here?"

"Vince does the cement work."

"I know, but you can do it."

"I *know* I can do it. Tell you what else I know," said Chuck hotly, "You think I'm gonna fall off the house and get myself killed."

Tom shook his head. "I need you on this stairway is all."

Chuck gave Tom a hard look. "I need my saw. You wanna help me up this plank?" Tom reached out but Chuck pushed his hand away. Tom noticed that he nevertheless chose his footing carefully.

———

About eleven thirty, Dave Balmer pulled up in his copper BMW. He stood in the middle of the street, avoiding the mud on site. "Tom?"

Tom looked up from his lunch. They were sitting in a bedroom on the third floor, enjoying the sun that had broken through the clouds.

"Ugh," said Vince. "It's Balmer. Now I gotta barf."

"Tom?" came a shout from below.

"Yeah! I'm here," yelled Tom, looking at his crew. "I need an advance, so don't give him any crap, okay?"

"He's the one that's full of it," laughed Vince.

"Hey, Tom," said Levitt, his voice tentative. "It's payday, remember?"

Tom was already halfway down the stairs so they didn't see him flinch. He was hoping they'd let him slide, but it was the fifteenth. His checkbook was empty and Balmer had already given him one advance and would hit the roof if he asked for another.

Tom climbed down the forms Chuck had been working on all morning. "Hi, Dave. How's things?"

Balmer was not happy. "What're you guys up to today?"

"Balcony and the front steps."

"You said you'd be starting the finish this week."

"The drywall hasn't arrived."

"What?"

"Plus we haven't got the final electrical yet."

"What?"

"The inspector hasn't shown. I called him twice Friday and once today. He's backed up with the rain."

"Tom!" exploded Balmer. "What in the—!"

"If he shows by Wednesday, we'll be okay. We got plenty to do in the meantime."

"Tom, you're behind schedule and it's not all the supplier's fault, nor is it the inspector's. What are *you* doing to make your deadline?"

Tom felt someone looking at him. Levitt and Vince were watching from the bedroom window. Dave leaned toward Tom. "When you're not here, do they do *any* work?"

"It always takes longer than planned. There are a thousand details, and—"

"You need to be on top of them. *Are* you?"

Something spring-loaded inside Tom snapped. *You're getting the best house on the hill. We added earthquake protection at the last minute; the balconies came into the plan late; and if your wife doesn't add any more bay windows, we just might make our deadline!*

"We're doing our best," he said instead.

"Well, do your best *faster*," said Balmer, slamming his door. The Beemer sped away.

Vince yelled, "Bite me, shylock!" and shook a fist.

"Well?" asked Levitt, rubbing his thumb and forefingers together. Tom crossed the street and opened his truck door. Fast food sacks and soft drink cans fell out, followed by loose change.

Chuck came up. "What you looking for?"

"My checkbook," said Tom, rummaging through the junk.

"It's in your pocket."

Tom pulled out his checkbook. He hadn't balanced it, but he kept a running total in his head and knew, more or less, how much was in the account. It wasn't enough.

Chuck saw his look. "I can wait."

Tom shook his head. "I don't want to get into that habit."

"It ain't a habit if you don't do it regular."

"You don't mind?"

Chuck hooked a thumb over his shoulder. "I'd pay them, though, if I was you."

"Are they worried?"

"They know you're good for it."

"I'll get you next time."

"Whenever. I trust ya." He walked back to his forms.

———

April burst into the lobby, past several clients, and ran down the hall to her office, slamming the door behind her.

A knock came at the door. Michelle slipped in, closing it behind her. "Running behind?"

April was writing on a legal pad. She nodded.

Michelle sat in the chair by the door, crossed her legs and waited, her acrylic nails tapping the chair arm. She was a shapely black woman who made men and women alike vaguely uncomfortable. But she enjoyed the attention her looks earned her and was renowned for her ability to get male clients to open up, for obvious reasons. "When's your next session?"

April looked at the clock. "Twenty minutes." She threw her pencil down. "I'm as organized as anyone, right?"

Michelle smiled.

"Then why am I always behind? My husband never makes a list, yet he comes out on top every time!"

"So use his system."

"He doesn't *have* a system! When a problem surfaces he just puts it on a shelf. He says worrying is God's job."

"Sounds okay to me," said Michelle.

April leaned back. "I didn't know you believed in God."

"What are you gonna do? These days, politicians, celebrities, and sports heroes are all corrupt. People need to believe in something."

April shook her head. "Do you use this line of reasoning with your clients?"

Michelle chuckled. "Of course not! I use terms like 'self-actualization,' 'finding your center,' 'releasing your angst' and such. But it's the same thing." She rose to go.

"Wait," said April. "I need to ask you something." She looked out the window. The fog had cleared and sparkling blue rectangles of the bay shone between the skyscrapers. "I went to a funeral on Monday."

Michelle raised her hands. "That's something for a priest."

"I can't discuss it with Tom. When I do I know he's sitting there, thinking, 'Who *is* this person I'm married to?'"

"I felt that way about my third husband."

"The funeral was for the wife of one of Tom's employees. I didn't know her well, but her passing is really affecting me.

"In what way?"

"I have a hard time when someone dies. I just don't buy the bit about 'if we remember them, they're not really dead—'"

"Star Trek," interrupted Michelle.

"Pardon?"

"*The Wrath of Kahn*. Spock dies saving the Enterprise. I think McCoy says it at his funeral."

"Figures. It sounded fake." She stared at the bay.

"Are your parents alive?"

"My father's dead."

"Tell me about him."

April glanced at the clock. It was ten minutes to two. Michelle said, "Let 'em wait. Tell me how your father died."

April sighed. "I was about ten. Dad was a jeweler. He had a storefront on Broadway, a few blocks from here. One evening a man came in and pressed a gun into his ribs, demanding all the jewelry."

Dan Carroll poked his head into the office. "April, your two o'clock is here." She didn't turn from the window. He asked, "Are you okay?"

April nodded.

Michelle said, "We're in the middle of something, Dan."

"Do you want me to meet with them?"

April shook her head.

"Okay." The door closed.

Michelle sighed. "He's got a thing for you."

"Who?"

"Who do you think? Old Dr. Dan there would write you love songs if he wasn't tone deaf."

April shook her head. "He hardly knows me."

"He sees you every day."

"Then I'm sure he can see this." She held up her left hand. A gold band glinted on her third finger.

"Doesn't matter. He thinks you're fine and that's that."

April sighed. "Do you want to hear this story or do you want to play matchmaker?"

Michelle sat back. "Fine, don't let me practice *my* specialty."

"Anyway, just then a woman came in to get a ring and saw the gun. She ran out screaming, so the robber shot my dad.

"Oh, April."

"That night my mom came back from the morgue with blood all over her dress."

"How did that affect you?"

"It was the first of a lot of things that convinced me that there is no reason to life. And I know I'm not the first to ask this but it's a still good question: If there is a God, how could he let something like this happen?

"You want the truth, or some therapist doublespeak?"

April smiled weakly. "Aren't they the same?"

"Okay, here it is: *I don't know*, neither does anyone else, and people who say they *do* know are liars. People believe in God because they can't bear the thought of believing in nothing."

"I don't believe in *nothing*," said April.

"But sometimes we realize that what we *do* believe in isn't enough. Weak minds turn to religion. But you're not weak. This will pass."

"Sometimes I feel like I'm in a deep, dark hole and every time someone dies, it gets deeper and darker."

"I should put you on Prozac and watch you float away, happy as a clam."

"Clams are not happy."

Michelle opened the door. "Then your only alternative is to hold onto the things that make life worthwhile: a good book, fine wine, and great sex!"

"Those are all good," said April, managing a smile.

"Love your man—even if he *is* superstitious, he's still sounds better than the other ninety-nine percent."

She left. April looked out the window. The sun was shining. *It's probably just the rain.* She picked up her pad and walked to the lobby to meet her two o'clock.

3

Sure enough, by Wednesday afternoon, not even the commute traffic could dampen April's spirits. She was listening to a Vaughan Williams CD, enjoying the soaring violin on "The Lark Ascending."

The sun was setting, casting long, blue shadows across the freeway. A few clouds flew eastward and the greenery in the median was dazzling. Spring was short here and she promised herself she'd enjoy every minute. Summer would soon be here, but for now, the evenings and mornings were cool and deserved to be enjoyed.

Since meeting Tom, she had gotten into the habit of looking at the sky. It affected his work and she alternately felt sad that he had to slog about in mud and jealous that he got to work outside in the sun.

She got off the freeway at Del Mar Heights Road. The sun was a red ball on the horizon. At dusk the wind subsided and the water was smooth. Surfers called it "evening glass." The waves rose from the surface and broke with very little display.

As the road wound around the hills, she saw surfers on their colorful boards, waiting for the next set. When a wave walled up, they would paddle furiously, but just the first one or two would catch it. The others would turn back and resume their vigil.

April didn't understand the appeal of surfing. The ocean scared her. She had seen *Jaws*. The idea of hungry sharks had always been

there, it's just that no one had ever really thought about those multiple
rows of sharp teeth until they were projected on a movie screen forty
feet high.

For April the beach was basically the strip of sand between the
parking lot and the water, a place where as a teenager she would go
with her girlfriends to work on their tans. She enjoyed watching the
boys surf, but going out there herself was out of the question. That
shark movie proved there was a hostile world below the ocean surface
and she wanted no part of it.

Tom was a different story. He could never sit on the beach or
read a book. He would stand, eyes scanning the water for a good
break. He was not a great surfer, but he loved it, and he never worried
about sharks. She loved to watch him but she was always relieved
when he came back safely, his board under his arm.

As she pulled onto their street, she was thinking about him
walking toward her across the sand, his hair slicked back, his brown
skin wet. She felt a warmth building. Tonight she'd make up for the
last few days.

Tom heard the door open. "It's Mom!" Josh cried, alerting the
neighbors. He tore toward the front door, brushing the palm planter so
it canted upward for an instant, then rolled around on its circular base
and settled back with a thump! The fronds waved but no dirt was
disturbed. Tom shook his head in wonder.

April came in with a load of books. Josh dragged a plastic
grocery sack along the parquet floor, heading for the kitchen.

"Hi, sweetie," said Tom.

April put a free arm around his neck and kissed him deeply.
Tom flushed. "Wow," he said, kissing her again.

"Wow," echoed Josh, looking up at them.

"Scoot!" said April, going into the kitchen.

Tom followed her, his eyes on the plastic sack. "What you got
there?" *It better be dinner because I forgot entirely.*

Seeing the full sink and empty stove, she said, "I kind of figured you might forget about dinner."

"Shoot! Is it Wednesday already?" asked Tom meekly.

"Already," repeated Josh, looking into the sack. His face fell as he brought out celery, lettuce, sprouts, a red pepper, and carrots. "What's this?"

"Salad, young man," said April firmly.

"And we're gonna love it," said Tom, going to the sink to start on the dishes.

April was already there. "I can do it," she said, her warm feelings cooling a notch.

Tom nudged her aside. "I'll do it. Josh has something to show you."

Josh was still looking forlornly at the salad fixings. April reached into her purse and with a flourish withdrew a Peppermint Patty. Josh yelled, "All right!" and reached for the treat.

April pulled it back. "After." She reached into her purse again. Out came another Peppermint Patty. She held it up for Tom to see.

He smiled. "What do you call those dogs that slobber when you ring the bell?"

"Pavlov's dogs."

"Yeah," he said. "That's us." Tom nodded at Josh. "Show Mom what we did in the back yard."

Josh's face lit up. "Oh, yeah! You gotta see!"

April gave Tom a look. "Do I *want* to see this?"

"Depends on whether you're an optimist or a pessimist."

"Come *on*, Mom. Look what me and Dad did."

"He did it," said Tom. "I just helped."

April followed Josh through the living room. Josh opened the sliding doors and ran outside, where he was met by Terrible Ted, their miniature terrier, who barked like Huns were attacking. They got Terrible Ted when Josh was two, and were wondering what to call him when Tom saw a Far Side cartoon with two panels, one of which was captioned "The names we give dogs," and showed a guy pointing to a dog and saying to another guy, "This is Rex, our new dog." The second panel was called "The names dogs give themselves," and showed a dog introducing himself to another, saying, "Hello. I am Vexorg, Destroyer of Cats and Devourer of Chickens." Tom had looked at the little frenetic puppy and said, "Let's call him 'Terrible Ted'—that's something he would call himself!" Whenever Tom wanted a laugh he'd say, "Stand back! Here he comes, Terrible Ted, Punisher of Chew Toys and Marker of Hydrants!"

Josh was running around and Ted was yapping at his heels. "Mom, Mom! Look at what we did!" He pointed to his bike.

April looked. It looked the same.

"The wheels!" yelled Josh. "We took off the wheels!"

"The wheels?" They were still on as far as she could see.

Josh rolled his eyes. "The *training* wheels! We took 'em off!"

In April's mind's eye she saw Josh careening down the gravel driveway, out of control, his face a mask of terror, his lips drawn back in a scream, heading for a busy street where black semis roared by belching great plumes of black smoke—

Tom was next to her, his arm around her. "It's gonna be great."

"Dad said we start on Saturday!"

April looked up at Tom. "Is he ready?"

"I rode a two wheeler when I was four. Evel Knievel here's five. I've been waiting for him to ask me to take 'em off. He's ready for a man's world!" He howled at the sky and beat his chest. Josh howled along with his dad.

"Are you sure?" asked April. "The driveway is steep, all gravel, and the street is so busy."

"Aw, honey, the drive isn't steep and the street is empty ninety-nine percent of the time. Right, Josh-man?"

Josh nodded vigorously.

"But the cars. That teenager down the street tears past here like a bat out—!"

"Okay, okay," said Tom. "We'll teach him at the park—nothing to fall on except grass. And when he learns, we'll enforce strict rules about riding in the street." He stuck his hand out to Josh. "Deal?"

Josh squeezed hard. "Deal." He ran away with Ted barking at his heels.

April turned to Tom. "Do we have to?"

"He's gonna grow up, no matter what. He's gonna fall and scrape his knees and all we can do is be there with the bandaids."

"He's growing up so fast."

"Yeah. But it's great to be reminded of what it was like to do things for the first time.

"He has no idea how hard life will be," said April, watching Josh play with Ted. "Scraped knees are nothing."

"But we'll be there, looking out for him, just like . . ."

"Just like what?"

He shrugged. "Nothing." He turned and went inside.

Later, Tom poked his head into the bathroom, where April was brushing her teeth. "There's something I want to ask you."

"Ask away," she said, brushing furiously.

"I'll wait 'til you're not rabid."

She wore one of his company tee shirts. Three years ago, when he decided to go on his own, he struggled with a company name, something solid-sounding like "Prestige Homes" or "Quality Construction." April shook her head. "Just call it 'Waring Construction'."

"That's boring. It's also kind of . . . pretentious. It sounds like I think I'm a big shot when I'm just a guy who got his license. I don't know if I'll even be able to make it."

"You oversaw the construction of almost every home in the Valle Alto subdivision. You know all you need to know."

"Those were cracker boxes. Custom homes are something else."

"Well, it has to be Waring Construction because I've already thought up the tag line." She raised her hands to show how big the letters would be. "It'll look like this: Waring Construction, in big red letters, block style, real strong-sounding." She indicated a place just below the name. "'Built To Last'. Get it? *Waring* Construction!"

Tom wasn't sure about the name, but the tag line sounded pretty good. "I *do* try to build things well."

"And it's catchy, too."

"'Waring Construction: Built To Last'." He mulled it over. "Tell you what. If you'll be in charge of advertising, payroll, the books, and hot lunches, we might stand a chance."

Now, April was rinsing.

Tom said, "Honey, Sunday is Easter." He watched her shoulders for signs of tightness. "I wish you'd come to services."

"Tom, please." She came out of the bathroom and sat on her side of the bed. Tom got in bed, saying nothing. She sat there for a long moment, her back to him. "I just can't," she said finally.

Tom looked at the ceiling. "You didn't mind going on Christmas. You liked the carols. There will be a big crowd, so no one will notice you and I'll protect you in case anyone wants to convert you." *There, I said it.* He wished he could see her eyes.

April got into bed. She lay with her back to him.

Tom said, "It would mean a lot to Josh." He regretted saying it the moment he did; he knew it was dirty pool.

April sighed. "I'll think about it."

Tom spooned up behind her, putting his hand on the rise of her hip. "That's all I ask," he said, kissing her neck. "I love you."

April felt his stubble on her neck. It was a long time before she whispered, "Me too you."

4

At breakfast Saturday morning Tom said he was taking the day off. "Are you sure?" queried April. His work ethic included every day except Sunday.

"I promised Josh I'd teach him to ride the two-wheeler."

"All right!" said Josh through a mouthful of Trix.

April wore a gray UCSD sweatshirt and cut-offs. "I'm surprised," she said. "I was gonna catch up on some files."

Tom said, "You've got enough nut cases here to keep you busy." He made a face at Josh. Ted sat by Josh's chair, his eyes following Josh's hand as it raised and lowered his spoon. Tom tossed Ted a piece of toast, which he caught in mid-air.

"Okay," said April. "Where are we going?"

"Where else?" smiled Tom.

They took the Coastal Highway north. In Cardiff, shoppers strolled, peering into antique store windows or sitting under red and white *Cinzano* umbrellas at trendy cafes. In Encinitas, they turned west toward San Elijo State Beach and parked. There was a large grassy area, shadowed by pepper and palm trees. Tom got out, his eyes scanning the ocean.

"You didn't bring your board," said April. "Nice offshore blowing, too."

Tom scowled. "Tempt me not. I came to teach Josh to ride a bike, not surf."

"That's quite a sacrifice for you," said April, laughing.

"Tell me about it," said Tom, hauling the bike out of the truck bed. Josh steered it toward the lawn. They walked to a table under some trees and April began unloading the picnic basket.

"But nobody said we couldn't *body* surf. Me and the Josh-man are gonna hit the waves," said Tom, pulling his shirt off. They ran across the sand. April watched them hit the water. Josh turned and bolted—it was obviously cold. Tom waded in, motioning for Josh to follow. Josh finally braved the water and Tom took his arms and spun him around in a circle, his body flying free of the water. April could hear Josh's delighted yells over the breakers.

She closed her eyes and raised her chin, feeling the sunlight on her face. She pulled off her sweatshirt. The warm sun and her guys playing in the surf were evidence that life was good. The storm clouds that had plagued her for the last week were finally gone.

When they came back, April had lunch spread out on the blanket. They ate ham sandwiches, dill pickles, carrot sticks, potato chips, and soft drinks. April, who had pieced on an apple, finished first and lay back on the blanket, placing a forearm over her face and feeling the sun on her legs. She imagined them strong, curvaceous and brown, with smooth knees and graceful ankles. Her legs were the opposite of Michelle's, whose legs were made for netted hose and spiked heels. And of course Michelle had a natural tan to beat all. April would have to manage with her freckles and bony knees.

She felt someone looking at her and opened her eyes. Tom was smiling, eating a celery stick. "What?" she asked.

"You're beautiful."

"Nice recovery."

"It's true."

"Prove it."

"Yeah, Dad, prove it!" echoed Josh.

"Josh, take Ted for a walk. See if he likes the water."

Josh jumped up. "By myself?"

April gave Josh a cold stare. "Just don't drown him."

He was surprised. "He could drown?"

April nodded.

"Wow," said Josh, looking at Ted with new wonder. Ted gave him a fearful look.

"Keep a hold of his leash," said Tom.

The boy and the dog bounded away. Tom said, "Prove it, huh?"

She nodded.

He leaned over and kissed her.

"Tom!" she said. "This is a bonafide PDA!"

"I know," he said, sneaking his hand under her. "I've had a change of heart. I'm into it now."

"What changed your mind?"

Tom ran his hand down her thigh. "No one notices anyway, and besides, you know I'm a big fan of *Private* Displays of Affection.

"So!" said April, rolling him onto his back, "You're ready for a serious *public* make out?" She straddled him, holding his arms over his head.

"I'm not sure I'm ready for a full-on make out just yet," he said, raising his knee and bouncing her off. He straddled her and held her arms by her side with his knees. "But . . . maybe I *am*!" He kissed her neck.

"Oh, Tom!" she giggled.

"If you're gonna laugh . . ." He walked two fingers slowly up her stomach.

"No fair!" she said, struggling. "I'll scream!" Her eyes flashed.

"No one cares if I tickle you until you scream. Or if I tickle you," he said, drawing a straight line up her chest to a spot under her jaw, "until you die!" He tickled her and she fell apart, laughing. She tried to get her arms free but he held them easily. Finally, he rolled off her. She nestled into the crook of his arm, spent.

"You are so mean," she said, pinching him.

"I know," he said, wincing. "I'm a bully."

"You are," she said, her head on his chest. "I hate you."

Tom put his arm around her. "Me too you."

When Ted and Josh returned, Tom grabbed the bike and walked across the lawn to an open area where he kneeled, eye to eye with the boy. April couldn't hear what he was saying, but she watched anyway. Josh looked at the sprocket as Tom pointed. Since April didn't have any brothers, she'd never seen first-hand how a father and son related, but she surmised from the families she counseled that too often those relationships were determined by stature: a father would order his son around until the boy got big enough to tell his dad to stuff it, and then war would begin.

But Tom always hunkered down to talk to Josh, erasing the physical distance. Tom knelt, his hand on the bike seat. Josh's hand rested casually on his father's shoulder as he listened. April felt a sudden tingly warmth.

She remembered the day she first met Tom. Her roommate Karen had graduated and moved out. Fortunately, she took her creepy boyfriend with her, but April didn't trust he'd stay away. He had been hitting on her the whole time he was seeing Karen, but April soon understood that he just liked to mess with her head. She was afraid he'd come back, so the Saturday after Karen moved out, April went to the home center to get the locks re-keyed.

The center was one of those huge stores that sold everything, and April was lost the moment she walked in. She read the signs, searching for something with "locks" or "doors" in it. The checkout lines were packed. She knew she'd have to find it herself.

She finally saw an aisle with dozens of doors stacked at an angle. She hoped to find handles and doorknobs as well.

Her first view of Tom was his scuffed yellow boots. He was walking toward her, carrying a door at shoulder height. She couldn't see anything of him but his khaki shorts and workboots. "Uh, excuse me," she said timidly.

He stopped. "Me?"

"Can you help me?"

He grunted. Obviously the door was heavy, but his voice was pleasant. "I don't work here."

She still hadn't seen his face. "Oh. I'm sorry."

Tom lowered the door. His blonde hair was long and pulled back into a ponytail. His nose was peeling and his eyes were blue. He hadn't shaved and looked kind of ragged in a faded yellow tank top.

"I thought you worked here," she said, looking away, wondering if he had noticed her staring at him.

Tom put the door down. "I'm in here enough, I ought to know where everything is."

She tried to speak but couldn't. He waited patiently.

"I need a lock," she said finally.

"What kind of lock?"

"Door."

"What kind of door?"

"Like that," she said, pointing at Tom's door.

"Hardware department."

"Where's that?"

"I'll show you," said Tom, leaning the door against a shelf and starting down the aisle. April followed as he wove his way through the crowd. He passed at least two people who knew him because before they got to the hardware department April knew his name was Tom and heard him agree to help a guy build a patio next weekend. Once, Tom glanced over his shoulder to see if April was still following him. She waved, feeling foolish. He disappeared down an aisle. She looked up. HARDWARE.

Tom stood in front of the lockset display. April joined him, opening her canvas bag and removing the lockset she had managed—after a frustrating hour—to get off a door. She handed it to Tom.

"This looks okay. Why are you replacing it?"

"My roommate moved out and . . ." *Why am I telling him this?*

"It's none of my business," said Tom. "But if you redo all the locks, it could get expensive. Are you sure you have to?"

April nodded.

Tom said, "I know a locksmith in Solana Beach. He might give you a—"

"I want you to do it," said April, surprising herself. She felt like putting her hand over her mouth. Instead, her knuckles whitened on the handle of her canvas bag.

"Pardon?"

Too late now. "I want you to do it. I'll pay you."

Tom was silent. He seemed uncomfortable.

"You know about these things."

"But you don't know *me*. I might be like the guy you're trying to keep out."

Smart, too. "You wouldn't say that if you were like him."

"So it *is* a guy."

"My roommate's boyfriend."

"Your *roommate's* boyfriend."

He looked at her for a moment, then extended his hand. "I'm Tom Waring."

She took it. "April Conway."

"I'll do it," said Tom, putting the lockset back into the bag.

April smiled. "I live in Del Mar. Is that too far?"

"No. Do you want to do it now?"

April looked down, feeling his eyes on her. It felt good, the way he looked at her, not leering or critical, just interested. She raised her eyes. "Now would be perfect."

At her house, Tom fixed the doors and she'd asked him to work on a few other things. He came back the next Saturday and while he worked, she made lunch and before the afternoon was over he asked her if she would like to go to the beach with him sometime.

She always thought it symbolic that when they met, Tom was carrying a door and she was looking for a lockset. He said it was fate, and although April didn't believe that, still she liked the symmetry.

She was watching him now, holding the seat as Josh pumped the pedals. It wasn't going well because when Tom let go, the bike wobbled out of control. Josh's wail came to her on the breeze.

Tom picked Josh up and held him, walking toward April, dragging the bike along behind him. Ted barked at the rear wheel.

Tom handed Josh to April, who rocked him gently. Tom crumbled onto the blanket. "I thought he was ready."

"I *am*!" cried Josh into his mother's neck.

"Sure you are," said Tom. "But I told you it was hard."

"That's right, sweetie," said April, stroking Josh's hair.

Josh's sobs let up and he raised his head. "It's too hard!"

April produced a napkin and helped Josh dry his eyes and blow his nose. "If it wasn't hard, it wouldn't be so much fun when you finally get it," she said.

Tom took Josh on his lap. "For a first time, you did good, Josh-man. I kid you not."

"I did not."

"Ted was so mad at the bike he about bit off the back tire."

Josh looked at Ted, who was looking up at him.

"Look at him," whispered Tom. "He *knows* you can do it!"

"Good old Ted," said Josh. The dog jumped up one his lap and gave him sloppy kisses.

"Good old *Ted,*" said April, smiling at Tom.

On the drive home, April leaned her head on Tom's shoulder. Josh was asleep next to her. She was sleepy, too. She closed her eyes, looking forward to soaking in the tub.

Tom's right hand lay on her leg. She counted a number of small scars. One wasn't so small. Before they'd met, Tom had sawn off the tip of his left forefinger. He was never self-conscious about it. Instead, he always held it up when he cautioned anyone about being careful.

"I was thinking," said April.

"Uh oh."

"I'd like to go with you to Easter services."

The road crested the hill and they got a magnificent view of the arc of sand along the blue water. Tom squeezed her knee with his imperfect hand, trying to be low-key. "That would be great."

5

They sat on the left, near the front. Sunlight poured through the stained glass windows and onto the pews, dust dancing in the shafts of light. The organist played a somber prelude as the choir assembled on the dais.

April knew many eyes were on her. The members of the Solana Community Church knew Tom, but they didn't know her. Josh sat by April in a white shirt and maroon bow tie, drawing crayon circles on the back of the program. Chuck sat by Josh.

As Reverend Heath walked up the center aisle, the congregation quieted and stood. He wore a black robe and shook hands, smiling, then took his place behind the pulpit. Everyone sat. On either side of the pulpit stood large bouquets of lilies and daffodils.

Heath smiled at the congregation. "Our thanks go to Brother Stanley, who has provided us with these wonderful flowers." The crowd murmured appreciatively. "It is appropriate that we have these flowers as a reminder of our Savior's sacrifice on this beautiful Easter morning."

April was looking at the shafts of sunlight. One fell diagonally across Heath, making him look pale and vague. She straightened her blue pleated skirt. It went well with her light blue blouse and thin gold necklace. Around her were dozens of bright, floral print dresses and some remarkable hats, the kind never seen outside churches. She suddenly felt underdressed and exposed as an unbeliever.

Heath welcomed the visitors, glancing at April. She felt like everyone in the room was looking at her. He made announcements about a food drive coming up next week, then he looked at Chuck and said, "Our lovely sister Carolyn Blankenship passed away last week."

Chuck sat with his head bowed and eyes closed, his mouth moving silently, apparently unaware of Heath's reference.

Heath continued, "A memorial service was held for her on Monday morning. Brother Blankenship has asked me to thank you all for your concern and help."

Chuck heard his name and looked up, his eyes glazed.

Heath said, "We are commanded to bear each other's burdens. It is pleasing to see how many have rallied around our brother in his time of need."

A woman leaned forward and touched Chuck on the shoulder. He nodded and touched her hand. Josh stared at Chuck, impressed that his name had been mentioned from the pulpit. Tom whispered to April, "Let's have him over for dinner, okay?" April nodded, feeling sadness once again creeping into her heart.

The choir sang a hymn and then Heath began his sermon. He started with Palm Sunday: Christ's triumphant arrival into Jerusalem, the last supper, and the garden of Gethsemane.

Tom thought about Jesus washing the disciples' feet, even as His own hard death loomed. Tom felt a fullness in his chest, which moved to his throat, where a thickness gathered—the warmth of the Holy Spirit. He remembered the first time he ever felt it.

Tom's father Don made no secret of his contempt for foolishness in all its forms—including religion. His mother Vivian was an alcoholic who spent most of her days alone in her room. Tom practically raised himself.

When Tom was twelve, Don moved out and ceased almost all contact with the family. Vivian withdrew further, drinking heavily.

By the time he was fifteen, Tom was going to school in a daze, confused by life, feeling alone and empty.

One day, while walking to school, he heard a voice say, "Stop." He hesitated and looked up as a truck turned the corner into his path, pushing the air past him, just inches away. Before he could move, the protruding metal mud flap brace behind the rear tires hooked onto his belt buckle and turned him around, then released him. He stood facing backwards, the hair on his neck erect and diesel fumes stinging his nostrils. He turned slowly, looking for the person who saved his life. No one was there.

In the days that followed, he thought a great deal about the voice. He should be dead; the truck driver never even saw him.

A group called "Campus Life" met once a week after school. He felt drawn to attend even though they were considered Jesus Freaks. He entered the back of a crowded room one day and heard Mr. Harlin, the biology teacher, encourage them to "listen to the Lord's voice."

Later, while he was walking home, Tina Morris asked him if he believed any of that garbage. Tom said, "Of course not," but in truth, he did believe it. All of it.

The next week Harlin gave him a small paperback copy of the New Testament. Tom read it cover-to-cover in a week. His conversion was total—he had found what he was looking for. The unpredictability of life, its complexities and mysteries, was swallowed up in the simple concept of grace. If you believed and gave yourself to God, He would take you by the hand and guide and protect you. Tom believed that was what had happened to him.

Heath was saying, "Christ said, 'these things I command you, that ye love one another'." Tom looked at April, who sat with her hands folded on her lap, her face blank.

Heath discussed the betrayal, Peter's denial and Christ's arraignment before Pilate. By now his voice, usually high and piping, had settled into an orator's tenor. The perfume of the flowers spread through the chapel and the sunlight shone through the stained glass.

Heath hurried through the crucifixion and Christ's final words, "My God, my God, why hast thou forsaken me? and came to the third day, a beautiful Sunday morning like this one, when the two Marys came to the sepulcher: "'And the angel answered and said unto the women, Fear not ye; For I know that ye seek Jesus, which was crucified. He is not here; for he is risen.'"

A woman in the choir, unable to contain the Spirit, said, "Praise the Lord!" Others echoed her. Heath paused, his hands raised.

Tom felt his spine tickle. He imagined the two women rushing past the angel, finding only the linen, not the body of Christ. The Spirit testified the truth of the moment and Tom felt full of light. He could barely feel April's shoulder under his arm. Josh looked around as people shouted "Hallelujah!" and "Praise the Lord!"

Heath bowed his head. "We thank Thee, Lord, for speaking to our hearts so clearly this day."

Amen, thought Tom.

"And now, Lord," said Heath, "Thou who sittest on top of a topless throne; Whose presence is everywhere; Who understands all things; Who knows the intents of our hearts; Who brings worlds into being; we praise Thy name."

"Praise be to God!" exclaimed a man in front of April, causing her to jump slightly in surprise.

"May we someday be found worthy," concluded Heath, "to be found on Thy right hand, amidst the concourses of Thine holy angels, to sing praises to Thy holy name, and to dwell with Thee in eternal joy forever and ever. Amen."

The congregation proclaimed "Amen!" and Heath sat down, his face red. He dabbed at his forehead with a hankie. The choir stood and the organ piped the familiar strains of Tom's favorite hymn:

I stand all amazed at the love Jesus offers me,
Confused at the grace that so fully he proffers me.
I tremble to know that for me he was crucified,
That for me, a sinner, he suffered, he bled and died.

Oh, it is wonderful that he should care for me
Enough to die for me!
Oh, it is wonderful, wonderful to me!

As they sang, tears filled Tom's eyes and he pulled a tissue from his coat pocket. All around him he heard sniffles. He folded the tissue over and studied his hands.

April watched Tom fuss with the tissue and felt her heart soften. Tom was the first man she had ever seen cry. A single tear escaped him on their wedding day as he placed the ring on her finger. On her other side, Josh was on his feet, ready to go. Chuck sat with his arms folded and his eyes closed.

"You okay?" said April, turning to Tom.

He put his arm around her. "Thanks for coming."

People stood and began conversing. Heath walked down the aisle, shaking hands.

Tom leaned across April and said, "Chuck?"

The old man opened his eyes, which April noticed were as dry as her own. "Very nice," he said without emotion.

April looked at Chuck. *He didn't hear a word of it.*

Chuck stood. "I guess we'd best get going," he said and sidled his way out the other end of the pew, followed by Josh.

Tom and April walked toward the back of the chapel. As the people cleared in front of them, they found themselves before Reverend Heath. He smiled at her. "Thank you for coming, Sister Waring."

"April," she said.

"I hope you felt the power of the truth today, April."

April removed her hand from Heath's. "I always respond to the truth, Dr. Heath."

"The Bible says, 'The truth shall make you free'."

Here we go, thought Tom.

April smiled. "Is that right? That's what Siddhartha said, too."

"Siddhartha?"

"The first Buddha. You know, the spiritual leader of a *billion* Chinese?"

"Oh," said Heath, perplexed.

Tom grabbed Heath's hand. "It was a great service." He looked over his shoulder at those behind them. "Well, we don't want to hold up the line!" he said. "Do we, honey?"

"Absolutely not," smiled April as Tom led her away.

Tom said, "There's Chuck. I'll ask him over for dinner." Chuck was standing by himself in the courtyard, looking confused.

April saw Josh running across the lawn with two other boys. "Josh! We're going!" she said, feeling loud and conspicuous. She touched Tom on the arm and headed toward the car.

"Chuck," said Tom, stopping by him. "Can you come over for dinner this week?"

Chuck nodded at the church. "What'd you feel in there?"

"What do you mean?"

"I can't feel her, Tom. I been consulting my *Spirit Guide*—"

Tom whispered, "That thing is full of witchcraft!"

"Says you."

"Chuck."

"Your mind is closed, Tom. Everything good is of God."

"But—"

"And if it *feels* good, then it *is* good," said Chuck, pulling his arm from Tom's grasp.

"Reading tea leaves and going to seances is sort of . . ."

Chuck raised his knobby chin defiantly.

Tom took a breath. "It's *creepy*, that's what I think."

"Who asked you?"

"What I meant is that you should try to reach Carolyn through more *regular* ways, like prayer."

"Done that," said Chuck with finality.

"Be patient."

"I could always feel Carolyn. Knew how she was feeling even when she was thousands of miles away visiting her sister Pamela.

Knew on the button when she was thinking about me. We'd compare notes and sure enough, I'd be right. But now she's gone and I can't feel her. I been praying but it ain't working. I think God will understand if I try some other ways. You would too, if you was me."

"You just gotta have faith."

"I got faith, that's why I'm trying these other ways! So don't pester me about 'em, or I'll quit talking to you all together."

Tom shook his head. "We aren't supposed to understand God's plan, we're just supposed to believe and let His grace guide us."

"So I'm just supposed to sit back and take it? Well, I'm tired of taking it!" he croaked loudly.

A woman nudged Reverend Heath, who looked over. Tom looked over to where April stood by the Nissan. "Just come to dinner Wednesday, would you?"

Chuck wouldn't look at him. He finally nodded and walked away. Tom felt all remnant of good feeling dissolve.

When Tom suggested they go for a drive, April agreed. She wanted to clear her head of all the nonsense. Tom drove the Maxima north on I-5. She knew where they were going—where they always went when they needed grounding: the Lot.

One evening during their first year of marriage, Tom took April for a drive. She was in the full throes of morning sickness, which hit her both morning and evening, so it was an ordeal for her to sit in a car for thirty minutes.

It was a warm August evening. She was hating pregnancy. She hated the way her stomach stuck out, even before she was pregnant. She lacked muscles there or something, and no amount of aerobics seemed to make a difference.

Tom drove into an upscale part of Leucadia. April's intuition jumped on her bladder and she began to get excited. She didn't know what it was, but she was pretty sure it was something for *her*, which meant Tom still loved her even though she hadn't let him come near her in a month. Tom had said he loved her anyway, and he had been very patient. She tried to feel romantic, but it just wasn't in her.

Tom took the truck up a steep hill, where the houses thinned out. He stopped in front of an empty lot with a big red and white FOR SALE sign on it. He didn't say anything. He opened her door and led her to the sidewalk.

April looked beyond the weeds and trash that accumulated on the lot to the spectacular ocean view.

"What do you think?" said Tom.

"It's nice. But we can see the ocean if we climb on top of Mr. Jenkins' house next door in Solana Beach."

"Yeah, but that's *his* view."

"It's ours whenever we want it."

"But it's not *always* ours."

"What are you trying to say, Tom?"

"I want you to have your very own view,"

"And you've given it to me," she said, looking at him.

Tom turned her around. "Not of *me*, dummy—the ocean!"

"Oh!" said April, turning back. "You mean you didn't bring me here to look into your blue eyes?"

Tom smiled. "Well, if you want to."

April folded her arms and turned away. "I don't."

Tom reached around her, pulling her to him. "I brought you here to compliment *you*."

April hugged his arms. "I'm listening."

"Well, for starters, even though you've never learned to take a compliment, still, I can't help it . . . I think you are beautiful."

April leaned back against his chest.

"In addition, I couldn't be happier that you're pregnant."

"*You're* not sick all the time."

"But you're generous enough to share *every* detail with me!"

April turned and put her arms around his neck. "It's been *awful*! I know I'm moody and distant, but I'm sick and I feel ugly and fat and I don't know why you still love me."

"Well, there's a limit, you know."

"Really? How close am I?"

Tom brought his forefinger and thumb an inch apart.

"I feel better. I thought you were gonna push me off a cliff."

"Maybe later," Tom said, starting toward the car. "But for now, we gotta go."

"Is that all you wanted to say? That you're glad I'm having a baby?"

"Pretty much." He opened the driver's door and got in.

April put her hands on her hips. "That's it?"

Tom started the engine. "Yep. Let's go."

April looked again at the FOR SALE sign on the lot. *You think you know someone*, she thought as she headed for the truck. Tom didn't get out to open her door like he usually did. *This is getting better and better.* She was about to get in when Tom said, "April, come here a minute."

April looked at him through the window. "Why?"

"Come here."

April grudgingly came around to his side. "What?"

"Take this." He handed her a hammer. "And these." He gave her a couple of nails.

"What am I supposed to do with this?"

Tom reached behind the seat and pulled out a piece of masonite. He handed it to April.

It said SOLD in big red letters. April gasped.

"Would you nail this to the sign over there?"

April dropped the sign, the hammer, and the nails. She pulled the door open and wrapped her arms around his neck. "Do it yourself!" she said, kissing him.

Someday takes its time, thought April as they pulled to a stop. The Lot was unchanged in six years except the weeds were thicker.

Tom got out, loosening his tie. "What a view!"

"It's beautiful," said April, taking his hand. Josh ran to the fort he and Tom had dug into the side of the hill. Tom had placed a piece of corrugated aluminum over the top as a roof and covered it with dirt. From the street you couldn't tell the fort was even there.

"Don't get dirty!" yelled April.

"I won't!" yelled Josh, disappearing.

"Good thing those pants are already black," said April.

Tom looked out to sea. It was a perfect spring afternoon, and the waves were peeling off in perfect form. "So . . . what did you think of the service?"

"You don't want to know."

"I do."

"Liar."

Tom took off his sunglasses and rubbed his eyes. "Okay. I already know. But I'm asking you anyway because I care what you think."

"Hey, Dad!" Josh was waving, just his head showing above the fort roof. "I see you!"

"I see you!" said Tom.

April sighed. "Well, since you asked . . ."

Tom held his breath.

"You *did* ask, right?"

He nodded.

"All right. Two things. The first is Jesus. I just can't buy his resurrection, although he did have some good teachings."

"But they're not original."

"They're not original," she echoed.

"But that might be because they are as old as the world, and God has given those truths to all great men, even that Siddhartha guy."

"Exactly. The 'truths' religions claim as their own are universals and even atheists believe them."

"You're not an atheist."

"How do you know?"

"I just don't think you are."

"So if *you* don't think I am, then I can't be one, right?"

"It's impossible to prove a negative, right?"

"I know where you're going with this," said April.

"I learned all about logic from you." Tom smiled tightly. "It's impossible to *know* there is no God because you can't prove His non-existence."

April said, "But that doesn't stop some people from being as certain that there is no God as others are certain that there *is*. It's all feelings anyway, isn't it?"

"It is. So, at best you're an agnostic. And you've got to admit, then, that He *might* exist—there's a lot of evidence."

She shook her head. "You mean like war and suffering?"

"*And* this perfect day, this incredible planet. There's an order to it all. It was designed by someone."

"I don't dispute the order, Tom. I just dispute the *someone*."

"Okay," said Tom. "What was your second point?"

April sat on the Maxima hood, which was hot through her skirt. "I call it 'He Gets It Both Ways'."

"Who?"

"God. He doesn't have a body, yet he sits on a throne; he's everywhere but nowhere; he and Jesus are the same, yet Jesus prayed to his Father in the Garden."

"Those are mysteries."

"That's a code word for 'It doesn't make sense'."

"So?"

"So, God gets it both ways: he's spirit and matter, love and hate, good and evil, Father *and* Son."

"And?"

"Those things are incompatible! They make no sense!"

"Like I said, those are mysteries."

"Life is hard enough without God playing hide-the-ball. He should just lay it out—tell us what the deal is. Even with all the answers, it would still be hard to live a good life."

"It's *His* test; He designed it. It doesn't have to make sense to us."

"Well then, I've got news for him. *This* is how *I* am. So, if he made me, then I'm *his* fault."

"I knew somebody was to blame," said Tom, shaking his head.

April threw her hands up. "He can't have it both ways. If he's omnipotent, why does he allow evil? If he's all-loving, why does he burn people in fire and brimstone?"

Tom lowered his voice. "We're supposed to have faith. You have to plant the seed and see if it grows."

"And if it doesn't?"

"You have to care for it. Nurture it and fertilize it."

"They sure did a lot of *that* today!"

"You have to believe, pray, and have faith. And then the seed grows and bears fruit that tastes good."

"It tastes bitter to me," said April.

Tom sighed. A dirt clod landed at their feet. Josh's voice called out, "Did I hit you?"

"If you had, you'd know it!" yelled Tom.

Another dirt clod sailed toward them, and Tom trotted down the hillside, growling, "I'll show you what a dirt clod tastes like!"

April heard squealing as Josh ran out of the fort and across the hillside. Tom lumbered after him, hooting like a gorilla. He caught Josh and scooped him up, placing him on his shoulders, dancing from one foot to the other. They were both scratching their armpits, hooting and howling crazily, making monkey faces.

I knew it, thought April. *Darwin was right.*

"You know," said Tom later when they were relaxing in the living room, "We gotta get going on the house."

April was reading Carl Jung's *Memories, Dreams & Reflections,* a biography of the psychologist who rejected Freud's sexual origins of dysfunction in favor of a more spiritual view of the psyche. April wasn't enamored with Jung's view, but he was in favor these days. She was glad Tom didn't know about Jung's belief in a Higher Force; if he did, she'd be outnumbered.

"We've gotta get going," said Tom again.

"Oh."

"You don't believe I'll ever build it, do you?"

April took off her glasses. "We'll build it someday."

"Code word for . . ."

"I mean *some* day. As in 'someday my prince will come'."

Tom left the room and returned with a set of blueprints. He cleared Josh's crayons off the coffee table. Josh was coloring on the floor. "Dad! I was drawing—"

"You get one place to draw at a time. Chose one. The coffee table or the floor."

Josh considered. Since they'd introduced choice-based parenting, Josh had gotten pretty adept at figuring out which door the tiger was behind. "The table!" said Josh triumphantly.

Tom scowled. "Fine!" He collapsed on the couch. April put down her book. Tom opened the plans, which were meaningless to her, just blue lines on light blue paper. "Why are they blue?" she asked.

"Because they're *blue*prints," he said. The plans were covered with red ink in Tom's hand.

"Maybe if we didn't call it our 'dream house,' we'd be more likely to build it."

"What's that supposed to mean?"

"Well, everything has to be perfect in a dream house, and you keep coming up with ways to make it better, so it's back to the drawing board." She laughed.

He scowled at her.

"I was laughing at how appropriate that phrase was. 'The drawing board'."

"You make your share of changes, too. Look." He pointed to the kitchen. It was a mass of red lines: new walls, lighting fixtures, a bay window.

"I just went over the plans like you asked me to."

"For *details*! You wanted a bay window? Fine, you got one. But then you move the dining room over here," he moved his finger to the other side of the garage. "It just won't work on the present footprint."

"Footprint," mocked April.

"Josh!" yelled Tom.

Josh looked up, crayon in mid-air.

"I thought you wanted to use the coffee table!"

"I did."

"Well?"

"Oh," said Josh, getting up. "You mean *now*?"

April laughed. Tom knew it was hopeless. He shook the plans at her. "I'm gonna build that house—bank on it!" He strode from the room.

"I know you will, honey, but put in a wheelchair ramp so I'll be able to get in it!"

Tom growled loudly from the office.

"I love you!" called April.

Josh turned back to his drawing. "Me too, Daddy!"

Tom switched on the bedside lamp. Josh stood in his Winnie the Pooh pajamas. "Ready?" asked Tom, kneeling.

"Okay," said Josh, kneeling beside him.

April heard them as she was carrying laundry down the hall. She stopped by the door, out of sight, listening.

"Dad, do you think I'll ever learn to ride my bike?"

"Sure. Like Mommy said, you have to be patient."

"She's patient with us, isn't she, Dad?"

April couldn't resist; she peeked around the casing. Tom kneeled next to the bed, his back to April. Josh knelt next to him.

"Pretty patient, I'd say," said Tom.

"She's a good mommy, but I'm mean to her sometimes."

"Well . . ."

"She makes me do things I don't wanna do."

Tom nodded.

"I wanna be better, I just can't."

"Well, when things are hard, I ask God to help."

"And He does?"

"Sure. Sometimes it doesn't seem like He's helping me, but I know He's smarter than me, so I do what He wants even if I don't understand why."

"So he's like a dad, only smarter?"

April laughed. Tom turned. "Eavesdropping?"

She came in and took Josh's face in her hands, rubbed noses with him and said, "Nighty night. Sweet dreams."

"'Night, Mom."

Tom said, "We were about to say prayers. You wanna join us?"

"I've got laundry to do."

Josh and Tom looked up at her expectantly.

April sighed and knelt down, pinching Tom's arm. He grimaced but said nothing. Josh closed his eyes. "Dear Heavenly Father, thanks for Mommy and Daddy and for Ted. Please help me learn to ride my bike so I can ride with Adam Garvey—he already knows how. And help me be better. Amen."

"Amen," said Tom.

Josh climbed under the covers. April tucked him in. "Love you, tiger."

Tom mussed the boy's hair. "Big day tomorrow." He and April went out, leaving the door slightly open. April picked up the laundry basket and began walking down the hall. Tom stopped her.

"What?"

"Where you going?"

"To do laundry."

He took the basket and dropped it on the floor.

"Tom!" She stooped to pick it up.

"It can wait." He took her hand and led her down the hall. He looked back at her, smiling in that way she recognized. She flushed and was smiling too, her eyes hooded, a little embarrassed, but sparkling nonetheless.

In the dark bedroom he pulled back the covers. She started undoing her blouse and he pulled her to him. "I can do it," she said.

He undid a button. "So can I."

When she slipped under the covers, a full moon shone through the high window, making everything blue. The sheets were cool. She shivered. Tom climbed in and pulled her to him. In the moonlight, her eyes were bright. She put her arms around his neck and they kissed. She felt his hand move slowly along her hips, then up, cupping her breast. She felt herself give way as he pulled her closer. He moved knowingly and time slowed as they traveled to a place where there were only the two of them.

Afterwards, she lay in the crook of his arm, a hand on his chest. Tom looked out the window. The moon sailed in the sky, filling the window, a white disk against a velvet background. "I heard something that might appeal to your logic circuit," he said.

"Mmm."

"Did you know the sun is four hundred times larger than the moon?"

"Is that right?" mumbled April, her eyes closed.

"It's also four hundred times farther away."

"That's nice."

"That means that they're the same size in the sky, so the moon can eclipse the sun."

April looked at the moon, its dry seas gray smears on its face. She yawned. "That's interesting."

"Carl Sagan or somebody said that we are probably the only planet in the universe where a total eclipse of the sun can occur."

"And?"

"Somebody put it there. For us."

April looked up at the moon moving in the emptiness and thought about a trillion planets moving silently in perfect arcs around a billion suns and in all that vast emptiness, this was the only planet where this kind man held her in his arms as she drifted off to sleep.

6

On Monday Tom drove to Chuck's to pick him up for work. As he turned on to Chuck's street, he promised to try to be of some comfort to him. Chuck's closest relative, a son, lived in Sacramento.

Chuck's house was a small stucco ranch with scalloped eave braces and an ivy yard. Twin junipers guarded the front walk. The house was dark except for a light in the bathroom window.

Tom got out of the truck and stretched, thinking about the day ahead. They had the rest of the roof to finish. The tar paper had sloughed off most of the rain but they needed to get the shingles on before it rained again. He walked right in, calling out, "Chuck!"

"Just a minute," called the old man.

The living room was a mess. Last week's papers lay in a pile, unopened. TV dinner trays filled the coffee table, except for a corner where *Tolkin's Spirit Guide* lay open. A small note pad lay on the book with jottings in Chuck's careful hand. By the book lay a string of rosary beads. Tom picked them up. He knew very little about the rosary, except that the beads were a help in remembering certain prayers. A crucifix hung over the fireplace. Books were piled by the lounger. They were various new age books about past lives, telepathy, and a paperback called *Seth Speaks*. He read the back cover:

WHO IS SETH?

Seth is a personality "no longer focused in physical reality"—who dictated his startling view of the universe beyond the five senses to the earthly body of writer Jane Roberts—and reveals these astounding facts: What to expect immediately after death. How to glimpse into past lives. Ways to contact dead friends and relatives. New revelations about the Dead Sea Scrolls. What really happened on Calvary. The three lost civilizations that preceded Atlantis. And much more.

Tom put the book down, shaking his head. He looked at the other books, more of the same, written by people who didn't like the simplicity of religion. "Love thy neighbor" wasn't enough for them, they needed some theatrical gimmick like space aliens delivering sacred writings on gold disks to some guy in a trailer park.

Chuck came in, still in his pajamas, looking anxious and confused. "You see the news?"

Tom shook his head.

"There was this guy who was working on a slump block wall at a Taco Bell yesterday, grouting the cells."

Tom nodded.

"He was walking along the wall, moving the hose, and all of a sudden the concrete stops. Somebody yells 'Watch out!' but before he can move, the kink pops loose and the mud spurts out and throws the guy off the wall—right into a ditch there where they was building a retaining wall. Only there's nothing but the footing poured, with about a hundred re-bar sticking up, and he lands right on top of 'em."

"Oh, man, that's terrible," said Tom.

"He was stuck through in about twenty places. It took 'em ten minutes to get him off the re-bar and all the while the guy's bleeding horrible."

"Will he live?"

"Don't know. Punctured his lungs. As I was watching, I got this feeling. When that reporter was telling about how they was lifting that poor guy off the re-bar and they was trying to plug up the holes in him

with their fingers like some kind of dike—I could see that guy's face
. . . and it was mine."

Tom understood. "Chuck, you've been on roofs all your life and
you never fell off. Besides, we've got to get the shingles on, before it
rains any more."

Chuck pulled on the wattles at his neck. "I just can't go up on
that roof today. I think something bad's gonna happen up there."

A creepy feeling tickled Tom's spine. "Sure, Chuck," he said.
"We'll manage."

"I want to thank you folks for having me over tonight," said
Chuck. "Tom's seen what I been eating, and it ain't pretty!"

April placed a large serving dish on a hot pad. Tom was filling
water glasses and Josh was gnawing on a roll. Tom said, "We figured
you'd like a little home cooking . . . in *our* home."

"Nothin' truer," said Chuck, fastening the napkin around his
neck. "Always liked your cookin'."

April retrieved a salad bowl. "You've had it exactly twice!"

Chuck nodded. "And both times it was memorable. The first
time it was spaghetti, and then it was Thanksgiving when Carolyn was
feeling poorly. You fixed a wonderful turkey dinner."

April sat down. "I'm impressed you remembered. I hope tonight
won't disappoint."

"Not possible," said Chuck.

He seems better, thought Tom. He'd been watching Chuck
closely all week. After their argument at church, he'd been afraid to
say much to him.

April dug a spoon into the serving dish. "We're having curry
chicken. It's made with onions, mustard, curry, and chili powder."

"Sounds spicy," said Chuck.

"It is, but the relish gives your tastebuds a reprieve," said April,
gesturing at the yogurt side dish with slices of cucumber.

"We have it when we need to clear out our pores," said Tom.

"Which is about once a week," said April. "Mr. Fast Food here is nuts for it. Hope you like it."

Chuck was loading salad on his plate. "Sure I will, almost as much as the company." His moustache turned up in a smile. He put a load of salad on Josh's plate.

Josh protested, "I don't want any. I don't like it."

Chuck was undeterred. "Too bad, 'cause it likes you. Keeps yer stools movin'."

April and Tom smiled. Josh's face lit up. "What's a stool?"

"It's what you set on," said Chuck.

"*That's* a fact," said Tom. When they'd quieted down, he said, "How about grace?" He looked at April for approval. She nodded. They rarely said grace when it was just them, but the odds were higher tonight, three to one.

Tom turned to Chuck. "Would you, Chuck?"

Chuck bowed his head. Everyone held hands. April could feel Josh's hand squeezing her left hand. Her right hand was held tenderly by Chuck's dry one. She could barely feel him.

"Lord," said Chuck, "thanks for this family and the way they've been looking after me. I wanna tell You I love 'em and wish 'em only the best, and I know that's what You wish as well. Bless this food; make it do us good. And please bless the dear heart that made it. She's awful good to us three good-for-nothing men and we love her for it. We know You do too. Amen."

They let go of hands and dug in. Tom snuck a look at April. She was a little too busy helping Josh fill his plate. Tom knew Chuck had touched her in his casual way.

Chuck teased all of them throughout dinner, mostly Josh, using expressions that Josh had never heard before, as his exposure to old folks was limited. Tom's parents lived in Yuma and although April's mom lived in Chula Vista, she might as well have lived in Sri Lanka, as emotionally distant as she was. Chuck was the closest thing to a grandpa Josh knew, which suited April fine.

Chuck crossed his knife and fork across the plate. "Lemme see your hand," he said to April, "I wanna show you something."

April held out her hand.

"See this line here?" said Chuck, drawing his fingernail across her palm from forefinger to heel. "This here's your lifeline."

April knitted her brow. "Doctor, how long have I got?"

Josh was craning his neck. Tom folded his hands on the table. *This is not good.*

Chuck said, "I'm no expert—I only just got my own palm read this week for the first time—but I picked up on a few things she said. If your lifeline is unbroken and runs all the way up here," he pointed to the pad just below her forefinger, "that means you're gonna live a long time." He leaned back. "You're gonna be a grandma a bunch of times!"

April turned to Tom, raising her hand. "A *grand*ma! Ha!"

Josh held out his hand. "Me, too! Do me!"

Tom cleared his throat. "I'd rather you didn't, Chuck."

"Why not?" asked April.

"Why not?" echoed Josh.

Tom didn't know what to say. *Why not? After all, it's just some side show act.* "It's nonsense, that's all."

April said, "If it's nonsense, then it won't hurt anything. Go ahead, Chuck, read Josh's palm."

Chuck took the boy's hand, gave it a quick glance, and mussed Josh's hair. "Gonna live forever, Josh!"

Josh raised his fist in victory. "All right!"

"What did she say about *your* lifeline?" asked Tom.

"Who?"

"The gypsy or whoever?"

Chuck folded his hands on his lap. "Said I've had a long life."

Tom turned to Josh. "Josh-man, have you fed Ted yet?"

Josh looked at April, who shook her head.

"Better feed him," said Tom.

Ted must have heard his name because he appeared from the living room, tail wagging and tongue drooping. He followed Josh out the garage door. Tom said to Chuck. "And what else did she say? Did she say you were going to die?"

April had an *I don't believe this* look on her face. Finally, Chuck said, "She didn't say I was sick or anything, only that my lifeline is kind of . . . choppy and broken up."

Tom grabbed Chuck's hand and turned it palm up. "This is a working man's hand, Chuck. It's full of callouses, scars, and wrinkles. You're old and so's your hand." He let go of Chuck's hand with a tinge of disgust.

"She told me she was gonna try to contact Carolyn next time."

Tom rolled his eyes.

April found her voice. "Is she a medium as well?"

Chuck nodded.

"And she's gonna try to get Carolyn to talk to you?"

"Ayup," said Chuck defiantly, looking at Tom.

"Well," said April. "I hope she reaches her." She picked up her empty plate and went to the sink.

Chuck looked flatly at Tom, who noticed a desperate strength in the old man's gaze. Tom picked up his plate. "Who cares what *I* think?"

After Chuck left, April came out to the garage where Tom was sharpening chisels. "I don't see what harm reading a palm can do."

Tom examined an edge. "It's not a legitimate spiritual gift. It may even be evil."

"How do you know—because the Bible doesn't mention it?"

Tom dug another blade into the wheel, making sparks fly. April waited until he was done. "You think *everything* is in that book?"

"All the important things."

"Really? I know something it doesn't talk about. It doesn't say a thing about what comes after death! And why not? Because no one knows! No one has ever returned! You believe in something no one has ever seen. Those that claim to have been there talk about white light and tunnels, but they don't *stay*, they come back!"

Tom turned off the grinder. The room suddenly got quiet.

April lowered her voice. "All these 'life after life' experiences are not about *life* after life at all! They *return*! None of them actually made it to the 'other side' or whatever you call it."

"Heaven."

"Okay, heaven. All we know is that people who are *about* to die see this white light and somebody tells them they can't stay and boom! they're back in their body again and I'm supposed to believe they know something about the afterlife? The only thing they know is something weird happened when they were near death; probably a short circuit in their brain!"

"What's this got to do with palm reading?"

"What does the Bible say about palm reading?"

"Nothing, that I know of."

"So how do you know it's wrong?"

Tom looked at the floor. A long moment passed. "All I know is that it *feels* wrong, that's all."

"Tom, I don't doubt your feelings. You've had some doozies, like the time you felt we should keep Josh home from pre-school and that day the kids got exposed to chicken pox."

Tom brightened. "That's right—"

"But," said April, touching his arm. "Sooner or later, Josh is going to *have* to get chicken pox and we shouldn't prevent it, even if we could! He *needs* to get it when he's still a kid, you know."

"I know," said Tom, deflated.

"Chuck is searching. Maybe he'll find some answers." She walked inside. The door shut behind her.

Tom gathered up the chisels and put them in the pouch. "But what *kind* of answers?" he asked himself. His stomach ached dully. *Every time we discuss religion I get heartburn.* He switched off the light and followed April inside.

7

Tom was straddling the cornice, humming to himself, installing shingles over the dormer windows. His shirt was off, the sun was shining, and he could hear gulls squawking above the cliffs. He heard the growl of a truck going into second gear and saw the yellow Boise-Cascade truck crest the hill, loaded with lumber.

"No way!" he heard Vince say from below.

"No fork lift?" moaned Levitt.

Vince growled, "We gotta haul it in by hand! This bites!"

On his way down, Tom passed Chuck, who was installing a newel post on the bottom of the staircase. "Looks like the stringers and banisters are here," he said.

"About time," Chuck said. "I'm running out of things to do."

"Should've said something!" Tom went down the stairway.

"No way!" called Chuck, grinning.

Vince and Levitt were sitting on the steps, watching the driver taking the straps off. "You could help him get it off," suggested Tom as he passed them.

"Like he's gonna help *us* haul it inside," said Vince.

The driver turned, saw Tom and smiled. Tom picked his way across the muddy front yard. "No forklift, Bill?"

Bill shook his head. "I knew your credit was tight so I didn't order it. Figured I'd help you haul it off myself." He winked at Vince.

"I don't know," answered Tom. "There's a lot here to move."

"That's why I brought Sam." He whistled and an Irish setter jumped out of the window and bounded over.

"We need all the help we can get," shrugged Tom, waving Vince and Levitt over. They reluctantly stood and walked slowly toward the truck.

Bill regarded them. "Real go-getters, huh?"

"When they get their minds around a job, they do okay."

Bill laughed. "But we don't got that long, Tom!"

The five of them unloaded the truck. While the crew hauled the lumber inside, Bill retrieved a clipboard. "Uh oh. It's C.O.D."

Tom was stunned. "Bill, I don't have a draw."

"I've got to get some money, Tom."

"I don't have any," said Tom, feeling stupid.

"I know you're good for it. But it's not me who decides, see? It's the company." He tapped the invoice as proof.

Tom frowned. He still owed Chuck his wages from last week.

Bill looked at Tom, then clapped him on the shoulder. "I'll just tell 'em I okayed the credit this time."

"Will you get in any trouble?"

"The computer puts a cap on accounts over a certain amount. It don't care what kind of guy you are."

"I'll get a draft Monday and bring it down the second I get it."

"Hey, *I* know you're good for it. And I appreciate you leveling with me instead of giving me some hooey about leaving your checkbook at home. But bring your account up to date or they might cut you off. I'd hate to see that happen."

"Me, too," said Tom. "Thanks."

Bill waved him off. He climbed into the cab and whistled for Sam, who jumped in. He tooted the horn and pulled away.

I've got to get a draft from Balmer, thought Tom. *It doesn't matter how mad he gets. I've got records to show where every penny went. I'll just tell him we need the money—*

"Tom?" Chuck was standing by him.

"Yeah?"

"You okay?"

"Sure," said Tom, heading up the stairs. "If anyone wants me, I'll be on the roof, looking for a place to jump off."

Chuck took his measurements for the banister. It was quiet. Vince and Levitt were outside, getting more drywall. He hadn't heard any pounding in quite a while from the roof. "Tom?" he called out. He walked up the stairway, listening.

On the third floor, he went over to the open skylight they used for roof access. An old aluminum ladder stood there. Chuck put his hand on the ladder and called out again, "Tommy!"

Nothing.

He hesitated, remembering the guy who fell off the wall, seeing graphic pictures in his mind. "Tom?"

No answer.

"Oh, Lord," he whispered, taking a step up the ladder, "please don't let me fall and if I do, let me land on my head so's I go quick."

He climbed the ladder slowly. He grabbed the skylight frame, pulled his head through the hole and looked around. No Tom.

He wiped his hands on his overalls and hoisted himself up. *Done this millions of times,* he thought as he made his way toward the crest. *He's probably in the john. Probably walked right by me, said, "How you coming, Chuck?" and I didn't even hear him.*

But as he crested the roof, a dread fell over him. The roof on the closest dormer was done. The second as well. But beyond the third dormer, Chuck saw a yellow work boot sticking up.

"Tom?" He couldn't take his eyes off the boot. "Tommy?"

As he moved forward, Tom gradually came into view. He was lying on his back, one foot pointing up, the other bent at the knee under him, his head pointing downward. His eyes were closed. Chuck crawled down as quickly as he dared. He came to a stop a foot from the drop off, even with Tom's head. "Tommy?"

Tom was unconscious, his face ashen and his breathing shallow. Chuck yelled, "Vince! Greg!"

After an eternity, Vince sauntered out the front door, looking up, shielding his eyes against the sun. "What is it?"

"Tom's sick!" said Chuck, cradling Tom's head in his lap.

Vince dropped his tool belt and bolted inside.

"I never saw it coming," said the fat man sitting opposite April. His neck so overgrew his shirt that his tie seemed to be choking him. "I never thought she'd just up and leave!"

April sat behind her desk, her legal pad in front of her. "She must have given you *some* warning."

Mr. Caldwell shook his head.

"Nothing?"

"Well," he said, gnawing a cuticle, "she's been sleeping in another room for three months."

April put her pen down. "You never mentioned this before."

"I thought it was temporary." He lowered his voice. "She said it was because I was too . . . *romantic* and she needed some space." He sat back, showing two rows of tiny teeth.

April jotted *check his medication* on her pad.

The intercom buzzed. April raised the receiver. "Yes?"

"Someone on the line for you."

"I'm in a session."

"It's about your husband."

April heard a click, voices, and a siren. "Hello?" she said, her stomach sinking.

"April? This is Chuck—"

"Chuck? Are you okay?"

"I'm at Palomar. Tom's sick. *Really* sick."

"I'll be right there." She put the phone down and picked up her purse. "We'll have to reschedule," she said as she opened the door. "Fine," said Caldwell. "I'll save the juicy stuff for next time." April was already halfway down the hall.

Tom lay on a gurney, wearing only his boxers. He had felt crummy all day, but he figured it was the flu. He remembered completing the roof of the second dormer. At about two P.M. he ate an apple, looking out across the haze that had settled over the beach.

When he was working on the third dormer, something happened in his stomach, like someone swinging a sharp pick, and he felt a pain so severe he saw double. Water squeezed out his eyes and he felt his gorge rise. His back and chest were next, attacked by striations of red pain. He must've passed out. Chuck said on the way to the hospital that he had fallen toward the drop-off; his head came to rest just a foot from the edge.

Dr. Devlin poked Tom in the stomach. The room went white and Tom gasped for air. He felt his stomach coming up his throat. He turned and vomited into a plastic bowl.

A nurse stood by, taking notes.

Devlin chewed the stem of his tortoise-shell glasses. "Let's see: mild edema, tenderness, and low blood pressure. Probably auto-digestion. I can't be sure until we get the ultrasound, but I believe you have acute pancreatitis."

"What is it?" asked Tom, feeling ghostlike and weak.

"Inflammation of the pancreas."

"No. What's the pancreas?"

Devlin pulled off his gloves. "It's a gland that secretes digestive enzymes into the stomach."

"Will I be okay?"

"The inflammation is usually temporary. But I'll order an ultrasound to get a better look, just to make sure."

He was out the door and didn't hear Tom ask, "When?"

April made her way through the doors. At the other end of the room Chuck got to his feet. She ran to him. "Where's Tom?"

"The doctor said they were going to do an ultrasound."

"Ultrasound?" She led him over to the admissions desk. A heavy-set lady with blue hair put down her magazine. "I'm here to see Tom Waring. He came in . . ." She looked at Chuck.

"About four."

The clock on the wall behind the receptionist said 5:33.

The receptionist began typing, then looked up. "He's in C-114." She pointed. "Go to the junction and turn left. It's about fifty feet."

April sprinted away from the desk, leaving Chuck trailing behind. Around the corner, she scanned doors. C-114 was empty. "Damn!"

Across the hall, a black orderly poked his head out. "Someone call me?"

"Where's my husband—Tom Waring?"

"You talk to admitting?"

"He was in here."

"Blonde guy?"

"Yeah. They were going to give him an ultrasound."

"Oh," said the orderly. "They do those in B-125." He pointed back to where they came. "Go past the junction. It turns into B wing."

April ran off. Chuck arrived and looked at the orderly's name tag. "Thanks, Mr. Lucky."

"Just Lucky. Real name's Jerome. Lucky's my nickname."

"Hope you're right," said Chuck.

Far down the hall, April turned a corner and disappeared.

"Hope so too," said Lucky.

April burst into the room, which was dark except for a light over the bed. Tom was lying on a gurney. A monitor stood nearby, playing gray snow.

Devlin raised his eyebrows. April moved past him. "I'm his wife." She touched Tom's arm.

He opened his eyes. "Hi ya," he said weakly.

"How's things?"

"Ask the doc," said Tom groggily.

Devlin said, "He came in complaining of stomach pains."

"And?"

"I thought it might be acute pancreatitis—an inflammation of the pancreas. We did an ultrasound to see if it was inflamed, and—"

"I'm pregnant," said Tom woozily.

Devlin smiled. "Percoset. He was in quite a bit of pain."

"Not any more," slurred Tom.

April felt Tom's forehead. It was hot. "Was it inflamed?"

"No, but that only means the ultrasound didn't reveal it."

"So what does that mean?"

"As I said, it was inconclusive. His stomach is tender and he's been vomiting. The next step is a computer tomography scan. It's like a super-sensitive x-ray."

"I know what it is," said April, her patience ebbing.

Devlin frowned down at her. "Right now, he's stable, the pain is manageable, and his fever is likely to break soon. He can go home and rest."

"Wait a minute," said April, shaking her head. "I thought you were going to do a CT. Why not now?"

"It's not an emergency. I've scheduled one for Monday. It may be nothing more than a very upset stomach."

"But—"

"He'll be fine," said Devlin, turning. The door shut behind him.

"Jerk," said April, turning to Tom.

"I'm sorry," said Tom, looking at her with glassy eyes.

"Not you, honey. The doctor."

"He's a nice guy," he said, closing his eyes.

April stroked his cheek. "You sure are."

April turned off the bedroom light. Tom slept a dreamless, narcotized sleep. She went to Josh's room. Josh was pulling off his sneakers. "Hi, Mom," he said, dropping the shoe.

April pulled back the covers. "Hop in, Tiger."

"I gotta pray first," said Josh, kneeling. He folded his arms. April knelt next to him, feeling vaguely hypocritical.

"Heavenly Father, please bless Daddy so he'll get better and so he can help me learn to ride my bike. Amen."

April got up, but Josh didn't move. "You're supposed to say 'Amen'."

"Oh, A*men*."

Josh crawled into bed. "Daddy's gonna get better."

"How do you know?"

"Because I prayed." He turned over.

April turned out the lamp. "Goodnight, honey." She went out the door, closing it almost all the way.

8

On Saturday morning Tom woke up groggy. He got out of bed around noon wondering if he should eat something. April made oatmeal and juice. It went down okay, but the orange juice looked too acidy.

By evening he felt better. April rented *Liar Liar* and they settled on the couch to watch. Josh was soon asleep. April drifted off, leaving Tom awake. He put an arm around her and the other around Josh and tried not to worry about his stomach.

By Sunday he felt better. Weeks ago, April had promised her sister she'd babysit while Joyce and Bob went to a luncheon. As she dressed, she told Tom she could still bail. Tom wouldn't hear of it. "I'm fine," he said. "I'll just lay right here and take it easy."

April stepped into her sandals. "You'll stay put?"

Tom nodded.

"You won't go out . . . not even to church?"

Tom crossed his heart. April kissed him and took Josh to his cousins'. Tom lay in bed, reading the paper. He popped the pills they gave him and slept all morning.

A little after noon, the doorbell rang. It took Tom a full minute to get out of bed and find his bathrobe. The doorbell rang again. He groped his way to the door. He opened it and saw Chuck in a western-style suit with fancy piping along the coat yoke.

"Tom!" said Chuck. "You all right?"

Tom nodded. "What's up?"

"Wanted to see how you was doing." Chuck walked in, taking off his tan Stetson, holding it in front of him. They went into the living room. Chuck sat on the couch. Tom sat across from him.

"So . . ." said Chuck. "How you doing?"

"Okay. They got me on some serious drugs."

"That's good . . ." Chuck drifted off. "I mean it ain't *good* to be on drugs, but it's good you're feeling better."

"What's up, Chuck?"

"We need to talk."

"Sure."

Chuck looked at the floor and began slowly. "When I found you on the roof, I was worried. And while they had you in the hospital, poking and prodding, I got to thinking and when I got off by myself, I prayed for you."

Tom was moved. "I'm sure it helped."

Chuck was still staring at the floor. "But while I was praying, I got a feeling like I needed to set some things straight between us."

Tom was touched. "I'm not going anywhere."

Chuck finally looked up. "I ain't talking about you—I'm talking about me."

Tom blinked once but held his tongue.

Chuck continued. "I feel like I'll be going soon, and though you think I'm soft about these things, I trust my feelings. Back in 1967, I dreamed my dad was going to die and he did, just a week later. In the months before Carolyn got sick, I could feel my heart growing more tender toward her. I even got her flowers one day for no reason."

"I remember," said Tom. "You brought 'em to work."

"All day long, I had this secret. I knew I was gonna make her whole day when I give her those flowers! It was a great feeling, and I'm glad I listened to it, because those little things I did for her meant

more before we found out she was sick. If I'd have started being nicer
to her after, it wouldn't have meant as much."

Tom nodded.

"Anyhow, I wanna give you a bit of advice."

"Sure."

"April's a fine gal. Just as sweet and good as my Carolyn. You
two got something special. I know you don't tell her no tales and I can
tell she don't tell you none. You got a good son and a lot of years
together ahead. What I'm saying is: trust her."

"I do," said Tom, confused.

"I mean trust her to find God in her own way. And trust the Lord
to show Hisself to her when He's ready."

"I'm scared He won't."

Chuck put on his hat. "Don't you fret . . . He will."

Tom shook Chuck's hand. "I'll work on it. Thanks."

Chuck opened the door. "You'd do the same for me."

By Monday morning, Tom quit taking the pain pills. They made
him feel muddle-headed. His stomach felt okay, but just in case, he
took a Tylenol bottle and stuffed it in his pocket.

On the job, the drywall was going smoothly. Levitt and Vince
had a system down. Chuck was moving along on the stairway. His
work was so precise that a painter once held up an empty tube of
caulk, saying, "I usually go through six or eight of these, but your fit
and finish is so good, I used just this one."

Tom made sure the guys heard about the compliment. They
were a rough crew, the kind of guys who had belching contests, or
cussed you out if you deserved it, but they got downright sheepish if
you gave them a compliment, after which they would do even better.

That morning at breakfast, April insisted on going with him to
the hospital, but Tom dismissed the idea. They were just going to run
tests. He doubted they'd find anything and if they did, he doubted
they'd tell him. On doctors' penchant for non-disclosure, April had to
agree. They decided to discuss it over dinner.

He left the job at one o'clock. At the hospital, Tom was unsure whether the knot in his stomach was nerves or something more. He went up three floors and down a hallway. At the end was a door labeled IMAGING CENTER.

Inside, dark paneling replaced wallpaper and thick burgundy carpet replaced vinyl tile. He stated his business and the receptionist asked him to take a seat.

Soon, an Asian woman appeared and asked him to follow her. He was led to a small room where he put on a gown. She returned and took him to a large, dark room. A giant white donut stood on end, through which a white plastic table passed. He was told to get on the table and lie on his back. The woman left. On the ceiling someone had pasted hundreds of tiny luminescent stars, which glowed like a night sky.

A technician gave Tom a glass of metallic-tasting grape juice. Tom lay back on the table. The tech told him to hold still. Tom held his breath. Something that sounded like ball bearings began rolling around inside the donut. Tom could follow it with his eyes; it took about two seconds to complete a revolution.

"Relax," said the tech. Tom exhaled.

They did this about ten times, then the tech switched off the machine and bent over a monitor for a long time. Tom craned his neck to see. On the screen was a mass of gray inside an oval on a black background. The tech finally looked over at Tom, then tapped a key. The screen went blank. "I'll be right back," he said, not meeting Tom's eyes, and left the room.

Tom looked at the stars overhead. His stomach hurt.

When the tech came back, he was accompanied by a man in a white coat with thick gray hair. He looked about fifty. He extended his hand. "Dr. Gardener," he said. "We're going to do another series, Mr. Waring, so we can get a closer look. It will just take a few minutes. Lay back and relax, like before."

This isn't like before. This is the "closer look" series. And I don't like the sound of that.

Gardener joined the tech at the monitor. In a moment, the whirring beads inside the donut began revolving. Tom held his breath.

When it was over, he was escorted out without a word. He dressed. He went back to the reception area, wishing he'd let April come with him after all.

Gardener came out ten minutes later with a manilla envelope. "I'd like to show you something." Tom followed him to a room with viewing boxes on a wall. Gardener removed films from the envelope and clipped them over the boxes, then switched the viewers on.

"This is an axial view of your mid-section, kind of like having a camera inside you looking down at your feet." He pointed to several objects. "This is your liver, this is your spinal cord, and this," he said, pointing to a pale carrot-shaped object, "is your pancreas. We think there is a problem here."

The pancreas was a white wedge near the stomach. It didn't look big enough to be a problem. "What kind of problem?"

"The films reveal an abnormality. Here." Gardener pointed with the pencil. Tom stared at a tiny off-white bulge.

"What is it?"

"We don't know. We need a tissue sample for a biopsy. I'm ordering an endoscopy."

"A what?" Tom's ears roared.

Behind a doorway labeled NUCLEAR MEDICINE, Tom was introduced to Dr. Brightman, a small thin man. Lying on a gurney, feeling the air conditioning on his legs, Tom looked out the window, where a warm California afternoon was progressing nicely without him.

They sprayed something minty into his mouth, deadening it. Then Brightman threaded a long, black tube with a tiny camera on the end down Tom's throat. They squirted purple dye into his stomach and sent him off to x-ray with the tube still down his throat. Strangely, the only thing Tom could feel was an odd fullness in his stomach.

After the x-rays, Brightman used tiny pincers on the tip of the endoscope to snip off a piece of tissue. The wand was removed and Tom lay on his side, feeling weak. He got dressed and walked slowly to the lobby. His lips felt rubbery and his throat was numb.

The receptionist gave him slip of paper. It said, "April Waring. Called at 2:35. Please call at work."

Tom looked at his watch. It was 4:50. He called her. "April?" he squeaked, his voice sounding alien.

"Tom? What's the matter?"

"Hospital," he managed.

"I know. What's wrong with your voice?"

"They stuck something down my throat."

"Yuck. Are you okay?"

"Okay," he said, trying to sound better than he felt.

"What did they find?"

Tom thought a moment. "Haven't told me anything."

"I'm leaving now. When are you coming home?"

"Soon."

"You want me to come get you?" She was worried.

"Nope. See you at home." He hung up and turned. There was Dr. Brightman.

"Mr. Waring?"

"What did you find?"

"Please sit down," said Brightman, motioning to a couch. Tom sat. Brightman stood before him. "The films reveal evidence of a tumor, Mr. Waring."

"A tumor?"

"What we don't know, is whether it's malignant or if it's metastasized."

"What's that?"

"In late stages, a carcinoma may spread to other structures, making surgery ineffective. The biopsy will determine malignancy, and we'll study the films for signs of metastasis."

Tom stared at him, uncomprehending.

"You may have cancer, Mr. Waring." He looked away, then back at Tom, whose expression hadn't changed.

"How long till you know for sure?"

"Within three days," said Brightman. He put his hand out and Tom took it numbly.

Even with the unexpected procedures, Tom got home before April, so he stopped by a neighbor's house where Josh spent his afternoons and picked him up.

Josh was oblivious to Tom's day and for that, Tom was grateful. Josh went into something about the monkey bars at school and a fat kid, which struck him so funny he could barely get it out.

Tom's stomach was settling down and he was actually hungry. He turned to Josh as they pulled into the driveway. "What say we surprise Mom tonight and make dinner?"

Josh was doubtful. "What could *we* make?"

Inside, Tom rummaged through the cabinets and fridge. He came upon several packages of noodles. "What about Ramen?"

Josh moaned. "What else is there?"

Tom found celery and carrots. He grabbed two cans of beef stew from the pantry. "We'll put this with the noodles and have stew."

"Yuck," said Josh.

"Ted likes the idea," said Tom, nodding to the doorway, where Ted sat, tail wagging.

"He'll eat *any*thing," pointed out Josh.

"So will you." He gave the boy a stern look.

Josh was crestfallen but resigned. Tom hated to see the little guy upset; he wanted things to go smoothly tonight, so it was important that Josh be in a good mood. "But for dessert," he said, opening the freezer, "we're having . . . ice cream!"

"Yay!" yelled Josh.

When April came home, Tom's dinner-making ploy almost backfired. "What gives?" she asked, looking around.

"Just trying to help out." He was stirring the stew.

April came up behind him and whispered, "How'd it go?"

"Later."

When later arrived and Josh was in bed, Tom wished they had talked sooner. His stomach was aching, sending needles of pain into his lower back. He went to the bathroom and snuck another Vicodin. He came back to find April sitting on the bed. "So what happened?"

Tom unbuttoned his shirt. Since leaving the hospital, he'd been having a furious internal debate. The doctors probed and used big, unintelligible words, but in the end all they really said was, "Wait and see." Sure, the words "tumor" and "carcinoma" were used, but Tom could barely stand to think of the implications himself. He didn't want the third degree from April; he was too tired for that.

"They looked at my stomach and said it was fine."

"I thought you were just getting a CT scan."

Tom shrugged. "That's what I thought too, but when we finished, they suggested that since I had time, I might as well do this other test now instead of later. You know how hard it is for me to take time off. I can't be running to the hospital every afternoon."

April was searching his eyes. He felt like a fraud. "So what do they *think* it is?" He could tell she was trying to be delicate, but there was an urgency in her voice.

"It might just be an ulcer. They took a tissue sample from my stomach. It will take three days before they know what's going on." He began pulling off his shoes.

"I thought they said your stomach was fine."

"I was under anesthetic. I can't remember what they said."

April regarded him. "Tom—"

"We'll know soon enough and still have time to panic."

"If you're keeping something from me, I swear I'll gouge out your eyes!"

Tom put his arm around her. "If that isn't true love, I don't know what is!"

9

Tuesday it was Tom who lay in bed while April showered. He said he had to do the books today, and so would hang around the house. Besides, he was still nauseated from the "gag stick"—as he called it—and wanted to take it easy.

April, consumed in her morning routine, accepted his explanation. She kissed him before leaving with Josh, telling him to call her if anything came up. Tom pointed to his head, his heart, then at her, one of their secret codes.

As the door closed, he ran to the bathroom and threw up breakfast. He washed his face. The pain wouldn't subside and he swallowed three Vicodins. He got into bed, curled up into the fetal position and closed his eyes.

The early sounds of traffic came and went, then things quieted down until about ten o'clock when he was awakened by knocking. The knock was unmistakable—it was Chuck.

"Just a minute!" yelled Tom. His stomach felt bloated, the pain roped off in the background, close enough to still be taking swipes at him. He splashed water on his face, then hobbled to the door.

There stood Chuck in his painter's overalls. "Thought you were dead," he said, stepping inside. "You're looking awful ragged, boy."

"Feel ragged." Tom led Chuck into the living room. His stomach was hurting. He sat on the couch, waving Chuck into the rocker. "How's it going?"

"As usual, Greg and Vince are acting like boneheads, but they got most the drywall done." He gestured with his hat. "What'd the doctors say?"

"They gave me some tests, but I passed 'em."

"You look like you ain't passed nothing, 'cept maybe a kidney stone."

"I'm taking it easy. After all, they stuck this cable as big around as your forearm down my throat."

"Endoscopy, huh?"

"You know about those?"

"What with Carolyn's diabetes and Pam's difficult pregnancy, I seen just about every procedure there is." He touched his throat and swallowed. "Nasty one, huh?"

Tom nodded.

"So you okay? Need anything?"

"Just some sleep. I think it's the pain pills."

Chuck stood. "Okay. Mind if I take your cell phone today? You can call me if you need anything."

Tom stood. "Yeah. I'll get it." He walked away, trying to stand up straight. He fetched the phone from its charger and handed it to Chuck, who said, "You call me if you start feeling poorly."

"I feel poorly *now*."

"If it gets worse, you call, hear?"

Tom opened the front door. "Get out of here. Don't let the guys goof off too much, but if they give you a good day's work, let 'em off early."

Chuck nodded gravely. "Feel better."

"I'm working on it." He shut the door.

By eleven thirty he was feeling better. He imagined the pain duking it out in his stomach and was amazed that something so small could be so ornery. At one point, he was lying on the couch watching TV and it occurred to him that he did not have a will. The idea irritated him; it was a cowardly thought. But like the pain in his gut, it just stepped out of the main circle of light and stood there, calling him a fool. After a few minutes of trying to redirect his attention, he gave up and turned off the TV, inviting the negative thought back into the ring to speak its mind.

You've got no will, no savings, and no plans for the future. You've been acting like a teenager, thinking you'd live forever. But now—and at this the thought pointed to Pain, which was shadowboxing just beyond the light—*this guy has changed all that. He's got you wondering.*

Tom shut off the voice and went into the backyard. The sky was cloudless. Ted bounded up, barking. "Perfect day, huh?" said Tom, stroking the dog's ear.

Ted agreed, slobbering on Tom's hand.

A gull wheeled overhead, then disappeared behind two palm trees. "Perfect day to be *alive.*" He went back inside, went to the closet and took down a black vinyl bag, then rooted around on the floor until he found the tripod.

He took another Vicodin. He was above the legal limit now—he should *definitely* not operate heavy machinery.

He set up the camcorder in the living room. He put Ted on the couch and focused on him. Ted looked at the camera, tongue lolling. Tom went to change out of his bathrobe.

He returned, dressed in slacks and a polo shirt. He sat on the couch, the dog on his lap. He pressed RECORD on the remote. The blinking light went solid red. He smiled, trying to see April in the small lens. "Hi, honey. I had some time today so I decided to make you a tape. Some of this is for Josh, so maybe you should go get him."

His stomach was quiet, but the pain was still there. He began. "Okay. Hey, Josh-man. This is probably the first time your old man has ever been on video 'cause I'm usually the one working it. I want to tell you a couple of things. First, I'm real proud of you."

He paused. His eyes had wandered from the camera. "Josh, we named you after a man who lived a long time ago. He led the children of Israel into the Promised Land. He was a man who loved God. There's nothing more important than doing the right thing, Josh, and if you're not sure what's right, ask God . . . and trust Him. I love you, Josh-man. I wish I could be there to help you ride your bike, but I might not be . . ."

There. I said it. "Obey your mom. She knows what's best. Don't forget your prayers. And always remember . . . your daddy loves you. More than anything." Tom paused the camcorder and leaned back, drained. He went to the kitchen and splashed water on his face.

Back on the couch again, he took a deep breath. He hit the PAUSE button. "April, you should watch this part alone. When Josh is older, he can watch it, but for now I want to talk to just you. I'm pretty bad off and I've got a feeling—you know, one of my feelings—that things are gonna get worse. There are some things I want you to know. One, as you know, we don't have a will, but this tape should make it clear that you and Josh get everything I have, which isn't much . . . I'm sorry we didn't get further along than we did.

"In addition, there are a few things I want to remind you of, because just telling you 'I love you' doesn't seem like enough. I remember the day we met. I was carrying a door to the check-out at the home center when I heard your voice. There was a kindness in it and even before I put the door down, I knew you were a good person. And when I saw you, your hair pulled back, those beautiful, brown eyes . . . well, I was smitten. I was also embarrassed. I looked like a low-life: my hair was dirty and I hadn't shaved. But you were nice just the same. I was trying to think of a way to ask you out when you asked me to help you re-key the locks.

"That's how it's always been. You always take the initiative. If it wasn't for you, I would've never gotten the courage to ask your name. You would have walked out of the store and I would never have seen you again. So thanks for being brave.

"When we got married, I was scared to meet your friends because they were all college-types and I nearly flunked out of high school. But you were never embarrassed by me, or at least you never showed it. You always built me up, even when I didn't deserve it.

"You went against your mother, your sister, and your friends and let me have a church wedding, which meant a lot to me. You were kind to my mom. She cares about you, even though she doesn't know how to show it. Please see to it that Josh knows his grandma Waring. She has a soft spot for him.

"Our honeymoon was another time you traded your dreams for mine. We couldn't afford Hawaii, so we went to Mexico instead. You never complained, even though there were fleas and bugs. We spent our honeymoon at the beach. I didn't know then how afraid of sharks you were, but you went with me into the water because you trusted me. I wasn't afraid of sharks back then . . . but now, I'm afraid one's got me."

Tom paused the camcorder, dizzy and nauseated. He put his head between his knees and stayed that way for a long time. Then he took another pill and hit the PAUSE button again.

"I was feeling pretty crummy there for a minute but I'm better now. There's one last thing I want to say, and it may be the most important. It's about Josh. Remember when you were pregnant? Sick morning and evening? I was no help. I was totally unaware of how hard it was for you. And you didn't complain much, even though I tease you about it now. You went right on making dinner and doing laundry and trying to be cheerful.

"You insisted on natural childbirth and your reward was *fifteen* hours of labor! I was yelling, 'Epidural!' but you said no. And then Josh came and he was pink and perfect and they laid him on your stomach and I fell apart—the two of you were so incredible! I knew that he was *exactly* what I'd been trying to say to you since the time we met. I watched you with him and something told me we'd always be together. You two have made my life worth living."

Tom felt light-headed. "Finally, I want to tell you how much I love you. I've never had to, but if I *did* have to, I would swim oceans, climb tall mountains, or cross burning deserts to be with you. You'll never know how much I love you, April, because I've never had a chance to show you. So try to imagine me doing something heroic. I would if I could. Goodbye, sweetheart."

His stomach was screaming. He pointed to his head, his heart, then at the camera, mouthing the words "I love you."

He got to his feet. Ted, who had been sleeping, raised his head groggily. He watched Tom go and then went back to sleep.

Tom drank a handful of water. When the cold liquid hit his stomach, a sharp pain doubled him over. He collapsed on the unmade bed and curled up until a blanket of darkness fell.

April picked up Josh from the sitters. She had called home all afternoon but got no answer. Thinking perhaps Tom had gone out, she tried his mobile. Chuck answered, saying he saw Tom earlier and he looked pretty bad. She cancelled her last appointment and hurried home. A bank of clouds had moved inland during the afternoon. She kept telling herself he had gone on some errands or was out in the backyard and didn't hear the phone. She hoped these things but didn't believe them.

She turned onto their street and craned her neck. There was Tom's pickup. Josh was tugging on her sleeve. "Mom, guess what?" She was wondering if the truck had moved since this morning. She parked and got out. Josh ran to the door, yelling for Ted. The dog's bark came from inside.

Josh went in first and was greeted by Ted, who acted like they'd been gone a week. April put her keys on the sideboard. "Tom?" As she started down the hall she noticed the camcorder in the living room. "Tom?"

Tom lay on the bed. He was gray as flannel and burning with fever. She shook him and he moaned distantly. "Tom!"

Josh appeared in the doorway. "What's wrong, Mom?"

"Stay out!" barked April. She shook Tom but he wouldn't wake up. She grabbed the phone.

"Is Daddy asleep?"

"No, honey," she said, squeezing Tom's unresponsive hand. It seemed like an hour before someone picked up the phone.

"Emergency Operator," said a voice.

April stood as Dr. Gardener turned the corner. He had a bundle of computer printout under one arm. "Mrs. Waring?"

April nodded.

Gardener gestured for her to sit. "This is the report from the yesterday's tests."

Three days my eye, thought April. "What does it say?"

"Dr. Brightman said he told Tom that the tumor might—"

"Tom has a tumor?"

"You didn't know?

April shook her head.

"It's malignant. Pancreatic cancer moves very fast. In many cases, the diagnosis isn't made until after. . . ." He looked away, then back. "But your husband is in excellent physical condition. It's a miracle—"

"I want to see him," she said and headed for the hallway. Her legs felt like popsicle sticks; she couldn't feel her feet on the floor. As she turned the corner she looked back and saw Dr. Gardener still sitting with the computer printouts on his lap.

She stopped outside Tom's room and made a quick self-inspection, smoothing her blouse and brushing her hair back. She opened the door. The room was dark except for a single light over the bed. It was dark outside and the light made the window into a mirror. Tiny raindrops spattered against the glass. Tom lay under a green coverlet, an I.V. needle in the back of his hand. His eyes were closed.

April took Tom's hand. He opened his eyes. "Hi ya."

"Hi."

"Pillow," he croaked.

As April lifted him to adjust the pillow, he gasped. She eased him back slowly. "Better?"

He nodded.

Dr. Gardener came in with a nurse. April said, "They told me."

"I asked them to."

"What are we going to do?"

"What everyone does . . . deal with it."

"Oh, Tom."

"But I want to ask you a favor."

April nodded.

Tom looked into her eyes, so unlike his own. His were a sensitive pale blue. Hers were large and brown, with tiny flecks of gold that he counted once as they lay on the beach. Seventeen flecks in the right iris and forty two in the left. He said she was "left-eyed," which was why she saw the world in her sinister fashion. She reminded him that sinister was Latin for "left-*handed*" so it was *he* who was sinister, because he was a lefty. He had kissed her then, tasting salt on her lips.

He came back to the present, in a hospital bed, hearing the I.V. drip. "Go home, hon."

She shook her head.

"I want you to."

"I don't care *what* you want!"

"But, honey—"

She placed her finger over his lips. He nodded. She raised her hand and placed it over her own mouth, blinking back tears.

"It will be harder for you if you stay," he said.

"I don't care. I'm not going anywhere," she said weakly.

"Like I said."

"Got nothing else to do."

"Slow day?"

"The slowest." She smiled a little. "For me, at least."

"I've got some excitement ahead of me."

April slapped her thighs, hard. "You can't! I forbid it!"

Tom took a deep breath. "I've been called."

"Is this about your God again? What kind of evil, cruel, sadistic "god" would take you away from your family?"

"Please, April, don't."

"If he exists at all, he's cruel. A world full of suffering people, starving children . . ." She took a breath. ". . . Husbands taken."

"Life is a test. Suffering is a part of it."

"Exactly. He *is* sadistic."

"It's how we learn to love. I can't hate God—He gave me you . . . even if it was only for a short time."

April tried to see him through welling tears.

"I don't know why this happened, but I'm willing to go when I'm called home."

"You *are* home! What will we do without you?"

"God will watch over you, like He always has."

"Oh, sure."

Tom sighed. It was hard to speak; the drugs were clogging his tongue. He touched her hand.

She looked at her lap. "Sorry."

"April. I know the power of faith is in you."

She shook her head. "It isn't."

"Know what I think?" he said. "I think most people know who God is, they just don't think He knows who *they* are."

"No. No. I can't stand this." She bent to hug him.

Tom hugged her and was rewarded with a blinding vision of red streaks. He struggled for consciousness, whispering in her ear. "If He loves you half as much as I do, He would do anything for you."

April pulled back and looked at him for a long time, her brow furrowed, her mind racing.

Tom sensed something. "What?"

April bent closer, her eyes looking directly into his. "Oh, Tom, you love me, don't you?"

Tom nodded.

"Then promise me something."

"Anything."

April looked at Dr. Gardener and the nurse, who were talking quietly, their backs turned. She leaned forward and whispered, "If there is something . . . or some*one* . . . promise me you'll come back and tell me."

Tom blinked, amazed. "Come back? From *where*?"

April smiled a little. "You know: *there*."

They looked at each other.

"Deal?" She held out her hand.

Tom squeezed it weakly. "Deal."

"Promise?"

"I promise."

She cradled his face in her hands and put her cheek next to his, blinking back tears.

He whispered, "God knows you and loves you. Never forget."

She felt his stubbly beard and smelled his shampoo. She closed her eyes and gauged his breathing, feeling his hand at her back, his chest moving slowly. Then something eased and his hand went limp. His chest settled and didn't rise. April drew back and looked into his eyes. They were glazed and hazy, open yet empty.

Suddenly, the EKG shrieked a continuous tone. Dr. Gardener switched it off. Silence filled the room. April hugged Tom fiercely, her arms around his neck. "No, no! Oh, Tom!" she sobbed.

Outside, rain struck the window.

10

Tom looked at himself. It wasn't *him*. The body in the bed looked like him, but it wasn't; it was just something that he had lived inside of. And now he was outside it, hearing the scream of the EKG, the drip of the I.V., and April crying.

He was dressed in a hospital gown. It was the same flimsy cotton. He was surprised. He'd always thought a spirit couldn't touch or feel anything. He reached to feel the blanket on the bed but his hand moved through it. He felt nothing.

Then a strange sensation caused him to jump aside as Dr. Gardener passed through him and switched off the EKG siren. Tom heard raindrops striking the window, each one distinct, a million tiny hands clapping.

April was sobbing, "No! Tom!" He passed through his own body, reaching to touch her. His hand moved though her hair. He felt nothing. He tried to touch her cheek but his hand moved through her.

Dr. Gardener and the nurse left. The door closed behind them. April remained bowed over Tom's body.

Someone whispered. Tom turned. There was no one, just April and himself. The whispering grew louder. The room grew lighter. In the corner where the walls and ceiling met, a pin-point of light was growing. It was impossibly bright, but Tom felt compelled to look at it. It threw off multi-colored sparks. Soon it filled the corner, pulsating. The whispering ebbed and Tom heard a voice ask a question—or rather he *felt* it ask a question, one that required a yes or no answer. He didn't know the question but he had already answered.

Yes.

The light expanded, flowing over him, leaking into his eyes and ears, trickling down his spine. He felt a pulling sensation at his sternum and was drawn toward the corner. For just an instant, his body passed through April's and he felt a familiarity, a knowing, beyond any connection they'd ever shared. As he passed, his fingertips grazed her shoulder. She continued to cry, unaware.

Tom turned to face the white light, exulting in its warmth. He looked at his hand. It was translucent. He could see every layer of skin and muscle, every cell, every nucleus and protein. He was amazed that his spirit body had every component of his physical body.

The grief he felt at dying began to flow out of him. He felt free and strong. Pulled upward, he passed through the ceiling, sensing the wood, gypsum and steel molecules moving aside as his own molecules pressed past them.

He passed through the roof. The buildings and parking lots fell away below. He stretched his arms out and passed between the raindrops themselves, continuing upward through the rain clouds. Above them, he could see the deep blue arc of the horizon. The moon cast its silver light over a sea of clouds.

Upward he flew, the earth soon shrinking behind him, a blue crescent on a black background. The moon rushed by, then shrunk and disappeared. The sun burst past him like a magician's flare, then withered and died in the far distance. Even the stars began to move, each in its own arc. Individual stars blazed by, surrounded by planets, some beginning the life cycle, others nearing the end. Worlds with blue seas and brown deserts. Worlds with a million lights twinkling on their night side. *People live there*, he thought, as if he'd known it all his life.

He moved past thousands of spinning galaxies until they began to crowd in upon him, dense accumulations of gasses, stars, moons, and planets. He felt himself nearing the Center.

And then suddenly he felt a firmness under his feet. His weight settled on his bones. He stood on a glistening marble stairway. On either side of the wide steps the light dropped off into blackness. He saw the curving stairs below him ending in a pinpoint of white light. Above, the stairway disappeared into white as well. The steps felt warm on his bare feet.

He climbed and thought about the people he knew, his father and mother, Chuck, April, and Josh. He was not surprised he still existed; he expected to be where he was now. Except, where was that?

He felt a draft and was reminded he was wearing a hospital gown. He reached back and held the gown closed with one hand, thinking, *Be grateful you didn't die in the shower.*

The top of the stairs was within sight. He ran up the last twenty steps. The stairway crested onto a white circular platform inset with gold geometric patterns. Gossamer curtains circled the platform, their tops disappearing overhead in a cloudless blue sky. The curtains moved in a fragrant breeze, revealing a lush garden landscape beyond.

Tom stepped onto the platform and walked toward the center. Straining, he could hear distant voices in conversation. And something else: music. The voices grew louder and the music swelled.

The curtains to one side of the platform stirred. A group of people appeared. They wore white robes and their faces and hands were almost too bright to look at. They seemed delighted to see him. Tom stood, one hand behind him holding his gown closed. He didn't know what to do with his other hand, so he waved. Several people in the group smiled and waved back. As they drew near, he scanned for a familiar face. He didn't see one.

The group arrived and a man with black hair grabbed Tom's hand. "Welcome, *Thomas*." The others crowded around. Tom tried to keep his backside away from them, which resulted in his moving away as they crowded around. He finally gave up.

Another man said, "Tom!" and shook his shoulder as if they were old friends. Others patted him on the back. The dark-haired man looked at him, waiting.

"Well," said Tom, "I made it."

"Exactly!" said the man.

"So, this is . . . heaven?"

They all laughed, nudging each other. "Not exactly," said the dark-haired man.

"You mean this isn't heaven?"

A thin man with slicked-back hair threaded his way through the crowd. Unlike the others, he had on a white three-piece suit with a white tie and white shoes. He had a sharp nose, high cheek bones, and a tall forehead. His eyes were flinty gray. The group quieted down as he came forward. He opened a white binder ceremoniously. "Thomas Philip Waring?"

Tom nodded.

"My name is Jonathan. I am your mystagogue."

"My *what*?"

"Your spirit guide." He extended a thin hand and gave Tom a perfunctory shake. His touch was light. He looked intently at Tom, sizing him up, then went back to his book. After a moment he smiled. "Very good," he said. "Ninetieth percentile!"

Everyone applauded. Tom felt like he should bow. People slapped him on the back. "What's that?"

"Come now, no false modesty!" said Jonathan. "Ninetieth percentile! Your life was, by our preliminary data, quite good indeed. Welcome to Paradise!"

Tom allowed himself to relax. "So this is heaven?"

"You're in *Paradise*, the last stop before the final judgment, when *He* will sort everything out. Until then, good people are here, while the others go . . . elsewhere."

"So I'm dead, but this isn't heaven."

"Right."

Tom didn't remember hearing about any distinction between
Paradise and Heaven. What was it the Lord said to the thief on the
cross? 'Today thou shalt be with me in paradise'? Weren't heaven
and paradise the same place?

A short man stepped forward. He was round and red-faced, with
large eyes. He grasped Tom's hand in both of his. "Tommy, Tommy,
my boy . . . oh!"

"Hello," said Tom, not recognizing him.

"You don't remember me, do you?"

Tom shook his head. "Sorry."

Undeterred, the man said, "Tommy—I'm your Harold, uh, I
mean, I'm your *Uncle* Harold. From down there!" He pointed to the
stairway.

"Harold?"

"That's right!"

Jonathan leaned in. "Right. Well met and all. Now, we must be
going." He took Tom's arm but Harold had still not released Tom's
hands. Tom was squinting at Harold, trying to place him.

"*Uncle* Harold . . . I don't remember any—"

"It's the trip! The *long* trip. Stars and galaxies! The infinite
stairway! New faces. Probably a bit conflused."

"Conflused?"

"Confused *and* flustered: conflused!"

Tom smiled. "Conflused. Right."

"Right-o," said Jonathan. He pulled on Tom's arm. "We must
be going now." He looked daggers at Harold, who bowed his head and
took a step back.

"I don't have any uncle . . . Harold."

Harold looked up, brightening. "Yes! Yes! That's me! *Uncle*
Harold! I knew you'd remember!"

Tom shrugged.

"Enough," said Jonathan, hauling Tom away.

Another man appeared at Tom's side. He crossed thick arms across a broad chest and looked Tom up and down. "That elbow ever set?"

"Elbow?"

"The one you busted on my porch." He glanced at the stairway. "See you made it up these without tripping. Good boy."

Tom felt a tickle in his spine. A thought came rushing out of the darkness. "Oh my God!"

"Easy," said Jonathan.

"Sorry?"

"Go easy on His name, please."

"Sorry." Tom turned to the man. "You're grandpa Waring!"

The young man nodded. "How's my Jessie?"

"Jessie . . . ? Oh, *Grandma*! She's good, pretty old, of course."

"*How* old?"

"Eighty-five." *Something is wrong here.*

"Eighty-five?" His face went white. He took a step back.

"What's wrong?" asked Tom.

"I've only been here a few cycles. I can't believe she's that old . . . How is she?"

"Well, she forgets sometimes."

"Oh. Sure." He seemed conflused, as Harold would put it.

Suddenly a beeping sounded and everyone reached to their midsections. Ben pulled out a pager and scanned the display. "Gotta go, son. Nice to see you. I mean, sorry to see you so *soon* and all, but we'll talk later." He shook Tom's hand and trotted across the marble floor, disappearing between the curtains.

Harold beamed. "It's nice to find family here, isn't it?"

Tom was drowning. "Sure."

Jonathan produced a gold pocket watch. Tom couldn't read it; there were no hands or numbers. "Fine. You've seen your family. Now it's time to—"

A female voice spoke. "Your attention, please. Next arrival in three minutes. Please clear the greeting platform. Thank you."

"As I've been *trying* to say . . . we should *go!*" Jonathan grabbed one of Tom's arms while Harold took the other. They led him toward the bank of curtains.

"Where are we going?"

Harold winked up at him. "Next arrival! Very exciting!"

Layer after layer of curtain moved aside as they walked, falling back as they passed. They descended several steps and entered a passageway. After a few steps, Tom noticed he and Jonathan were alone. The others had turned into a doorway labeled OFFICIAL GREETERS ONLY. Uncle Harold stood outside, drinking out of a paper cup. When their eyes met, he raised his cup in a salute.

Tom looked through a split in the curtains. An old woman ascended the stairway. The greeters gathered behind the curtains. Someone gave a signal and they moved forward, led by Uncle Harold, who extended his arms toward the startled new arrival, calling out cheerfully, "Welcome to Paradise!"

They walked down the bright passageway, Jonathan a half-step in front. He looked back at Tom, gesturing for him to move faster, but Tom was in no hurry. He was wondering what the sparkling floor was made of and where the light behind the walls originated. The passageway was joined by several other passageways. Entering their path ahead of them was a man in white, holding a small boy's hand.

"Who's that?" asked Tom, pointing at the child.

"New Arrival. We have numerous stations. Your station serves your geographical area on Earth."

Soon there were many people walking along, each with an escort. They passed through an arch and entered a huge chamber, full of people. There were scores of conversation areas, made up of two or three ornate chairs and a low table, around which sat spirit guides and their charges. At the far end of the room was a raised platform with a white desk, behind which a woman sat writing in a book. A female New Arrival stood before her with her escort.

"Admissions," said Jonathan, as if that explained it all. He sat and opened his book. Tom sat down, trying to make sense of it all.

A voice from overhead said, "Darren Newson. Step forward."

To Tom's left, an old man struggled to his feet. Like Tom, he wore a hospital gown, but it was stained red. Jonathan snorted, "He obviously went during an operation."

The old man ascended the steps with the help of his escort. The woman at the desk asked him something. He nodded and she wrote something in her book.

Jonathan sat, his back rigid, concentrating on his binder. Tom craned his neck to see what was in it, but Jonathan shut it and fixed Tom with a cool stare. "You have a question?"

"Ah . . . no."

"Don't hesitate if you do," said Jonathan. He opened his binder again, holding it so Tom couldn't see inside it.

"Well, I was wondering—"

Jonathan let out an exasperated breath. "What—"

"Thomas Waring. Come forward." The voice echoed.

Jonathan rolled his eyes. "We stayed too long at the Gate."

"We did?"

Jonathan pointed to the platform. "Go ahead."

The woman at the desk was looking at Tom.

"Off you go."

"Will I see you again?"

Jonathan laughed, a high laugh that wasn't the least bit merry. "Of course!" He strode ahead of Tom, waving at the woman, who raised her chin in recognition.

At the platform, Jonathan stopped and urged Tom onward. Tom ascended the steps. The woman was turning pages in a large white book. She read for a full minute before she looked up. "Thomas Philip Waring?"

Tom nodded. On the wall behind her was a large gold square, about two feet on a side, inside of which was a giant check mark.

"Mr. Waring?"

Tom looked back at her. "Yes?"

"I asked you to sign in." She turned the book to face him. There was his name in bold caps, followed by Jonathan's name, and a blank space. She handed Tom a pen. "Please."

Tom stared at it.

"Sign, please," said the woman again.

"Hey!" said Tom, bending his forefinger. "I got my finger back!"

The woman tapped the book. "That's nice. Now, will you *please* sign the contract?"

Tom signed, never taking his eyes off his forefinger, complete with fingernail and everything. It was perfect. He showed it to Jonathan.

"Very nice," said Jonathan, inspecting his watch.

The woman studied his signature as if it might be a forgery. Without looking up, she said, "You see the icon behind me?"

"The square?" Tom couldn't get over his finger. He stuck it in his mouth, tasting it.

She began speaking in a sort of practiced sing-song one hears at the DMV. "That is the Paradise logo. It is symbolic of your life up until this moment. You have shown proficiency in learning and obeying the rules of your mortal probation, and although you are no longer mortal, your probation continues. If you do well here, you will be rewarded. If you do not," she said, finally looking up, "you will be quite unhappy here. Do you understand?"

Tom nodded, scratching his neck with his new finger.

"Fine." She turned the book to him again. Underneath a paragraph of the speech she just recited was a blank line. "Please sign, indicating that you agree to abide by what I have just told you."

Tom signed.

Jonathan smiled unctuously at the woman. She nodded almost imperceptibly, then turned her attention to her book.

Another name was called by the voice and Jonathan escorted Tom away. They turned toward a new set of doors. Beyond was a smaller room with a counter along a wall and people bustling behind it, disappearing between shelves and returning with white bundles.

"What's this?"

"Unless you'd like to trot around Paradise with your bottom exposed, you may exchange your fine apparel for something else."

Tom reached and held his gown closed, reddening. They got in line. When it was his turn, a woman said, "Name please?"

"Thomas Waring."

She consulted a screen and disappeared between two shelves. In a moment she returned with a bundle and gave it to Tom. She looked over his shoulder and said, "Next?"

When he emerged from the dressing room, Tom wore a white tunic with half sleeves of a fine, silky material. It looked like fabric, but he couldn't detect a weave. A belt held the front closed. He also wore a pair of white sandals. He lifted one up to show Jonathan. "Birkenstocks!" he laughed, wiggling his toes.

Jonathan sniffed. "Once in a while, mortals come up with something worthwhile. We've only been using them for a few cycles." He pointed to his white wing tips. "I prefer more traditional footgear."

"So you guys keep an eye on us," said Tom.

"That is one of our two great priorities here."

"What's the other?"

"You will soon find out." He headed for another doorway.

"Where are we going now?"

"Orientation," said Jonathan as they threaded their way through the crowd. They passed a pretty woman with auburn hair and brown eyes who reminded Tom of someone. He turned suddenly, walking back toward the admissions hall. "Where are you going?" asked Jonathan.

Tom broke into a run. "Home."

11

Once again, April stood by a grave, looking into the darkness.

Reverend Heath stood at her side. He was talking, but she didn't hear him. The day was warm and sunny.

Josh wore a black suit that April's mom had bought him against her wishes, because what's a five year-old going to do with a black suit? It seemed ludicrous and unimportant, as did most things in the days following Tom's death.

His parents stood opposite April, united for the first time in twenty years by the death of their son. April had spoken with them but she couldn't remember a thing they said. They came into town the day before yesterday. Vivian was staying at April's while Don stayed at the Marriott in Carlsbad.

Tom's friends from church had been bringing in meals and tending Josh. April barely left her bedroom before yesterday when she went to the mortuary to pick out a casket.

Since they had no burial plot, Chuck suggested the cemetery where Carolyn was buried, the one with the view of the ocean. April had agreed numbly.

The night Tom died she lay alone in their bed. One day he's fine and the next he's dead. Just like that. She could still see the doctor's face, that look of inevitability, when she finally got up off her knees by Tom's bed and went outside.

She went home to an empty house.   Josh was staying at the neighbor's.   She didn't undress, but fell onto the bed.   Her eyes wandered to the window and she watched the moon move while her mind raced.   After an hour, she drew the drapes.   Tom was wrong about the moon. It wasn't unique. There were a million moons in the universe, hanging over a million planets where a billion wives mourned the loss of their husbands. The most plentiful substance in the universe was not hydrogen, as the scientists claimed. It was grief.

An open house followed the funeral. April sat in the kitchen while people offered mumbled condolences, then split off into small groups, talking quietly, occasionally looking at her.   There were strangers, people from Tom's congregation and the building trade. Vince and Levitt were there, looking uncomfortable.

Don and Vivian Waring hadn't spoken to each other since before the service, and only then did they exchange short hellos. Don didn't bring his young wife and child from Arizona. Vivian stood as far away from him as she could. When April was making up the sofa bed for her the night before, Vivian commented angrily that it wasn't fair that Don should stay at the Marriott and she had to impose on April. Her anger was so vitriolic that April suddenly felt alive in comparison. Later, when Vivian apologized for her bitter comments, April felt her superiority ebb and thick grief washed over her again.

She was thinking about that now, how another's practiced, time-sharpened anger could actually make you feel *better*.   She felt uncharitable. After all, Vivian had fended for herself for twenty years while Don had a dozen girlfriends, finally stumbling into a relationship with a young attractive woman and having another family, ignoring his first one. It was unfair, even though April saw elements in Vivian that would drive anyone away. Vivian would never know that it was her bitterness as much as Don's abandonment that had pushed Tom toward the California horizon. If not for that angry woman April might never have met Tom. She suddenly felt compassion for Vivian. She crossed the room and gave her a hug, right in front of Reverend Heath.

Heath had been looking for an opportunity to speak to April all day. "Thank you for allowing us into your house," he said, treating each word like explosive ordnance.

"Tom would have wanted you to do the service." April was surprised she could say the words without bursting into tears.

"It was an honor. And I hope the members of the congregation have been helpful."

"They've been wonderful. Since I don't know most of them, please thank them for me."

"Even better, I could introduce you."

Vivian put her arm through April's, the ice clinking in her glass of fruit punch. "April is overwhelmed right now. Trying to remember new people's names would be difficult."

April had no defense mechanisms to protect against Heath's sincerity. *This is how they get you. They comfort you and then you believe whatever they say.* She wished for Tom's lack of subtlety; the way he would just state his faith forthrightly. Then she could deconstruct it. Without him, she was left to deal with people like Heath who would try to trick her into believing.

"Was the service acceptable?" asked Heath.

Vivian took a sip. "If you like mumbo-jumbo."

April felt the room warming.

"Tom always enjoyed spiritual discussions," said Heath.

Vivian sniffed. "We all have our superstitions." She met Heath's gaze directly. The glass in her hand shook slightly. April suddenly had a revelation. Somewhere in Vivian's bags was a bottle of vodka, the alcoholic's drink of choice, it being odorless. She suddenly felt protective toward the small man. Compared to Vivian Waring, he was an innocent.

"Dr. Heath," she said, guiding him away. "Let me ask you something."

He beamed at her, eager to help. "What is it, Sister Waring?"

April overlooked the familiarity. "What do you think of the fact that the moon is four hundred times smaller than the sun and is four hundred times closer to the earth?"

"That's fascinating."

"They're the exact same size in the sky."

"Is that a fact?"

"So it results in full eclipses. I imagine that particular juxtaposition is rare, don't you?"

"I imagine so, but in a universe as big as ours . . ."

April suddenly felt sorry for him. *He only believes in pre-packaged faith. If I told him these facts strengthened Tom's belief, he'd see it as a sign, but since it's coming from an unbeliever, he doesn't even see the connection.* "I just wondered if you knew that." She patted him on the arm.

"Hmm," mumbled Heath.

"It's a big place, the universe," said April.

"Yes it is," said Heath. "There is room for everything . . . and everyone." He nodded at Vivian, who was glaring at Don across the room. "Even those who feel they must drown their pain." He looked at Vivian, his eyes full of compassion.

You old fox! Not as dense as I thought. "Reverend Heath," April said, suddenly filled with kindness toward him. "If Josh wants to keep going to church, I am not opposed."

"And you, Sister Waring, are always welcome. I hope you know that."

"I do," she said, feeling a tiny bit better.

When everyone had left and Vivian was asleep, April poked her head into Josh's room. He was pulling off his shoes. He still had on the white shirt from his new suit. "Hi, tiger," she said.

"Hi, Mom," he said without emotion.

She put her arm around him. "How're you doing?"

He shrugged.

"You feel okay?"

He shrugged again.

She pulled him close. After a long moment, something gave and he started to whimper. Soon he was crying, and she with him. They cried, sobs followed by sniffles and fumbling with tissues, until April could finally speak. "It's not fair."

He nodded.

They pondered the truth of it.

"Mom?"

"Yes, hon?"

"Mom, I wanna pray."

April heard herself say, as if from a great distance, "I don't know, Josh."

"Mom, I wanna know why God took Daddy away."

"So do I."

"I'm gonna ask Him." He began unbuttoning his shirt. April helped him and his hands fell to his side, his face turned up to his mother's. She didn't dare meet those trusting eyes. Instead, she concentrated on the buttons, then pulled the covers back. Something inside of her was bending, about to break. She stood and put her hand on the door frame to steady herself.

"Mom?" Josh was kneeling, his fingers laced together.

April felt herself drowning in darkness. She shook her head. Tears flew from her cheeks. "I can't, Josh. I'm sorry. I just can't." She fled the room. Only her grief had survived, and it lay on her, pressing down on her like gravity. She got into bed and cried into her pillow.

Josh could hear his mother crying. He shut his eyes. "Heavenly Father, Daddy is gone and Mommy is sad. Please help her not be sad. Please let Daddy come back and live with us again. If it was my fault he died, I'm sorry. I don't know what I did, but I'm sorry and so please forgive me and send Daddy back. Please, God, let Daddy come back. Amen."

He crawled into bed, listening to his mommy cry in the next room, fighting back his own tears.

12

Tom raced down the passageway, dodging New Arrivals, his sandals slapping the floor. He saw April's face in everyone he passed, pleading him to come back to her. He turned a corner and there stood Jonathan, arms crossed, his jaw set. "What's this about?"

"How'd you do that?"

Jonathan sniffed. "You're not in Kansas anymore, Thomas."

"I can't stay here. I gotta go . . . back."

Jonathan took him by the elbow. "In due time, if that is His will. All things in their proper order. But for now, come with me."

They walked through a door and found themselves outside. Behind them, the Admissions Center dome rose twenty stories into the air. Before them, a wide path wound through an incredible garden, disappearing over a small knoll.

Tom tapped the pathway with his sandal. "This isn't gold."

"Of course not," said Jonathan. "Why would it be?"

"I thought the streets of heaven were paved with gold."

"So I have heard as well. But as I keep saying, we are *not* in Heaven. We are in Paradise, and," he looked at his blank watch again, "we are late!"

The sky was uninterrupted blue. Everything exuded light. As they passed a flowerbed, Tom noticed that each flower, each petal, each leaf, glowed with a halo effect. The elms that bent over the pathway shone, as did the neatly clipped lawn that rolled over the curved hills.

"Everything gives off light," said Tom, picking a leaf off a sycamore branch. It lay in his hand, humming with energy and light.

"That is so."

"But there's no sun."

Jonathan motioned for Tom to catch up. "All your questions will be answered in due time. Come *on!*"

"How come there's no sun?"

"Everything here is pure spirit. Spirit is matter, but it is more refined than mortal matter. Your mortal eyes could not perceive spirit matter, but your spiritual eyes can. There is no sun, Thomas, because it is superfluous in a realm where spirit is revealed. Everything glows because everything has a spirit."

They crested a hill. The path ran down the far side under the boughs of leafy trees. A crystalline lake glinted in the distance.

"It seems almost alive," said Tom, still examining the leaf.

"Everything *is.*"

"Everything?"

"To a tiny degree. Everything has a degree of awareness and yearns to realize its full potential."

Tom plucked a blade of grass. "Am I hurting the spirit of this grass if I chew on it?" He put it in his mouth.

"I suppose one of its uses is snack food," said Jonathan flatly.

Embarrassed, Tom spit the grass out. They were abreast the lake now. A flock of white swans took flight. Beyond the lake was a huge, ornate building with silver windows. A broad marble staircase led to gigantic golden doors, which were thrown open. Hundreds of people were ascending the stairs.

"The Great Hall," said Jonathan proudly.

The architecture was unlike any Tom had ever seen, with arched roofs and cut stone embellishments. At the foot of the stairs, cutting into several steps, was a pediment upon which stood an immense alabaster statue of an angel with wings lifted high overhead. It loomed over them as they approached.

"I knew it," said Tom, craning his neck up at the angel.

"Knew what?"

"I knew they had wings!"

Jonathan laughed. "Oh, my boy! They most certainly do *not* have wings! That's just a bit of the old theater!"

As they ascended the stairs, Tom asked, "Who is it?"

"The Archangel Gabriel."

"*The* angel Gabriel?"

Jonathan shrugged. "There's only one."

They passed through the lobby. Dozens of chandeliers hung overhead. A bank of golden doors stood open as people filed in. Tom and Jonathan found themselves in an enormous hall, with tier after tier of balconies hung with red and gold tapestries. Rows of red velvet chairs filled the floor, which sloped down to a red-carpeted stage. The room was dark, except for guide lights in the aisles and a spotlight focused on center stage.

They found two empty seats. The room filled with New Arrivals, accompanied by their spirit guides. Many appeared to be old friends already. Their conversations filled the room with a friendly hum. Tom looked at Jonathan, who sat with his nose in the air.

The doors closed, darkening the room. The last people took their seats. Tom asked, "What's next?"

"Shh," whispered Jonathan. The spotlight dimmed and went out. Tom looked at his hand, which glowed faintly. He looked around. Everywhere, he saw glowing people. A hum arose as others made his discovery.

A whisper began at a low register, rising as it increased in volume. Tom felt his spine tickle and goose bumps rise on his forearms. He could make out voices rising and falling in a toneless melody. The tickle moved up his spine.

High overhead, tiny lights on an immense spherical chandelier winked on one by one, until it burned like a sun. The voices rang out now, their cadence steady, their words rising and falling rhythmically.

Tom was unable to take his eyes off the chandelier. His skin tingled. He felt apprehensive, yet peaceful; he felt himself letting go of a lifetime of cares. Suddenly, he realized he was singing with the voices. He looked at Jonathan, who sang with the others in a brittle tenor. As his own lips formed unlearned words, Tom saw that everyone was singing, some of them with a surprised look on their faces, others with eyes closed, as if remembering a childhood melody.

After several minutes of transcendent praise—for that is what it was—the music slowed, growing fainter, until it whispered into stillness. The chandelier dimmed, the lights going out one by one, until once again the room was dark. But the people, energized by a song long forgotten, glowed brightly.

Suddenly, the stage exploded in a blinding fireball. Tom felt the expanding heat corona press past him. He shielded his eyes. The fireball hit the rear wall, then collapsed back, drawing the light after it. Tom felt the hair on his neck stand on end. The light pulled into itself and coalesced around a human form. Tom made out a tall, finely proportioned man with flowing white hair and bronze skin. Light poured from his eyes, which were two almond suns. Tom got to his feet along with everyone else. He looked at his hands—he was applauding.

Tom had never seen this person before, yet he felt hot tears on his cheeks. He wiped them away, surprised by his own visceral response. Beside him, Jonathan's face was unreadable. The person on the stage raised a hand and the clapping stopped. Tom leaned toward Jonathan. "Is that . . . ?"

"It's Gabriel."

"Oh," said Tom, disappointed.

"You expected . . . ?"

Tom looked away. Jonathan laughed. "Oh, Thomas! *He* doesn't come around *here*! He's much too busy!"

Tom looked at the luminous person on the stage. *If* this *isn't Him,* he thought, *then* He *must really be something.*

Gabriel motioned for the audience to sit. "Welcome," he said in a voice like distant bells. "I am the Archangel Gabriel. Welcome to Paradise. Well done!" He extended his hands toward the audience. The crowd burst into applause. Tom saw people hugging their spirit guides. He looked at Jonathan, who sat with his arms folded, his eyes hooded.

Gabriel began to walk the stage. He was so bright that Tom had to squint to make out his features. "Congratulations, all! Only the righteous dwell in Paradise!" He walked down a couple of steps and stopped, surveying the crowd.

"It is my privilege to remind you of things you once knew as well as your own name. I will tell you about yourself: a story that has no beginning, no middle, and no end—a story that each of you has written over eons of time. On this glorious day, I will answer the three great questions: who you *are*, what the purpose of your life *is*, and what lies *ahead*!"

Thunderous applause erupted.

Gabriel sat down on the steps, draping an arm over his knee casually. "Now listen carefully. Existence takes place on a continuum—an endless path. Your spirit, the part of you that quickened your body in mortality, has always existed. Before you were born on Earth, you lived in a world of pure spirit, children of eternal parents, sons and daughters of God!"

The audience murmured among themselves, turning the idea over. Tom felt a warmth on his lower spine. He had always suspected such a thing. He remembered the day he first held tiny newborn Josh in his arms and just *knew* this child came from somewhere. Somewhere *else*.

"Your legacy is noble, as is your destiny—to walk in the footsteps of those who precede you on the Continuum. Your life on Earth was but one in a series of experiences designed to prove you. This time, the element of mortality was added to your experience.

"You received a body, which is a powerful tool if used wisely. Before we were born, we never imagined that eating a meal could be so satisfying; that a bath after a long day could be so refreshing; or that the touch of a loved one could be so fulfilling. These are the blessings of a physical body.

"But there are burdens as well. Most of the troubles vexing mankind—lust, greed, and envy—are a result of not governing the body's passions. But with varying degrees of success, each of you has harnessed your body to assist your spirit, not inhibit it."

He stood. "I lived on Earth thousands of years ago. I died and was resurrected. I am an 'Immortal,' a spirit clothed in a perfected *physical* body. You see my brightness. In the darkness before I came, you saw the light of your own spirit. What you see is a difference in *degree*, not of kind. God himself possesses a body like mine, but many times more glorious. I find it difficult to gaze upon Him. The light that He exudes is a function of His virtue. It is He who lights the very universe; the sun itself merely reflects His glory."

Slow down, you're losing me! thought Tom.

"I dwell in the presence of God. Wherever God is, *that* is Heaven. It is not a place so much as a *quality* of life, where the opportunities for progression are limitless. God rules the universe we dwell in. But there are many universes, and many gods. Our God scatters the stars in the vast emptiness of space and creates worlds upon which His children live and are proven.

"You find yourselves once again on the cusp. You have departed one world and entered another many times before. This is why this all seems familiar to you. But do not misunderstand. We are moving along the Continuum, a road that stretches before us into the eternities. We pass each place just once. Your time on Earth has ended and you are poised to enter a new world.

"This place is called 'Paradise.' Here you will continue your progress toward 'Heaven,' a circumstance where you may someday organize worlds for your own children, and be called 'God' by them." Gabriel stopped, letting this sink in.

There was a murmur in the crowd. Tom noted that some people were nodding their heads, others were scratching theirs. Tom fell in the middle. *This is too much. It's too far out, and yet . . .*

Gabriel's voice became quiet. "Now, there is another place where the souls of those who hate the light await judgment. When the end arrives, all will be resurrected and receive a body that mirrors the light within them. Many of you will receive eternal bodies that will rival the sun in glory and will allow you to progress further along the Continuum. But there are many who prefer darkness. *This* is Hell, my brothers and sisters: to *choose* to not progress. And the misery of those who choose darkness is a grief that swallows the very soul."

He turned, shaking his head to erase the image. Tom felt his hands gripping his armrests. Jonathan was doodling in his binder.

Gabriel looked up and smiled. "But *you* have proven yourselves worthy. Because of your love of truth, you will be privileged to taste a bit of what awaits the righteous! Paradise is your new home! You will learn more in one day than you learned in your entire lifetime on Earth! You will be busy and sometimes weary, but you will be progressing along the Continuum! Well done!"

The doors behind them opened and light sifted into the room. People came down the aisles with large boxes. One was placed next to Tom's row. It was full of white binders and rectangular objects. Someone handed Tom a binder, nodding for him to pass it down the row.

Gabriel continued. "Since Paradise is an extension of mortality, you are still limited in some ways. The binders you are receiving are one way you may overcome these limitations."

Tom opened his. It had pages for scheduling appointments, comments, and journal entries.

"The Record is indispensable. You will soon find that you feel naked without it!" He held his own aloft. "Your communications devices are similar to cell phones, but they transmit a kind of hologram." He held his up, his face radiant. "Give praise to God!"

"Hallelujah!" shouted the multitude.

The light surrounding Gabriel began to draw in on him until he was too bright to see. Then suddenly, it went out, and he was gone. "Showoff," smirked Jonathan.

"What?"

"I said, let's shove off."

"What now?"

"The Naming Ritual." Jonathan stepped past Tom, who was juggling his new possessions. Outside, they walked across a great tiled square toward a number of smaller domed buildings. Jonathan consulted his Record.

"So these are important," said Tom, turning his own over in his hands.

"Couldn't get along without it," said Jonathan. "Ah, here we are." They stood before one of the domed structures. Jonathan consulted his watch.

"What's going on?" asked Tom.

"We're waiting for your grandfather. He's notorious for being late." Jonathan surveyed Tom. "I hope it doesn't run in the family."

Tom was late for everything, even church. He shook his head. He instantly felt bad. *I'm here one hour and I'm already telling fibs.*

"Good. Like anywhere else, success here requires punctuality."

Tom nodded. "I'll try."

"That's my point," fretted Jonathan, "It's not enough—"

"Hello!" came a voice. Tom's grandfather was trotting toward them. Jonathan glanced at his watch, his lips pursed.

"I know, I know," said Ben, raising his hands. "I'm late. You probably know that from my profile. Sorry!"

Jonathan's hard stare silenced Ben. "Benjamin, are you prepared to escort Thomas through the Naming Ritual?"

"Yes," said Ben gravely, winking at Tom when Jonathan glanced at his Record.

Jonathan looked up and said to Tom, "When you are finished, I will meet you in front of the Great Hall. Understood?"

Tom nodded. Jonathan walked briskly away. Ben watched him go. "Stuffed shirt, that one," he said, slapping Tom on the back. "But no worse than some I've seen."

"I can't get over how young you are," said Tom.

"And I can't get over how old *you* are!" said Ben. He led Tom into the small domed building. The room was circular, no bigger than a living room. The domed ceiling was dark. Fans of light bloomed from sconces along the curved interior wall. In the center of the room was a gold altar with a padded knee rest. White curtains covered the wall behind the altar. Ben gestured for Tom to kneel. Tom did so, resting his arms on the cushioned top, which was gold velvet.

A woman passed through the curtains and stood behind the altar. She had long hair and appeared to be a mix of European and Hispanic ancestry, about thirty years of age. She produced a binder and opened it, scanning it quickly. "Thomas Philip Waring?"

Tom nodded. The wall sconces dimmed. On the domed ceiling, thousands of tiny sparkles shone like stars. Tom thought of the stars on the ceiling at the hospital.

The woman's voice was pleasant but her manner was business-like. "You have attended Orientation?"

Tom nodded.

"Please vocalize, so your answers may be recorded."

"Okay. Ah, yes, I did."

"This altar is a symbol of your humility and desire for further knowledge. Who presents you?"

Ben said, "I am Benjamin Waring, his grandfather."

"Very good. The chain remains unbroken." The woman looked at Tom solemnly. "You have always existed. You are uncreated. Mind has no birthday and memory has no first."

Tom felt mesmerized by those great, expressive eyes.

"Throughout all eternity, you have always been you. No self can change into another. Identity remains. Nothing is something we never were and never can be. Do you understand?"

He didn't, but he said "Yes" anyway.

"As an eternal being, you have passed through many stages and have had many names. On Earth, you were known as Thomas Philip Waring. Is this true?"

"Yes."

She looked into her Record. "Yet you have another, older name. Would you like to know it?"

"Yes."

She placed her fingertips on his forehead and closed her eyes. "Your old name is known to you. Do you recall it?"

"No."

"It lies within."

Tom tried. "Sorry."

She removed her hand. "Mortality still holds you."

"It's because of my wife, she—"

"When mortality ceases its hold on you, you will remember your old name, at which time you will return to this place to receive it formally. Do you understand?"

"Yes."

"Now," she said, gesturing to the curtains behind her, "I will give unto you a knowledge of the Veil of Forgetfulness. During each stage of existence, the memories of the previous stage are veiled, in much the same way these curtains veil what is behind them. Because each stage on the Continuum is a test, memories and learning from the previous stages must be veiled.

"When you were born, your memories of your pre-mortal life were gradually veiled until you no longer remembered it. In the same way, the memories of your mortal life may interfere with your life here. Living in the past is never constructive. Therefore, a veil of forgetfulness will cover your mind; you will find it hard to recall experiences, events, and even people from mortality."

Tom was thinking about April, wondering how she was doing. Since he'd just barely died, she was probably still at the hospital. His heart grew heavy. He looked up at the woman. "I miss my wife."

She nodded. "Your heart aches for loved ones left behind. When you were born, you left loved ones, people you have since forgotten. Those memories will now begin to return."

Tom pulled his eyes free from her hypnotic gaze. "Huh?"

She smiled. "Welcome to Paradise, Thomas Philip Waring."

He took her warm hand. Ben said, "Welcome home, son."

The woman gestured toward the veil. Tom felt Ben's hand on his elbow as he came around the altar. The woman pulled the curtains aside, revealing a dark tunnel at the end of which a bright light burned. After a few steps he found himself outside on the plaza. Ben was by him. "How do you feel?" he asked.

"I forgot my—"

"Here it is." He handed Tom his Record. "Lots of input," he said, gesturing toward the domed buildings. "Easy to forget things."

"Grandpa, what's your old name?"

"I can't tell you."

"Why not?"

"Well, you chose to keep your Earth name, and that means your heart is still there. It would be wrong to tell you to things you don't yet wish to know."

"But it's just a name, isn't it?"

"It's more than that, it's a mind-set. But don't worry, as you get acclimated, you'll remember your old name and a lot of other things, too. Well, gotta go!" He grabbed Tom's hand, pumping it.

"You do?"

"I'm due somewhere. Your mystagogue will be back in a minute. He'll give you the grand tour."

He took off at a trot. He seemed so unlike the gray, stooped man Tom remembered. He realized he'd never really known his grandpa as anyone but an old man who held him in his lap and smelled of tobacco. He never knew a thing about him.

"Thomas!" Jonathan was striding toward him, reading his Record as he did. "So, you still prefer 'Thomas'?" He frowned.

"For awhile, I guess."

Jonathan said nothing, but began to walk. They passed the sculpture of Gabriel. "That will change," he said. "Soon enough."

April turned from the sink, her hands dripping. "Josh, you were supposed to clear the table!"

Josh ran into the room. "But I was watching—"

"I know what you were doing, mister!" snapped April. "I told you it would have to wait until your chores were done."

Josh began stacking plates, hurrying. He bumped a glass and it fell, shattering. April grabbed his arm. "Josh!"

"Oww! That hurts!" he wailed.

"I'll give you something to cry about! I tell you and tell you to do things and you ignore me, and then—this!" She picked up glass shards. Ted was licking up spilled Hawaiian Punch. "Get him out of here!" yelled April. "He'll swallow a splinter!"

Josh grabbed Ted's collar and hauled him away. He was sniffling, rubbing his arm where April grabbed him.

"Well? Clear the table!" She threw the glass in the trash, then thrust her hands into the sink of soapy water, feeling the heat rise up her arms. In a moment, she was in tears.

Josh started crying as well. April went to him and he backed away. "No, honey." She scooped him up. She pushed her hair from her face. The doorbell rang. "Great," she said flatly, walking to the entry and looking through the peep hole. It was Chuck. She set Josh down and dried her eyes with the dishtowel. Josh was hiccupping tears. Ted sat by the fridge, looking guilty.

April opened the door. Chuck was wearing a flannel shirt and jeans, his baseball cap pushed back to his crown. He had a stack of papers under his arm.

"Hi, Chuck," said April.

"Howdy," said Chuck, stepping inside. He looked at her red eyes and flushed cheeks, then at Josh, who was whimpering at her side. Chuck picked him up. "Hey, Josh-man," he said as he carried the boy into the living room.

"My daddy calls me that," sniffled Josh.

"I heard him call you that many a time," said Chuck, dropping the papers on the coffee table. He produced a hankie and held it to Josh's nose. "Blow."

Josh obediently honked into the hankie.

Chuck put it away. "Just the ticket for the blues." April stood in the doorway, feeling embarrassed and inept.

"Sit on down, honey," said Chuck. "Looks like you two are having a bout of the griefs."

April watched as Chuck cradled Josh just as natural as could be. She was amazed that such a bony old man could make such a comfortable seat for a child. Josh's thumb snuck into his mouth. "Just the usual," she said.

"Know what you mean," said Chuck, rocking Josh.

"More invoices?" asked April, nodding at the papers.

"Keep finding them all over the site. When we cleaned out the truck a couple of weeks ago, I thought we'd got 'em all."

"That's what I thought when I cleaned out the den," said April. "He had quite a filing system, didn't he?"

"If you could call it that."

They considered that for a moment in silence, then April found herself blinking back tears. She felt her lip quiver. "Not again."

Chuck stood and put Josh on his hip. He pulled April to her feet and put his arm around her. "There, honey."

April said, "Will it ever pass?"

Chuck thought of Carolyn. "I don't know, honey." His eyes were dry but they had a distant look.

"You must miss her so."

"I do. Surely do." His voice quavered. April took Josh in her arms. Chuck seemed gaunt, like he had been treading water for quite a while. "We're a sad bunch, aren't we?" she asked.

"We're lonely cusses, that's a fact. Sure do miss 'em."

April nodded. "Yeah. We sure do."

13

Chuck lit the candle on the dining room table and sat down. In front of him was his large leather-bound *Spirit Guide*. He'd been struggling through it for two months now. It was a compendium of religious history and occult practices. In it, he learned about the *I Ching*, the "Book of Changes," an ancient Chinese divination tool. He liked the theory of opposites, the *yin-yang* concept. As a carpenter, the concept of balance felt right to him.

He read about Hinduism, which promised transcendence through meditation. He was unsure about *karma*, where the deeds of one life influence the next, but he'd been practicing a form of *yoga*, meditating while seated on a cushion on the floor.

Then he became fascinated by Haitian voodoo, where adherents walked on hot coals, and Australian aboriginal creation myths. He liked the idea that the entire world is a temple in which to worship.

But the section on spiritualism caught and kept his attention. He read with fascination the exploits of famous "mediums," gifted people who entered trances, spoke to the dead, and levitated tables. He had even gone to a lady who billed herself in the phone book as a "Psychic Reader."

When he'd entered her back room, he sat on a folding chair in front of a card table with a red velvet drape over it. The woman, who called herself "Frieda," shook his hand. He could feel her long fingernails on his skin as she let go. She wore a black dress and a string of pearls. Her long hair was gray and her eyes a piercing blue.

She told him why he had come to see her. It was quite amazing. She knew he'd lost his wife; that she had died after a long illness; and that it had happened recently.

He expected crystal balls or incense sticks. Instead, they sat in the back of a storefront on Levy Avenue in National City, and he heard a teenaged girl out front talking on the telephone the entire time.

Frieda asked him what he wished. Before he could answer, she reached out for his hands. He felt kind of foolish, but she'd already proven her abilities by telling him things he had not mentioned on the phone when he made his appointment.

She read his palms, telling him that he would "approach another level of existence" soon. He figured she meant he was going to die. The thought didn't bother him.

Frieda closed her eyes and hummed. She still had both his hands in hers and his elbows were starting to ache from leaning on the table. He felt his neck getting stiff and turned his head. She squeezed his hands. "Don't move."

She continued humming, occasionally whispering, "Carolyn." Then she listened. Chuck found himself straining forward, listening as well. All he could hear was the girl on the phone.

"You're not concentrating," said Frieda.

"Sorry," said Chuck, impressed.

"Carolyn," she murmured. "Come from the other side. Your husband calls you. Speak to him."

Chuck closed his eyes. *Carolyn, please come. Please. I need to talk to you.*

"Silence!" said Frieda suddenly.

Chuck was unaware he had said anything.

"I feel her. She is coming toward us."

Chuck shivered. He wanted to open his eyes, but who knew what combination of seating arrangements, chanting, and hand-holding had drawn Carolyn here. He didn't want her to leave.

"Carolyn is here. Speak to us," commanded Frieda.

Chuck's heart quivered in his chest, afraid to beat.

"Chuck," came Frieda's voice. It was different, thinner and kinder. It *did* sound like Carolyn. "Chuck, I am here."

"Carolyn?" He opened his eyes. There was no one but himself and Frieda. Her eyes were closed and her face was peaceful.

"Speak to me," said Frieda in Carolyn's reedy voice.

"Oh, honey," said Chuck. "Is everything all right?"

"Everything is beautiful. I am at peace. What do you want?"

"I just wanted to know if you were all right."

"I am well."

He didn't know what else to say. All his words tumbled into heaps on the floor of his mind. His mouth opened but nothing came out. Finally, Frieda opened her eyes. "She is gone." She let go of Chuck's hands. They tingled where she had held them. She spoke in her own husky voice. "What did she say?"

"Don't you know?"

She shook her head.

"She said she's all right."

Frieda clapped her hands. "Wonderful!"

"She seemed upset at me for calling her back," said Chuck, just now realizing it.

"They often are, the first time. They are unused to piercing the veil. They need to get used to it, just as we do."

Chuck nodded.

"You had other questions for her?"

"I forgot them."

"That's only natural. Next time you will do better."

She gestured toward the door. Chuck backed out. "Jennifer will make another appointment for you," said Frieda.

Chuck left that day elated but confused. Elated that he'd made contact with Carolyn—of that there was no doubt—but confused that it had been so unsatisfying. He blamed himself for being tongue-tied, making a mental note to write down some questions for next time.

That was Saturday, three weeks ago. In the interim, Tom had died and Chuck broke the next appointment He now thought about death all the time, and even imagined himself lying on a table and someone pulling a white sheet over his face. He didn't mind. When Tom died so suddenly, he felt like the balance had been tipped toward the next world. Already, most of his circle was over there.

When he went back to see Frieda the next week, she couldn't reach Carolyn. She said his grief was a wall. He needed to have a more positive attitude, she said.

The next session was scheduled for Monday but he couldn't wait. He was sure he could reach Carolyn by himself. So here he was, Sunday at 1:30 A.M., sitting in the dark, trying to contact her.

He turned a page in the *Spirit Guide* and came upon a chapter about contacting the dead. Ouija boards, automatic writing, table rapping, even leaving a tape deck on RECORD at a preselected place and time. In Japan they worshipped their dead ancestors. He'd read about American Indian peyote ceremonies which contacted departed spirits. Afraid of drugs, he'd settled for a glass of sherry and a cigarette. He felt warm and muzzy. It was now or never.

He stared into the candle, visualizing Frieda and how she did it. He let his eyes go out of focus and laid his hands palms down on the table cloth. He whispered Carolyn's name.

He felt the evening coolness on his bare feet. He recalled Carolyn's image: her light blue eyes sparkling, her crisp, tight curls tucked under a gardening hat, her hands in dirty garden gloves, her knees black where she'd been kneeling on the ground.

He shook his head. What kind of an image is that? *That's not the way I'd want to be remembered*, he told himself sternly. *Think of her more . . . attractive.*

But he couldn't. In fact, the image of her gardening on a fall afternoon was the only image he could find. Her face would disappear below her hat brim and reappear as she looked up, asking him something. Her mouth moved but no words came out even though he could hear the crunch of the leaves under her knees and the trickle of the water leaking from a hose.

Chuck changed course. "Tom," he said quietly. "Tom. Speak to the living. Come from the other side and speak to me."

He visualized Tom wearing jeans and a tee shirt, his battered tool belt around his waist. He held a clipboard in one hand and a red pencil in the other. "Tom," said Chuck again. "Tom, hear me."

Tom stopped writing and looked at him. "What is it, Chuck?"

Tom stopped and looked around. "Someone just called my name."

"I didn't hear anything," said Jonathan. "We really have to be going. Your Naming Ritual went long and now we are behind schedule." He pronounced it "shed-you-ul."

Tom walked around the statue of Gabriel. "Someone I know."

"There's no one. Come *on!*"

Suddenly, it dawned. It was Chuck's twangy Texas drawl. "What is it, Chuck?" Tom asked the empty air.

Jonathan shook his head.

Tom listened. Nothing. He shrugged. "I could swear I heard a friend of mine call my name."

They began walking again. In the distance was the city skyline. Their route would take them back through the garden, toward the city center. Jonathan was walking fast, apparently upset.

"What's wrong?"

"Nothing."

"Okay," said Tom, shrugging, still looking for the source of Chuck's voice.

Jonathan shot Tom a hard glance. "If you must know, I'm tired of waiting on you. You seem to think everything here is on your schedule."

"Where were you born?"

"How is *that* relevant?"

"I just wanted to know. England, right?"

Jonathan sighed. "London. Nineteenth century."

"What did you do there?"

"Why do you want to know?"

"Just interested." He pointed to Jonathan's Record. "You know everything about me. I don't know anything about you."

"That is on a need-to-know basis."

"What?"

"It's none of your business. Too much personal interaction between a spirit guide and his charge breeds a lack of respect."

"Why?"

The road was busy with people, usually in pairs, often in deep conversation. The trees were green, the grass was manicured, and the air was sweet with the scent of flowers.

"Are you listening?" asked Jonathan.

"I'm sorry."

Jonathan shook his head. "You ask me questions and then you don't listen to the answers. I'll not be toyed with, young man."

"Sorry."

"My job is to get you acclimated. You will make new friends here and rediscover old ones."

"You don't want to be friends?"

"It's not that. That's just not my job description."

"You are pretty concerned with your job, aren't you?"

"My job is important!"

"I'm sure it is. You just don't seem to enjoy it very much."

"That is not true!"

"Well, you don't *act* like you enjoy it."

"A job isn't meant to be enjoyed. It's meant to accomplish a purpose. You will see—soon you will be assigned a job and you may wish you had a prestigious vocation like mine!"

"I wasn't knocking your job. I know it's important. But you don't seem to have much fun at it."

"What does fun have to do with it?"

The city skyline was a crisp cut-out against the cloudless sky. The buildings were tall and beautiful. Tom spread out his arms. "We're in Heaven, Jonathan! Think of it! We were right! On Earth we tried to do what was right and we've been rewarded. I'm not too clear about this Continuum stuff, but the fact is, I'm *here*! It's good to know that the small voice that guided me wasn't wrong!"

"Of course it wasn't."

"And I'm happy I made it!"

"You haven't 'made it' yet. Paradise is an extension of Earth. You're on probation—you could still falter."

"How? I've only been dead a couple of hours and already I know more than anyone on Earth! Gabriel told us the purpose of life! Why would anyone turn their back on the truth?"

"It happens."

"Who wouldn't want the things that have been promised us if we just do what's right?"

"People are still people, and some are contrary by nature."

"Well, it is a *little* obsessive here, but—"

"Watch yourself, Thomas. It's *not* obsessive; it's *perfect*, and the sooner you understand that, the happier you'll be."

Tom plucked a flower from a planter, inhaling its fragrance. "I don't think I'll have any problem with that."

Jonathan took the flower and tossed it into a trash receptacle. "I certainly hope not."

The city center was big, like New York, with skyscrapers and boulevards busy with people, but it was clean and there were no automobiles. Everyone had on tunics, except for business types like

Jonathan, who wore suits. The crowd surged around them, faces of every color. Everyone looked like they were coming home from a family dinner, satisfied and hopeful about humanity. But he noticed something. "How come there aren't any children or old people?"

"There are, they just don't look their age."

"What do you mean?"

"Well, people die at all ages. But here you get to choose your age, and naturally most choose their prime. About your age."

They stopped in front of an immense skyscraper. Huge letters over the entrance proclaimed COUNCIL BUILDING. Jonathan admired the impressive facade. "Tallest building in Paradise," he said proudly.

"What happens here?"

"This is where the Council meets—the ruling body."

"I didn't think you'd need leaders. I mean, there's *Him*, and then there's us."

"Even He delegates. What do you think a guardian angel is? We all share the load." He didn't wait for Tom to answer, he just strode on ahead.

They walked down a street bordered with trees shading sidewalk cafés. People were eating, served by white-coated waiters bearing trays of all kinds of food. Tom suddenly was hungry. "When do we eat?"

"Anytime you wish."

"Great. I'm famished."

"No, you're not."

"What?"

"*You* aren't famished—your physical body is."

"But my body's on Earth."

"While your spirit dwelled in your body, it became habituated to certain appetites. Eating is one of them. Sleeping is another. Although you don't *need* to eat or sleep, you may feel like you do."

"What's the point of that?"

"It's a reminder that the body's passions are strong. You might consider how much of your time is absorbed with the phantom needs of an absent body."

"Feels real," said Tom, eyeing a man carving a steak.

"I never eat. I prefer to use my time in better ways."

"Do you sleep?"

"Only when I need a break from incessant questions."

"You make it sound like a sin."

"Well, in *my* opinion, eating and sleeping are minor vices which signal a proclivity for self-gratification—along with some other more *intimate* activities I don't wish to discuss."

"You mean . . . ?"

"Please, Thomas, don't be crass."

"I just wondered."

"If your spouse is here, then certainly. But I prefer not to. It's base and unevolved."

That's probably what she *says.*

"I heard that," said Jonathan scornfully.

"Heard what?"

"Strong thoughts are communicated here. Anyone may eavesdrop if you are not careful. It is best to avoid emotional areas, including rude asides."

"Sorry," said Tom. "This is gonna be hard, having everyone listening in on my thoughts."

"You learn to keep them shielded. Excessive passion, positive or negative, will be heard by others. Best to keep on an even keel."

Tom spotted a boy in the crowd. His back was to Tom; he was looking up at an adult, licking a popsicle. "Josh?" Tom stumbled toward the little boy. "Oh, Josh, what are you doing here?" He turned the boy around. It wasn't Josh. The man who held the boy's hand was wearing a white suit. Tom couldn't take his eyes off the boy. His hair, his eyes, his mouth, all were so much like Josh, but it wasn't Josh.

"I'm Eric," said the boy, smiling.

"New Arrival," said his spirit guide, a tall black man.

"Oh," was all Tom could say. Jonathan steered him away. Tom said, "It looked like Josh."

Jonathan consulted his Record. "Your son is still on Earth."

"How do you know?" He reached out for the Record but Jonathan pulled it back.

"I have some basic facts, that's all. If a family member were to arrive, I would be notified, as would you."

Tom suddenly remembered his promise. He turned to face Jonathan. Eye to eye, Tom outweighed the Englishman by at least fifty pounds. "I've got to go back," he said evenly. "It's important."

"It's impossible. Prime Directive."

"What's that?"

"A key law."

"But I said I'd return and tell my wife that God exists."

"Indeed."

"She doesn't believe in any of this. She's an agnostic."

"Agnostic," sniffed Jonathan.

"I promised."

"Out of the question."

"Why?"

"It just *is*. Forget about it."

"I can't," said Tom miserably.

"You will," said Jonathan, walking ahead. Tom followed, his mind in turmoil. As they walked along, Jonathan kept a step ahead. Walking fast was apparently his way of not dealing with it. But Tom could think of little else. They passed fountains, parks, and massive buildings, but Tom walked with his head down, filled with guilt. He had forgotten his promise during most of this eventful day. April crossed his mind a few times but he was easily distracted. And when he *did* make it an issue, Jonathan flatly said "No." No discussion, no reasons, just "No." Jonathan didn't even want to know why Tom had made such a promise. Who ever heard of such a thing? Promising to come back from the *dead*? That alone should have piqued his curiosity. But not only was he uninterested in Tom's promise, he didn't seem to care about Tom at all. He strode ahead, his back bent defensively.

Tom wished for his grandfather and pulled out his phone. The face was blank; no keys or numbers. He shook it but nothing happened. He spoke his Ben's name into the plastic block. Nothing. Finally, he stuffed it back in his tunic, disgusted.

Soon they found themselves on the outskirts of Paradise City, standing in front of a sparkling white skyscraper with thousands of mirror-like windows. "Your new home," said Jonathan.

The lobby was like an expensive hotel, with thick carpeting and dark paneling. Mirrors reflected the glass entry. Jonathan stopped in front of a bank of elevators, holding the door open as Tom reluctantly entered. As they rose, Jonathan fixed his attention on the digital counter. The door opened on the 42nd floor and they walked down a featureless hallway. Jonathan stopped before a nondescript door. It didn't even have a knob.

Jonathan pushed the door open and Tom walked in. A tiled entry, a living room beyond, a kitchenette to one side. To the left was a bedroom and bath. Glass doors opened onto a balcony. Beyond, Paradise City rose magnificently into the sky. The light felt like late afternoon. "Will it get dark?" asked Tom, uninterested in the answer.

"We have day and night. Some people prefer the evenings, which are warm. Streetlights come on; the streets glow. Quite pretty."

Tom stepped out on the balcony. The city spread out, an oasis in a featureless emptiness that stretched to the smooth horizon.

Jonathan said, "You've had a busy day. More tomorrow. I shall meet you downstairs in the morning. 8 A.M.—sharp."

"I don't have a watch," said Tom listlessly.

"I'll give you a wake-up call."

Tom leaned on the railing, his head down. "Whatever."

Jonathan almost said something personal, then checked himself. "Don't hesitate to go downstairs. There are some nice restaurants. Go for a swim in the pool. There's even a shopping mall."

"For those of us with consumer addictions," said Tom icily.

"Just take it easy. Enjoy yourself. Soon enough, you'll be busy working and attending class. You'll feel better then."

"Right," said Tom, watching the ants below walking in and out of the building.

Jonathan left. When the light changed from gold to red to cobalt blue, Tom went inside and lay down on the bed. He stared at the ceiling. No one had bothered to glue stars to it.

He thought about April. He had died no more than twelve hours ago. She was probably home now. Tom hated to think about her and Josh being alone. April had probably called Vivian with the news. He could just imagine the questions Vivian would ask, all sorts of extraneous concerns that danced around the real issue of how April was doing. He imagined April trying to maintain, trying to stay calm and rational while Vivian asked her what clothes she planned to bury him in.

It occurred to Tom that he would miss his own funeral. He always believed that the dead were present to hear the nice things people said. But he didn't even know *where* he would be buried. *Oh well, I suppose that's something I'll find out when the time comes.*

He pulled a pillow over his face and imagined them lowering his coffin into a dark hole. He felt entirely alone. The irony was bitter: here he was in Heaven, feeling like Hell.

14

April's ten thirty was a teenager named Steven Menikoff, who had been in and out of rehab and recently assaulted a school teacher. He sat in the waiting room, making the receptionist nervous. He was a tall boy with spiked black hair and an earring. Like so many troubled kids, he wore the uniform: baggy jeans, Dr. Martens, a black tee shirt with something unprintable on it, and self-inflicted tattoos.

April had met with him three times and hadn't made any progress. She felt badly; the expense came out of the pockets of the people who were sitting in front of her: Roger and Sherry Menikoff.

Today was their first face to face. They had spoken on the phone, but after making no progress with Steven, she asked them to come in.

They told April about themselves without prompting. He was a stock analyst and she was a housewife. They had two other children. Steven was the youngest; the first two had been no problem at all. April watched their body language. Roger let Sherry enter first, found her a chair and then pulled another close so he could hold her hand. They let each other speak without interruptions. As they talked about their family, April could detect no dysfunction.

She queried them about drugs: pills, alcohol, etcetera. No, they didn't even drink coffee. They didn't know where Steven got his predilection for drugs. He was a connoisseur, having bragged of his experiments with everything from toluene to angel dust.

"I'm an advocate of the nurture theory," said April, closing her notebook. "Family problems can usually be traced to the parents' attitudes toward each other. Children learn to love by watching them."

"That makes sense," said Roger.

Sherry said, "Our children are our first priority. We check out their friends, set limits, and reward proper behavior."

"And it worked with the older kids," said Roger. "Three kids is a lot these days, but we've adjusted so we could be there for them: sports, school programs and all."

"It's perplexing," said Sherry, blinking back tears.

"It is," said April. "I expected to see some reason why Steven is so rebellious, but it doesn't seem that you are contributing to it."

"He scored in the ninetieth percentile on his I.Q. test," said Roger. "He's very smart, but he doesn't seem to care about anything."

"Or anyone," said Sherry.

April tapped her pencil on the blotter. "Thank you for coming in. If I think we need to talk again, I'll ask you back. For now, though, I'll continue with him alone."

Steven glared at April. "We can do this for as long as you want," she said, trying to remain calm. It wasn't easy; he'd just spit at her. "I hope you can express yourself better than that."

He laughed.

"I asked you about your family."

"I just told you," he sneered. He fingered his earring.

"You still thinking of running away?"

He shrugged.

"You've got it pretty good here."

"What's that supposed to mean?"

"Only that it must take a lot of energy to be so mad at people who care about you."

"They don't care. They just act like they do."

"What's the difference?" said April. "We are what we do. So if we act as if we like someone, then we probably do."

"That's crap," said the boy. But he was thinking.

"But you've told me your parents are morons."

"That's for sure," said Steven.

"Then they're probably not smart enough to fool you, right?"

He looked at her. *Go on*, said the look.

"If they're that stupid, then what they say is probably the truth—what they really think."

"They're idiots," reaffirmed Steven.

"It's rare for people to be straight forward. It's a good quality. You have it. But that's not all there is to you."

"I'm not telling you nothing."

"I'm sure there are things that make you happy, but all we've talked about are the things that upset you."

"That's just about everything," said Steven, tugging at a crucifix hanging around his neck.

"Are you a Christian?" She surprised herself with the question.

He laughed. "It's just a thing I wear."

"My husband was one." *April!*

"One what?"

"A Christian."

"So what?"

"He died last month."

"No way!" He leaned forward. "How'd he die?"

"Cancer." *Why am I telling him this?*

"Wow," said Steven. "I think about dying."

"What do you think about it?"

"It might not be so bad. The world's pretty wasted. The next place has got to be better."

"So you believe in an afterlife?"

"If there isn't, then who's to blame for all this? And if this is all there is, then *nothing* matters. Why not off that jerk who cuts you off in traffic? Why not shoot heroin?"

"Why not be kind to people?"

"Right," he laughed. " Good or bad—it doesn't matter."

"If there's nothing more."

He raised an eyebrow, amused. "Yeah."

April closed her book. "That's all for today."

"Now *I've* got a question."

"What is it?" It was the first time he'd initiated anything.

"Do you miss him?"

April nodded. And though this was the last place she thought this could happen, she could feel tears building behind her eyes.

"You think you'll see him again?"

The sixty four dollar question. "No. I mean, I don't know."

"But you hope so, right?"

"Yes."

"Hey, Doc, know what I think? I think *you're* the one who needs therapy. I don't believe in nothing and that explains me. But you—you kinda believe, but not really. At least I'm consistent: I *think* it's all meaningless. You're just *afraid* it is."

April knew she'd broken a taboo, bringing her personal life into a session. Since Tom's passing, her judgment had been lousy and everyone's attempts to console her didn't help. She must've heard "if you want to talk" a hundred times from her co-workers. But she didn't want any advice, she just wanted someone to hold her and let her cry.

The door opened. It was Dan Carroll. "Busy?"

She waved him in.

"Any progress?"

"Today went well. He opened up a bit."

"Yeah? About what?"

"The meaning of life. He says there isn't any. He asked me if I believed in an afterlife."

"And you said?"

"'No'."

Dan whistled. "Not the best answer for a kid like that."

"What would you have said?"

"I would have said there's a God in heaven who punishes drug-using psychopathic miscreants."

"I think he's a little past scare tactics, Dan."

"Then he's the first. Most of us hope there's a God so we'll be rewarded for the good stuff we do. But at the same time, we're afraid there's one because of all the stunts we've pulled. But you can't have it both ways. And so most of us—me included—try not to think about it at all."

"But what *do* you think?"

He looked at her for a long time. Something in his eyes made her look away, feeling exposed. He finally said, "I'll tell you everything I know . . . over lunch."

"Lunch?" *How did we get here?*

"So . . . ?"

"I'd better not."

"Okay. But I *do* have all the answers, you know."

"Maybe another time. It's too . . ."

"Okay. No hidden agenda. All right?"

"Okay."

The door closed behind him. April stared door, hoping there was an afterlife; it would take her that long to figure men out.

By mid-May, April's birthday had come and gone. Fortunately, almost no one knew. Tom's mom sent her a Mother's Day card with a photo of Tom when he was about Josh's age. Josh was standing close by and it was all she could do to get into the bathroom before the tears came. She shut the door and sat on the edge of the tub looking at the picture. Tom was standing in a wading pool, holding a squirt gun, a spray of water arcing toward the camera. He held a fudgesicle in his other hand. Then Josh knocked on the door. She put the photo in her pocket and dried her eyes. When she opened the door, there stood Josh in a pair of shorts, looking just like his dad.

On Sunday morning, Mrs. Kugler was honking her horn out
front. Josh sat, dressed for church, his face set. "I'm not going."

"Why not, Josh-man?"

He stared ahead.

"It's just for today. Next week Chuck will be back from his trip
and he'll take you. Mrs. Kugler is nice, you said so."

His eyes were fierce. "I don't wanna."

"I thought you liked church."

"Not without Daddy."

"But Daddy would want you to."

He looked at her defiantly. "*You* don't want me to."

"That's not true, Josh."

"Then why won't you go with me?"

Her eyes fell on a load of laundry. "I've got laundry to do."

"We're not supposed to work on Sundays."

"I'll go another time."

Finally, he said, "Okay."

Outside, Mrs. Kugler honked again.

Josh smiled. "Dad said it was impossible to get you to go. But
I just got you to," he said proudly.

"I said I would. I keep my promises."

"You better."

After he left, April rearranged her morning. She was going to eat
a leisurely breakfast and read the paper, but now she knew she'd better
do some laundry. Josh would notice. She decided to take Josh to the
beach this afternoon. The sun would do her good. She was pale and
felt like her entire life was going to and from work.

As she folded a batch, lost in the rhythm, her eyes moved across
the fireplace mantle. On it were family pictures—and the camcorder.
She wondered what it was doing there.

That eventful Friday, the evening sun came through the patio
doors. The camcorder tripod cast a shadow across the entry. She

headed for the bedroom, calling Tom's name. She didn't see the camcorder again after that—someone must've put it away, perhaps her mom.

April picked up the camcorder. There was a tape inside. One reel was empty. The bag lay in the corner. She fished around and found the cords.

She had never hooked up the camcorder before. Tom had been in charge of electrical things. He would untangle the cords, plug them in the right slots, all the while talking about something totally unrelated. And in minutes they'd be watching the video.

Tom took a lot of videos of Josh, saying he regretted not having many pictures of himself as a boy. April looked at the one of Tom with the squirt gun, now tucked inside the frame of a family portrait. After she got used to the new picture, she showed it to Josh. He laughed at how fat his daddy was at his age and asked her to put it by a picture of him. Side by side, they looked like brothers: blonde hair and big eyes.

April pulled the television out and fumbled with the cords. She finally got an image. There was Ted on the couch, watching something off-camera. He yawned, put his head on his paws, and closed his eyes.

The scene continued that way for a few minutes, then the camcorder kicked off and April heard the rewind whir. She wanted to stop and see what this was all about, but when she reached for the STOP button she had a feeling she should wait and see it from the beginning.

After a couple of minutes she heard a click and the camera was silent. She pushed PLAY, her heart in her throat. She tucked her feet up under her. The screen was gray snow. Then there was Tom, sitting on the couch in slacks and a polo shirt. Ted's muzzle was on his lap. Tom looked into the camera. "Hi, honey. I had some time today so I decided to make you a tape . . ."

April wanted to jump up and run around, sparked by the incandescent reality that here was Tom, talking to her. But she was also terrified—she was almost certain this was not something she really wanted to see. Unable to move, she let the camera run.

Tom began by talking to Josh. He reminded him he was the namesake of the prophet Joshua. April was glad she'd encouraged Josh to go to church today.

The image shifted in a quick edit. Tom was flushed and his eyes glistened. He talked about how they met, their wedding, and honeymoon. And sharks, at which point April had to stop the tape; she couldn't see him through her tears.

He ended by talking about what a miracle Josh had been and how he was moved by the birth. April wiped her eyes with a dish towel. Finally, he looked into the camera for a long time. April felt his eyes penetrate hers. He pointed to his head, his heart, then to her, silently mouthing the words "I love you."

April pointed to her own head, heart, then to the televison. "Me too you," she said, tears in her eyes.

As if he'd heard her, Tom smiled. Then he got up slowly, grimacing, his hand on his side. Ted watched him leave the frame, then yawned and went back to sleep.

No sooner did Tom lay down than the phone rang—or so it seemed. Jonathan informed him that they were to meet downstairs in thirty minutes. Tom showered, then took the elevator down. Outside, the light had a bluish morning quality, but he couldn't be sure—there was no sun in the sky, just a whitening at the horizon.

Jonathan asked Tom if he'd eaten. Tom said no. Jonathan said they had time if he wanted to. Tom wanted to, but didn't want to admit he was hungry. His mind was on April, Josh, Chuck, his mother—all the people he knew. He was homesick.

As they walked, he looked at Jonathan's Record, sure that any negative vibes he emitted would find their way into that book.

They arrived at a huge structure, almost as big as the Council Building. It was incredibly tall (gravity seemed to be a law low on the hierarchy here) and ornate. Fluted columns marched along the front.

Broad stone steps went up to doors standing open under arched portals. It looked like the biggest Greek temple in the universe.

"The Great Library," said Jonathan. "It contains all the knowledge of the human race, as well as all of the records. We spend a great deal of our time here compiling the data. History, science, genealogy, mathematics, philosophy. All here." He handed Tom a white card. It said BASIC PARADISE SKILLS: ROOM 4547."

"What's this?"

"They'll train you in the Record and communications."

"Oh."

"Try to be enthusiastic. Your first full day in Paradise. Good luck." He started to go.

"You're not coming?"

"I have another arrival in exactly half an hour. I hate to be late." It sounded like a reprimand.

"Will I see you later?"

"Drop by after your classes. I'm in the Council Building. Inquire of the receptionist, she'll give you the number."

He nodded crisply and headed away. Tom looked at the columns. He could make out a frieze atop the triangular cornice. He took a few steps back to get a better view. It showed several tunic-clad people in various poses: reading, lecturing, writing, pondering. In block letters it said, INTELLIGENCE IS ALL.

"Boy," muttered Tom, shaking his head, "am I in trouble."

Lecture Hall 4547 was a half circle that sloped dramatically down to a small platform. The room filled with people. Presently, a young boy entered and stood behind the pulpit. In a high voice, he introduced himself as Galamiel. He said he lived about three thousand years ago on the island of Crete.

Tom wondered why a boy was teaching the class. As if on cue, Galamiel said, "I died as a child of diphtheria. Since I never enjoyed the opportunity of growing up, I decided to grow up here in Paradise. I've been here about two hundred cycles and I'm about ten years old. Is that about right?"

Heads around Tom nodded.

"But I've discovered that it's difficult for people who've lived a long life to take me seriously. I assure you that intellectually, I am older than any of you. It is only my body which is young."

He continued. "Some of you may wish to try it. You are not limited to the age of the bodies you now possess. You may choose any age you wish. Of course there are considerations. If you choose an old body you may be treated with more respect, but you may not be able to play leap frog. If you choose a child's body, you may find it hard to see over heads." He jumped up and down, craning his neck, to demonstrate. Everyone laughed, including Tom.

"I've found that having a child's body with adult perceptions is quite exhilarating. It keeps my mind open to new ideas, since I am experiencing new things as my body changes. Right now I am nearing puberty. It is quite exciting! I encourage you all to give your spiritual body some thought," he concluded.

Tom figured he'd probably just keep things as they were. He considered his restored forefinger. *I guess I'll keep this.* He pinched his stomach. *But I wouldn't mind being a little skinnier.*

Galamiel explained the Record, which received constant updates from the central computer. To receive updates you had to fill out a questionnaire. The questionnaire itself was an inch thick. Tom groaned as he flipped through it.

The instruction on the phone went faster. It seemed that technology here was roughly at the same stage as on Earth. Galamiel explained that it would do little good to have technology that no one knew how to operate. He said when the first computer scientist arrived, there was a parade!

Someone asked why they had crude technology like the phones when there were things in Paradise that defied science, like choosing the age of your body, for example.

Galamiel said the Council made those decisions. There were many things that could make life easier but it wouldn't do to run before you could walk. They were progressing in technological terms, yet the limitations were reminders that technology is not an end in itself, but rather a tool to lead us to God.

Tom scowled at his Record. *Could've fooled me. This whole place seems to worship technology and organization.*

Galamiel looked at Tom. "You have a comment?"

The other students looked at Tom. He shook his head.

Galamiel continued. "Our friend here"—he consulted his book—"Mr. Waring, thinks we are over-concerned with technology and organization. Is that true, Mr. Waring?"

Tom was mystified as much as he was embarrassed. "I didn't say anything."

"Thoughts are powerful communicators. When you focus, they are easy to hear."

Tom felt his cheeks burning.

Galamiel turned away. "As I said—and I will reemphasize for Mr. Waring's benefit—all these things are *tools*. The Continuum requires knowledge in order to progress. How many of you noticed the words above the building entrance?" He looked at Tom.

Tom looked away.

"Mr. Waring did," said Galamiel.

Leave me alone. I'm sorry already.

"What did it say?"

Tom sighed. "Something about intelligence being everything."

"'Intelligence Is All'," corrected Galamiel. "Intelligence is light and truth. Truth can be used wisely or unwisely. The wise use of truth is *wisdom*—light—the key to progression on the Continuum."

People looked at Tom, their brows furrowed.

"How about you, Thomas? Do you subscribe to this credo?"

"I guess."

"Because if you do not, then life here can be quite . . . *limiting*. And to be limited is be what, class?"

A woman raised her hand. "To be limited is to live in Hell," she said, glancing at Tom.

"Quite correct. Hell is not a place—it is a state of being, where a person no longer desires to move forward, but prefers instead to sit down and rest."

Tom couldn't help himself. *Sometimes you need to.* He was afraid to look up. When he did, Galamiel had his head down, reading something in his notes. *Whew! He didn't hear.*

For the remainder of the class, Tom kept his thoughts quiet. It wasn't until he'd left the room with a card that said INTRODUCTION TO THE CONTINUUM: ROOM 7632 that he allowed himself to think freely. *It shouldn't be bad to ask questions. Anyone who doesn't like questions can't possibly like answers, either.*

The thought made him feel guilty. He felt like he was in high school again. He didn't do well there, either.

After classes, Tom trudged the main thoroughfare, heading toward the Council Building. His arms were full of books. He felt overwhelmed. The amount of information they threw at him! However, it occurred to him during one class that the attraction principle of particle physics wasn't so difficult after all, if you thought about it. Then it struck him: before entering that room he didn't even know how to *spell* "physics." Indeed, most of the knowledge he gained in school, outside of wood and metal shop, had been forgotten.

But though the classes were interesting, his mind wandered back to April and Josh. At times his heart was so heavy he could barely breathe. Everyone else seemed delighted to be here, almost impatient for more knowledge.

In a courtyard before an arc-shaped building, Tom sat on the rim of a fountain. He thumbed through his Record and found today's page, which had updated itself to include his homework assignments. By each entry was a small square, where a check would appear once he'd finished the assignment. He didn't even need to turn them in—he had only to finish them and enter the fact in the proper place and the city computer would credit him. It was based on trust, the only thing here that made sense to him so far.

He knew he'd have to forego sleep to finish his homework. He hated the idea of returning to that sterile hotel room they wanted him to call home. His home was a million light years from here.

He wondered what Dan Balmer would do now that he was dead. *I've been here two days. I died on Friday. That would make today Sunday.* Too soon for any changes yet on Earth. But when he did find out, would Balmer fire his crew and hire another contractor to finish? Chuck could handle the job but Tom figured he wouldn't get the chance. And what about the other guys?

Tom furrowed his brow. He couldn't remember their names. He could picture them, one tall and skinny, the other one short and dark. The tall one's name was . . . Levitt. Greg Levitt. But what was the other guy's name? He and Tom had surfed together a hundred times. He *knew* his name. It . . . was . . . right . . . .

This was impossible! They'd known each other ten years! Tom could see him yelling at a kid who cut him off on a wave, paddling after him, shaking his fist, scaring the kid silly, then lazily paddling back.

"What is his name?" His anger was choking off his thinking. "What was it? Ben? Bennie?" He said the names out loud, not recognizing any of them. Then a door opened. "Vinnie! VINNIE!"

The name was a linchpin. All the other information about Vincent DiCapo flooded back: where he was from (Valencia, California), his girlfriend's name (Naomi), his building skill (cement finishing). Tom hated the hole his absence had momentarily left in his memory.

Then he felt a surge of anger. That memory was *his*, and he resented someone covering up his memories or maybe even taking them away from him. He would see about this.

The Council Building elevator stopped at the 158th floor. Tom found Jonathan's office. There were three secretaries behind gray metal desks, all writing in their Records, all wearing white power suits. Tom felt underdressed in his tunic.

He was told to take a seat. He thumbed through a *Paradise Times* magazine. It had graphs and charts with ascendant lines. The people in the pictures had on big smiles. They looked hypnotized.

He was surprised at the vehemence he felt. Just then Jonathan stepped from an inner office and waved him inside. His office had an incredible view. City streets stretched out like spokes from the Council Building hub. In the distance a black gash cut diagonally across the view and something glistened.

Jonathan sat at his desk. Tom wanted to remain calm; just state his case diplomatically. "They're stealing my memories!"

"They're *what*?" Jonathan steepled his fingers.

"I tried to remember a friend's name and I couldn't!"

"You were informed about this during the Naming Ritual."

"But they're *my* memories!"

"And what do you want me to do about it?"

"Stop it!"

Jonathan shook his head. "Impossible."

"I have to go back."

Jonathan sighed.

"To Earth."

"Yes, you told me before."

"But I promised."

"You don't know what you're asking."

"It's important."

"You think you're an important man, don't you?"

"No. But the promise is."

"Do you think you're the only one who wants to go back?"

"I don't know."

"Well, you're not. Many wish to return. They all have unfinished business: children to raise, lovers to comfort. Even revenge to exact."

"So?" said Tom. "There must be a policy to cover it then."

"Oh, there's a policy all right." Jonathan opened a drawer and withdrew a stack of papers an inch thick. He tossed it to Tom. It was titled REQUEST FOR FORMAL POLICY CHANGE.

"There you are. Fill it out and I'll see that it gets into the proper hands."

"Whose hands are those?" asked Tom, hefting the stack.

"Mine, to begin with. Then it goes to my supervisor, then to hers, then to his, and up a few levels more."

"Who makes the final decision?"

"The Council."

"Can't I just talk to them directly?"

"Those are the channels."

"This is too complicated."

"If you want to change a policy that has stood for six thousand years, you'd better be prepared for some work," Jonathan said firmly. "We will see how important your promise is. What price are you willing to pay?"

15

By the time April pulled to a stop in front of the Lot, it was sunset. Josh was sleeping over at Jeremy's tonight and April couldn't bear the thought of spending another Friday night alone. She had started driving with no destination in mind but she wasn't surprised when she found herself here.

To the west the sun was sandwiched between black clouds and ocean. The sun's last rays heliographed bronze off shoreline windows. Out to sea, near the horizon, hung curtains of gray rain. Soon it would be raining here as well. April didn't mind the gray sky; it echoed her feelings exactly.

When at last the sun sank, April focused on the Lot. "Not a great building lot," Tom used to say. It would be difficult to build on. The roof of Josh's fort had been pulled off a couple of months ago and they hadn't been here since to repair it.

Over the ocean, a finger of lightning crackled. April counted, waiting for the thunder. A distant boom sounded. Four seconds. She didn't know how far away that meant it was. Tom would know. He knew things like that, practical things that would mean the difference between staying dry and getting soaked.

The thunder reminded her of San Simeon. It was early in their marriage. They spent the weekend there and went on all three tours.

Tom took a zillion pictures. He was amazed at the massive colonnade surrounding the indoor Olympic-sized pool. The furnishings and statuary impressed April only in their ostentatiousness, but for Tom, the opportunity to build anything he wanted, at any cost, was his idea of nirvana.

They stayed at nearby Cambria, in a motel perched on cliffs overlooking the turbulent ocean. The clerk suggested they watch the video *Citizen Kane*, which was based on William Randolf Hearst, the newspaper tycoon who built San Simeon. It was Orson Welles' *tour de force.* Many thought Welles would be ruined for libeling such a powerful man. He was and he wasn't, said the clerk. Hearst never laid a hand on him, but didn't need to; Welles wrecked his own career, a victim of his own astonishing talent and hubris.

April had seen the movie but Tom had never even heard of it. They watched the video in their room. They had trudged up and down a thousand stairs that day. Before long, April was asleep. A thunderclap woke her. The movie was ending. Workers were tossing furniture into a huge fireplace. A man threw a sled into the fire and flames ate the word "Rosebud" stenciled thereon. The last shot was smoke pouring out of a chimney.

Tom turned off the TV. April asked groggily, "What do you think?" wondering if he had slept through it as well. Tom went to the window and pulled the drapes. It was raining and lightning crackled out to sea.

"He had it all."

"Yeah, but he blew it."

"You think we'll blow it?" He turned to her, his face concerned.

"We don't *have* anything to blow! We're paupers!"

"I mean, how do we know we won't blow . . . *us?*"

April heard worry lines in his voice. "We won't."

"Everyone has their weakness. For Kane it was money."

"I don't think we'll have to worry about money coming between us," said April lightly.

Tom sat on the bed. "It could be something else."

"No way." She pinched his arm.

"Ow!"

"That's for doubting us."

"I don't doubt *us*. I doubt the world." He rubbed his arm. "But we've got an edge on Charles Foster Kane—we're not in a movie! We don't have to follow a script."

Tom said abruptly, "What if you get tired of me?"

April rolled her eyes. "When we were walking around the castle, I was watching you. While everyone else was lusting after the tapestries, the furniture, and the idea of hundreds of servants—"

"Not to mention owning all the land as far as the eye can see."

"Yeah. While everyone else was wishing they were rich, you were just admiring the workmanship."

"What's not to admire? It's an amazing structure."

"But you'd rather meet the guys who built the place than the owner, right?"

"What's that got to do with us?"

April patted the bed. He lay down, facing her. "The reason I'll always love you is that you are *grounded*. Of all the people I know, you are the most unaffected by that kind of external junk. You don't care what other people say or think or like—you like what *you* like."

"I like you," said Tom, winking.

"Well I'm nuts about you . . . in case you wondered."

"But sometimes I feel pretty . . . *clunky* around you. I mean, I might know how to nail wood, but I don't know much else."

"Don't know much about history?"

Tom raised an eyebrow.

"Don't know much biology?"

Tom smiled and started singing in his tuneless baritone. After the first line April joined in.

> *But I do know one and one is two,*
> *And if this one could be with you,*
> *What a wonderful world it would be.*

April laughed. "Boy, we are *horrible* singers!"

Tom lay back. "We cain't sang, but we gots heart."

Leaning against the warm car hood, April began humming "What A Wonderful World" and thrust her hands deeper in her coat pockets. She looked at the darkening sky. Rain was coming. She made up her mind. She didn't care what the realtor offered her. She would hold on to the Lot so she could come here and look at the ocean on nights like this and remember Tom. That was reason enough.

By late September, April had gotten back into her life, at work at least. Home was another matter. Josh was cranky and demanding. He seemed to hold everything against her; she had never seen him nurse grudges like this. When he would pout and pitch fits she would remember how much her own father's death affected her and she was twice Josh's age at the time. But when she'd put her arms around him to calm his fussing, he would break away, blaming her for his anger.

She was thinking about this when Michelle came into the lunch room. "How's things?"

April reminded herself to be cordial. She liked Michelle, but lately she didn't have much to say to anyone. As the silence stretched out, Dan walked in. He went to the fridge, pulled out a brown paper sack, sat down at the other table and began reading a newspaper.

A minute later, Trish bopped in. She was popping her gum, her bleached hair a wiry nimbus around her face. "Hi, Dr. Carroll."

"Hi, Trish." He went back to his paper.

"Can I sit here?"

Dan squinted at Trish through his half-glasses, then over at April and Michelle, then back at Trish. There were two tables. He couldn't get the math right. "Sure," he finally said, moving his *Union-Tribune*.

Trish spread her stuff on the table. Dan tried to go back to his paper. She put an end to that. Her voice was tinny, wound up a notch too high. Dan tried to be a good sport. She was yammering and he was nodding, his brow furrowed.

April heard herself say to Michelle, "I want to ask you something."

"Okay, but remember, I only play a doctor on TV."

April lowered her voice. "Before he died, I made Tom promise me something."

"What?"

"To come back from the dead."

The moment it was out, she regretted it. It hung there absurdly in the air, neon and garish.

Dan looked over. So did Trish. Her mouth was full but she was still talking around a bite of sandwich. She turned back, pulling Dan's attention by sheer force of will, if not by reason.

Michelle leaned close. "Excuse me?"

April closed her eyes, mortified. "I made him promise that if there was a God, he'd come back and tell me."

Michelle said flatly, "From the dead."

"Yes." *This is what being mentally retarded feels like. I ought to take notes.*

Michelle considered, then smirked. "So? Has he?"

"Of course not!" April felt her cheeks reddening.

"And what does that mean?"

"I don't know!" April looked at the table. She whispered, "I shouldn't have told you."

Michelle laughed. "Did you think he *would*?"

"Of course not. I'm just wondering what got into me. I mean, what was I thinking?"

"Maybe we should ask the head shrink." She turned to Dan.

"No!" said April. She could feel Dan's and Trish's eyes on her. Out of the corner of her eye, she saw Dan collecting his papers self-consciously, trying not to look at her.

"Ooh! What happened then?" asked Trish. "I read this book about a woman who—"

Dan touched her arm. "Trish, can I ask you a question?"

Trish's gum popped. "Sure, Dr. Carroll. What is it?"

Dan turned her away. She looked back, hoping to hear more. They disappeared through the doorway.

April was burning with embarrassment. Michelle mimicked Trish's brittle drawl. "So, what happened then?"

April rose and walked out the door.

Tom walked out of Jonathan's office with the REQUEST FOR FORMAL POLICY CHANGE form under his arm. On the elevator, he thumbed through it. It was a hundred pages of small headache-inducing print. A tall man standing by him said, "That'll be the day."

"What?"

"'Policy Change'—that's a good one!" he said jovially. He smiled at the woman standing next to him.

"Poor thing," she said sincerely.

"What?" asked Tom again.

The small woman dug an elbow in the man's ribs.

"Ow! Marina, what in the devil . . . !"

"Don't mind him." Her voice was tiny and frail, like her.

"Far as I know, ain't never been a Policy Change," said the tall man, stepping away from Marina's sharp elbow.

"Why not?"

"Guess they don't want any."

"Can't think of anything I'd change," added Marina.

"How long have you been here?" asked Tom as the doors opened on the first floor. The tall man walked out ahead and Marina fell into step beside Tom. They crossed the airy lobby.

"We've been here twenty cycles. "We're from Nebraska territory, in the United States of America."

"Gracious, Marina, he knows that. He speaks English."

"I thought everyone spoke English here," said Tom.

"Oh, no. Without you even noticing it, your mind translates. But if you watch people's lips, you'll see that sometimes they don't match what you're hearing."

"That means they're talking a different language," said Marina helpfully. Her mouth was full of scattered teeth.

"Nebraska territory?" asked Tom.

"I was an undertaker. Saw many a man to the grave. If I'd known how nice it was here, I'd've taken more joy in my work."

"Imagine, an undertaker in Paradise!" said Marina, as if such a thing was impossible. She reached to shake Tom's hand. Her husband bowed. "Good luck." They walked toward the street, his arm draped across her narrow shoulders.

Tom suddenly felt dizzy and almost fell down. He found a bench and sat, holding his head in his hands. After a long excruciating moment it passed.

A beep came from his Record. He opened it. In block letters at the top of the page it said, "Cycle 2: Thomas Waring." Below that, a red entry blinked. It said STUDY PERIOD: GREAT LIBRARY. The word MAP blinked in red. Tom touched it and a box appeared containing a detailed map of Paradise City. A dot blinked next to the Council Building. Another blinked a few streets away.

Tom looked across the nearly empty plaza. Magnolia trees ringed the square. The fountain gurgled quietly. Tom remembered passing here yesterday, when it was crowded. The fountain was on high then. Now, with no one around, it was almost still.

He started toward the Great Library. *Why is everything called 'great'? It's like they don't trust you to be impressed; they've got to hit you over the head with it.* Paradise was the most obvious place he'd ever seen, full of over-done buildings and millions of rules. He flipped through the Request Form as he walked. *Another prime example.*

He passed many people. Without exception, they smiled or said hello, but they seemed in a desperate hurry. He found himself slowing down, thinking how this place made him want to be contrary. He wondered if that would pass, along with his memory. That made him slow down even more.

The Library was a huge hall. The distant ceiling was covered with cherubs and angels, like the Sistine Chapel. *Of course. Michelangelo is probably here.*

The hall was a hundred yards across, ringed by bookshelves, with tables and chairs in the center. People were scattered about, studying. On either side, broad marble stairways switchbacked up to the higher stories, which overlooked the main floor. On each floor he saw row after row of books.

Tom sat at an empty table, scanning the Form. They wanted to know everything about him, but they *already* knew everything about him. *They can read my thoughts, for crying out loud!* He looked around. No one looked at him; everyone was apparently lost in their studies.

But an old woman behind a desk *was* looking at him. Tom avoided her gaze. When he looked up again, she was standing in front of him. Her white hair made tight curls around her face and her blue eyes had crinkles at the corners. "May I help you?" she asked pleasantly.

"I don't think so." Tom placed both hands over the Form.

She stuck out her hand. "I'm Helen."

Tom shook it. "Tom."

The silence stretched out.

"If you don't want company," she said.

Damn mind readers!

Helen's mouth made a little "o." "Sir, please!"

"Sorry. I'm still not used to people reading my mind."

"I certainly don't try. In fact, your . . . *comment* about mind readers was the first thing I heard."

"Oh. Then why did you come over here?"

"You don't have to be a mind reader to see that you're feeling blue. I thought you might want someone to talk to. But if you don't, then *I'm* sorry."

"No. I'm sorry. Please, sit down." He tried to smile. She sat down. Tom's hands went to the Form, covering it.

"I see you have some homework," said Helen.

Tom nodded.

"I can help. I'm a librarian. I know where everything is."

"It's a big place," Tom said stupidly.

"It is indeed. All the Earth's accumulated knowledge! Why, I could spend an eternity here!"

Great. Then checking himself, he thought, *That's great!*

Helen read him well. "Of course it's not for everyone. To most people, knowledge is just a tool. But for me, learning itself is the most fun." She lowered her voice. "You see, on Earth I was illiterate."

"Really."

"In my time, almost no one could read. There was hardly any writing at all where I lived."

"Where was that?"

"Northern Europe. You're a New Arrival, aren't you?"

"I got here yesterday."

"You're on your second cycle. Just a baby!"

"How long have you been here?"

Helen somehow produced her Record out of thin air. She flipped a few pages. "Two hundred and fifty five cycles."

"Is that a long time? Do you like it here?"

"Oh, yes! This is *my* idea of Heaven! I find a good book—say something by Thomas Hardy—he was a wonderful writer, do you know him?—and a soft chair with a footstool, and I read him cover to cover. Have you read *Jude the Obscure?*"

Tom shook his head. "I've heard it's good, though," he lied.

Her face lit up. "Do they still read Mr. Hardy . . . down there?"

"Sure," said Tom, digging deeper.

Helen's face was rapturous. "That's wonderful! He's so profound." She placed a hand over her bosom, calming herself. "But enough about me. How are *you* finding Paradise?"

Tom almost said he didn't know it was lost, but she didn't deserve his sarcasm; she was a sincere soul. "It's hard," he ventured.

Even that was too much for Helen. "Hard? In what way?"

"I feel like I don't belong here."

She patted his hand. "Oh, don't be silly. They don't make mistakes like that. Of course you belong here!"

"I mean, not yet."

She looked at him blankly, then recovered. "Oh! You mean you went early—that it wasn't your time?"

"Maybe I'm supposed to be here; maybe it *was* my time. I don't know. But I *do* know that I've got to go back to Earth." He showed her the Form. "That's why I'm doing this."

Helen scanned the title, her eyes wide. "Oh my."

"Yeah," said Tom. "But I hear they never approve these."

She nodded slowly.

"You've been here a while. Have you ever heard of a case?"

"Well, there are a few, but they always come from . . . Upstairs," she said, looking up. "Things *never* go up. They come down from On High."

In frustration, Tom shoved the Form. It slid across the polished table and stopped, balancing on the edge. *If it falls, it's a sign.*

"That's superstition," said Helen. She fetched the Form. "If you feel that strongly about it, you shouldn't give up. I know you wouldn't want anything that was wrong."

"How do you know?"

"Well, if you weren't a good person, you wouldn't be here. But, aside from your mysterious 'mission' on Earth that you won't tell me about—"

"I just—"

"I don't want to know about that. That's private and you've probably discussed it with your mystagogue. But I've got a feeling that even without that you'd still be unhappy. Is that right?"

Tom nodded.

"Cheer up! It takes time! It's a big change! My goodness, what a change Paradise was for *me*! We lived without electricity, plumbing, computers, automobiles, or nuclear energy. I lived in a rock and thatch hut my whole life. Fortunately, we *did* have fire!" She smiled.

"I don't fit in with the people. Everyone is happy; I'm not."

"You should be! I hear the *other* place is full to bursting with miserable people."

"It's just not how I thought Heaven would be."

"What did you think it would be like?"

"I thought they'd give me a harp and I'd sit on a cloud and take it easy, kind of like Club Med."

Helen looked at him blankly. "Club Med?"

"Forget it."

By the time Tom finished the first ten pages of the Form, it was dark. He was tired, but he was glad he'd met Helen. When he told her he had to practically write his life's story, she took him upstairs and pulled out a nondescript black book. On the cover, in white lettering, it said:

THOMAS PHILIP WARING
son of Vivian and Donald Waring
b. August 11, 1963 at Yuma, Arizona, USA
d. April 19, 1997 at Solana Beach, California, USA

"What's this?"

"Your life's story has already been written!"

Tom turned the book over in his hands, amazed. "You people work pretty fast," he said, flipping through the pages. It contained all the events of his life, even the private and embarrassing ones. He shut the book and looked at Helen. "Who wrote this?"

"Your guardian angel. But it's not complete yet."

"It isn't?"

"One of your duties is to finish your story. As you can see, it doesn't contain any of *your* opinions about things. Just the facts. It's your job to flesh it out, to explain things."

Seeing his name on the cover, with his birth and death dates, gave Tom vertigo. He stared at it. "So I'm really dead."

"But not finished," added Helen. "You've got a lot of work to do! Look here!" She pulled out a volume that was three inches thick. "This man has been working hard on his story!"

"But what's it all for?"

"It's one of the books we'll be judged from!" said Helen brightly. "The people Upstairs keep a set, and your guardian angel wrote this version, to which you will add your explanations." She was beaming at the symmetry of it all.

The book suddenly looked menacing to Tom. "Then this is my defense at the final judgment."

"It's more like an *interview* with God. But you won't be alone. Your family and friends, your guardian angel, and all the people who've known you will be present as well!"

Tom suddenly felt sick. "Sounds crowded."

"It will be a wonderful day! The books will be opened, the stories—*your* story—will be told and an accurate version will be recorded. *That* book will be placed in the Celestial Library."

"Have you been there?"

"Oh, no, honey. It will be built in the eternal worlds, not here in Paradise. But I hear it will be beautiful, with crystal chandeliers and marble floors! Every book will be white with gold lettering—a book for everyone who has ever lived!"

"Wow," said Tom.

"And what stories! For a person like me, it *will* be heaven! Reading about people's lives, then meeting them and discussing what they've done!"

"So this place here," said Tom, looking around at the stacks full of thin, incomplete books, "is like a branch library."

"It's a pale reflection of what will be, that's true."

"You said my guardian angel wrote this?"

"Yes."

"Where is he? I want to talk to him."

"You'd have to ask your Guide. But he's probably on Earth. When you died, he was given another person to watch over."

"How do you know it's a he?"

"It makes sense."

"How do you know about all this?"

Helen stood taller. "I was once a guardian angel."

"You were?"

"Most people choose to do it for at least a little while. Some people really love it and keep at it. But most, like myself, find it too taxing, to stay on Earth amid all the wickedness. I did my time as an angel, but when the time came, I was happy to come home. Still, there are many who find it exhilarating, doing battle with the Dark Spirits."

"Dark Spirits?"

"Those who rejected the Plan and chose to stop their progress on the Continuum. Haven't you been taking notes in your classes? They discuss all of this."

"I may have missed a couple of classes."

"Well, you should go! The Dark Spirits are souls who were basically lazy and when the opportunity came to go to Earth, they said no thank you. That would have been fine—everyone has the right to stop if they want to—but when God told them that if they didn't come to Earth they would never have mortal bodies, they rebelled, claiming He had no right to stop them. And then there was a war, you know."

"I knew about the war. I never knew what it was about."

"Well," said Helen, "go to class! And come back any time!" She walked away, head held high.

Tom read his book straight through. The light faded, the Library emptied, and the chandeliers glowed. Tom read on. When he finished, it was dark and there were only ten people left in the Library. He looked at Helen's desk. She was gone. In her place a brown-skinned woman sat reading.

He refiled his book and worked on the Form for awhile, then left, walking down the dark streets. A few people strolled along, but most moved with a purpose. Tom went to his room, his brain overloaded. He had spent the evening reading about his own life, yet it seemed like the life of a total stranger. The book did lack emotional content, but not details, even if they were external ones. He had forgotten about the time he caught a water snake and took it home, where it died three days later. He was devastated and thereafter never had much interest in pets. It wasn't until April insisted on Terrible Ted that he had another pet, only because she said she'd be responsible for him.

There were also a few places where he closed the book, embarrassed to read further, and even more embarrassed at the thought that *others* might read it. All his activities were chronicled, *all* of them, good and bad, including small sins like cheating on a spelling test in seventh grade. But so was his fumbling with Sara Hill's bra strap behind the gym after a high school dance, as were his more "private" sexual experiences.

Early high school was a bad time, with puberty and his parents' divorce. At this point, the book began to wear Tom out and he closed it, disgusted at himself for living such a small and inconsequential life. He considered stealing the book so no one else could read it. That idea gave him another. He went to the shelf and pulled out another book. The cover said:

ALLYN WARNOCK
son of William and Elisabeth Warnock
b. June 22, 1575 at Devonshire, England
d. August 13, 1601 at Devonshire, England

He grasped the cover and pulled. It wouldn't open. He tried digging his fingers between the pages. He couldn't penetrate them. It simply wouldn't open. He looked at the book, relieved. *No one but that guy can read his book. I hope that's true with mine as well.* The thought gave Tom some solace. *Still, if God can read my book, who cares who else reads it?*

And one day God certainly *would* read it. What a day *that* would be.

Now, back in his room, Tom walked out onto the balcony. The city was bright against the darkness. A breeze fluttered the curtains. Hundreds of memories he'd forgotten (or wished he could have forgotten) roiled in his head. He went inside, pulled the drapes, and lay on the bed. He couldn't get his mind to be still. It kept going over the memories, explaining and rejecting things he'd done on Earth. He was a fraud. He knew he had no excuse; he'd had an easy life. He never went hungry, never fought in a war, was never sick, never lost anyone close. Life had been one long buffet and he'd gorged himself, never considering who prepared the meal or what it might cost. He was considering now. He had the feeling that his early death was no accident. Soon, they were going to present him with a bill. He mentally searched his pockets—they were empty.

16

"Daddy?"

Tom came into the room. "Yes."

"Daddy, can you hear me?"

"I'm right here, Josh. What is it?"

Josh looked right through him. "Daddy!"

Tom knelt by the bed. "Daddy's here. What is it?"

Tears welled in Josh's eyes. "Daddy, where *are* you?"

"I'm right *here*, Josh."

April walked in. "Honey, what's wrong?"

Tom stood. "I don't know what's bother—"

"Honey," said April, ignoring him, "what is it?"

Josh's eyes were full of anguish. "Mommy!" April pulled him into her arms.

Tom came around the bed. "What's wrong with him?"

April held Josh close. "It's all right."

"Daddy," sobbed Josh.

"What?" asked Tom, "What about me?"

"It's okay, Josh. I know."

"Know what?" asked Tom. "What's *wrong*?"

"He won't answer," said Josh.

"Josh!" yelled Tom. "I'm HERE!"

"I know," said April. "He's gone. I'm sorry,"

"I'm NOT gone!" said Tom. "Look at me! April!"

April seemed different. The skin around her eyes was bruised-looking. Tom touched her cheek but she didn't react. "April," he said.

"Oh, Tom," said April, rocking the boy.

"April!" Tom tried to connect with her eyes.

"Why'd you have to go?" she asked the wall.

"I'm here," said Tom, his hopes sinking. "Right here."

"Why aren't you here?"

Because I'm dead.

He awoke. It was night and he was in a hotel room, on an impossibly hard bed. He got up and washed his face, looking at himself in the mirror, demanding an answer. None came. Finally, in disgust, he turned away. *Liar.*

Jonathan stood outside the door, tugging on his shirt sleeve. His watch said 11:47. He knocked again. Inside, someone stirred.

Tom opened the door. His hair was uncombed and his eyes were bleary. "Oh, it's you," he said, turning away.

The room was a shambles. The bed was unmade. Crumpled paper was strewn on the floor. The drapes were closed. Outside the day was bright; in here, it was dark and stuffy. "What's all this?"

"I'm working," said Tom, sitting down, writing.

"It's nearly noon."

"Is it?"

"Yes, it *is*," said Jonathan. "You've interrupted my schedule. I'm a busy man," he added, looking for a place to sit. He pushed some papers aside and sat on the bed.

"I'm almost done."

"You missed your classes!"

"I'll make 'em up."

"This isn't high school!"

"It's beginning to feel like it."

"I resent that!" said Jonathan, standing.

Tom collected sheets of paper. "Don't take it personally. You're just doing your job."

"That's absolutely right!"

"I don't blame *you*," said Tom, scooping pages off the bed.

"Blame *me*?! Now look here, young man! You miss your classes and they notify *me*, and I have to drop everything—including a *very* important meeting with my supervisor—and come over here because you won't answer your phone—"

"It's on the balcony. I didn't want to be disturbed."

Jonathan sputtered. "So I have to come all the way over here to see why you've missed your classes! Didn't you know that this morning you were to receive your work assignment?"

Tom ordered the pages he'd collected.

"You cannot thumb your nose at the regulations, Thomas! It just isn't done! We all have our duties! Yours is to attend your classes and do your assignments!"

Tom handed him the sheaf of paper. "Okay. Here's my first one."

"This is not an assignment."

"It is to me. It's my Policy Change Request Form."

Jonathan dropped it on the desk. "I know full well what it is."

"I hope it won't take too long."

Jonathan stood. "You have the cheek! You put me out and then you ask me to hurry and do *your* bidding?"

Tom sat on the bed, giving Jonathan the height advantage. "I meant I hope you can *find time* to look at it. It's—"

"Important! Your earth-shattering, all-important promise!"

"I would appreciate it," said Tom. "Really."

"You are becoming a thorn in my side, Thomas Waring. Be warned. I am a patient man, but I do not brook insubordination. Things are *expected* of you."

Tom felt better now that he'd finished the Form. The awful dream he'd had of Josh was beginning to fade.

Jonathan picked up the Form. "I'll tell you again: this is unlikely to be approved." He shook the papers for emphasis.

"I know," said Tom. "That's what everyone says."

"Well?"

"But I hope you'll pass it along anyway."

Jonathan shoved the Form under his arm. "You should concentrate on the *present*, not the past."

Tom held out his hand. "I'll try."

Jonathan ignored it. "I'll do what I can. On one condition."

Tom nodded.

"Go to class! Now!"

Tom smiled. "Thanks, Jonathan. You're a real friend!"

Jonathan found himself in the hallway, walking toward the elevators. "Friend indeed," he huffed.

For several days after the lunchroom incident, April felt like Dan was avoiding her. At first she was relieved at his sensitivity—at least she hoped that's what it was. But she was afraid that he was simply embarrassed for her. When a week went by and he barely spoke to her, she began to suspect that her stock had fallen with him.

On Monday, nine days after the incident, April couldn't stand it anymore. She had to know what he *really* thought. The realization that she cared so much about his opinion surprised her. She had never given Dan a thought. He was nice looking, but she knew little about him, only that he was an excellent therapist who knew how to pull the truth out of people. He said people knew what to do; they just needed the courage to do it.

In her own sessions, April found it difficult to focus as patients rambled on about insignificant things. She wanted to get them on track, to deal with their problems. Dan, on the other hand, would listen for an hour and never even ask a clarifying question. And people would gush out their most intimate details. He had the gift.

I'll say, she thought as she found herself outside his office. *Here I am, ready to spill my guts, dying to know what he thinks of me.* She had to know. She knocked.

"In," came his voice.

She opened the door. Dan wore a blue pinstripe shirt with braided maroon braces. He had his back to her, hunting and pecking at his computer. "What is it?" he said.

"Dan?"

He turned and pulled off his glasses. "April!" He caught himself and pulled back, lowering his voice. "What can I do for you?"

"I need to . . . talk to you."

He shuffled papers on his desk. April felt an impulse to bolt. Then he said, "I'm sorry."

"For what?"

"For avoiding you."

"You've been avoiding me?"

"Yes. And you me."

"I guess," she said. "But I'm the one who should apologize—"

"Nonsense!" said Dan. "Sit. Please."

April shook her head. "I might need a quick getaway."

"From me?"

"No, from the situation. I'm embarrassed."

"Don't be."

"It's just that . . . now that you know what happened . . ."

"I didn't hear much, but it sounded personal."

"It was."

"Then don't tell me. I was embarrassed *for* you, not *at* you."

"You didn't think what I asked Tom to do was . . . bizarre?"

Dan looked carefully at her, measuring his words. "Not really. In fact, I've thought a lot about it and I decided that it was a very rational thing to ask, kind of like a scientific experiment."

"I felt like I was giving in."

"Giving in?"

"To believing there's something more."

"That's a sad way to put it. Of course there's more."

"Like what?"

April was wearing a gray suit with a charcoal gray blouse. Her auburn hair, recently cut, curled loosely around her face. She looked pretty and vulnerable. "Loving someone is something more," he said, striving for simplicity.

"But is there something more than that?"

Dan shook his head. "Isn't that enough?"

April sighed. "Not when they're gone."

"April, I'm sure your husband understood what you were asking. You loved him; he knew that."

"Thanks," she said. "I was afraid you might think I was . . . you know . . . *clinical*."

"You are the most rational person in this room."

"Thanks for not judging me."

"Oh, I judged you, all right," said Dan, coming around his desk. "And you were not found wanting." He put his arms around her. She allowed herself to hug him back, and suddenly tears were falling.

"Your shirt," she said between muffled sobs.

"Doesn't matter," he said, stroking her hair lightly.

They stood like that until April pulled away. "A hug between friends, nothing more," he said, giving her a tissue.

April dabbed her eyes and left quickly. Dan leaned against his desk as the door closed behind her.

Over the next week, April avoided Dan. She believed him when he said it was just a hug between friends, but she couldn't be sure. Maybe even he didn't know how he really felt. She was certain that she didn't know how *she* felt. She caught herself—twice—remembering how it felt to have him hold her. Up until then, she felt like she would fly apart at any moment. But when he hugged her, she felt like her parts might settle back into place . . . maybe. She discounted the feeling as the simple need to be held and put Dan Carroll into the background.

A couple of days later she came to work and found an envelope on her desk. She opened it. The note inside said:

> *Dear April: I'm sorry about what happened. It was*
> *inappropriate. But sometimes a hug is good therapy. I hope you*
> *understand. If you want to talk, I'm available. Maybe sometime over*
> *dinner—as friends.*   *Dan*

April put the note down. Here she was, someone who spent her days counseling others about dealing with real issues and not inventing false ones, and she was imagining that Dan had intimate feelings for her, when the truth was he just wanted to help. She was amazed anyone would care at all, the way she'd been acting. She picked up the phone and dialed Dan's extension. It rang, then clicked to his voice mail. After his greeting, she heard a tone.

"Dan, it's April. I'm sorry I've been acting so . . . weird. It's not your fault. I've just been . . . wallowing in you-know-what. Maybe a dinner with friends is what I need."

She paused. Something felt wrong. "I mean, *as* friends. You know. I hope so, at least."

This was getting worse. *'I hope so'?* And now it was on tape! She had to end it, and soon. "Anyway," she said, hurrying, "sometime is okay. Thanks for being concerned. You're a friend. Bye."

You're a 'friend'? she thought crazily as she hung up. *What kind of lame thing is that to say? 'A friend'? Like he isn't a friend already? I should've said 'a* good *friend,' or something casual like that.* She looked at the phone, then buried her head in her hands. "I am such an idiot."

For the next two days Tom tried to keep up with his schedule. He had classes in astrophysics and quantum mechanics, and—most amazing—he understood some of it! Maybe he wasn't stupid after all. In addition, he had no difficulty recalling things he once knew.

During a biochemistry lecture, the instructor mentioned something about symbiosis. Tom recalled seeing a film in high school about sharks and the tiny fish that clung to them. He remembered their name: remoras. Then every detail of the room came into his mind's eye. He saw Jackie McCall, the willowy blonde cheerleader. She was wearing a print blouse and Levis. That day the teacher, Miss Richards, had worn a brown skirt and a white blouse with a scoop neck. Tom could even see his own Adidas tennis shoes tapping the tile in boredom.

When he came back to the present, the instructor had moved on to discuss things that even the greatest Earth scientists hadn't imagined yet. It felt odd to know things that no one on Earth knew. Yet Tom also knew he was one of the slowest people in the class. The boy next to him was taking notes, muttering, "Makes sense" over and over. Tom thought about the advantage all that knowledge would give a young person. He began to regret that he hadn't read more. *They'll cure me of that if they get their way.*

It was like that in all his classes. His mind absorbed things with astonishing rapidity. In his Pre-Mortal Existence class, the discussion of transformation from pure intelligence to proto-physical spirit-being elicited a glimmer of recognition. He felt sure what they were saying was true. It *tasted* true. In this regard, he was pleased. On Earth he had been at a loss to explain why he felt he *knew* things. Here, those same feelings of certainty confirmed the truth and he didn't need any more convincing than that.

Walking out of the class, he felt a shimmer of hope: maybe his gut responses would help him overcome his intellectual shortcomings. It was difficult, though. There were people in the class far smarter than he and the result was a visible *change*. He thought about a girl in the row in front of him. He noticed her because she looked like a teller at his bank. She was plain as an empty ledger sheet. But on the second day—the second day!—she glowed! She didn't even take notes; she just leaned forward, listening intently, her eyes bright. The knowledge was making her somehow *brighter*. Looking around, Tom detected that some people were brighter than others, as if they had a higher wattage bulb inside.

Tom wondered how he looked. On the street, he would seek his reflection, to see if he too was growing brighter. He couldn't see any change. He tried not to worry about the progress of his Policy Change Request or if it was still sitting on Jonathan's desk. He was afraid of what he would do if that was the case. As he thought this, he saw his reflection in a window. His face was dark with worry. *In a world without a sun, where the people give off light, I'm actually growing darker.*

He didn't look in another window the rest of the cycle.

On the afternoon of the fourth cycle, he sat in a café across from the Great Library, drinking lemonade and feeling vaguely guilty. His phone rang, startling him. Thus far, no one had called him and he'd almost decided not to carry it anymore. He pressed SEND. Instantly, Jonathan—or rather a remarkable likeness of Jonathan—was sitting across from him. He assessed his location, frowning at Tom's lemonade glass.

"Thomas. How are you?"

"Fine." Tom felt as transparent as Jonathan's hologram.

"You're between classes, right?"

"I've got Heavenly Hierarchies class in an hour."

"Meet me by the fountain in front of the Council Building."

"You have news? My request?"

"Twenty minutes," said Jonathan and switched off. His image dissipated like smoke.

Tom felt heavy and light at the same time, two emotions battling. Twenty minutes! It was too long.

Five minutes later he was at the Council Building. He considered going up to Jonathan's office but maybe Jonathan hadn't called from his office. *I'm so nervous I've just got to move.* He started toward the building, but something in the fountain caught his eye.

Sheets of water fell in curtains from angular stainless-steel projections. Tom could see muted shapes of people on the other side.

But in the smooth wall of water, he saw something else. Himself. But it wasn't a reflection; the perspective was impossible. He stood between the fountain and the Council Building. By all rights, the columns and stairs should be behind him. But in the water, his reflection stood on an empty plain, flat to the horizon. And he was looking up at something.

Tom followed his double's line of vision across the street to a gray building. On the second floor were a dozen identical oval windows, all empty, except for one. A woman with dark shoulder-length hair rested her forearms on the sill, watching the people.

Tom looked back at the fountain. Now his twin was looking right at him. He felt a chill course down his spine. This wasn't his image in a mirror; this was a *different* person. He didn't know what to do, so he raised his arm . . . and waved. The reflection laughed, then pointed at the woman in the window. Tom looked, his arm still raised. The woman waved back. He took a step forward and she disappeared. He turned back to the fountain. His reflection was gone. Instead, the columns of the Council Building undulated in the water.

"Thomas!" came a voice. There was Jonathan, striding toward him with an envelope under his arm.

"What's with that thing?" asked Tom, pointing at the fountain.

"The fountain? Why?"

"I just saw something in it."

"Perhaps it was a penny."

"It was like a vision. Of myself."

Jonathan frowned. "Perhaps in your vision you were faithfully attending your classes and behaving yourself."

"I was on a plain, looking at something. When I looked where my reflection was looking, I saw a dark-haired woman in that building." He pointed at the oval windows.

"So?"

"Have you heard of such a thing?"

"A woman in a window? Why, yes. I think there *is* precedent."

Tom's temper bumped up a degree. He pointed at the package. "That for me?"

Jonathan was instantly all business. "Yes, it is."

Tom took the envelope and opened it.

"I'm afraid it's not good news," said Jonathan.

Tom pulled out the REQUEST FOR FORMAL POLICY CHANGE form. In red block letters across the first page it said DENIED. "Why?"

Jonathan sighed. "As I said, it's a Prime Directive: no one may return to Earth except for extraordinary reasons."

"'Extraordinary,' huh?"

Jonathan nodded. "I'm afraid yours was rather . . . um . . . pedestrian."

"You mean 'ordinary'."

That's what pedestrian means," said Jonathan automatically.

Tom glared at him. "I just wanna know one thing," he said, tossing the Form at Jonathan, who caught it clumsily. "Did *you* recommended it?"

Jonathan clutched the Form to his chest and raised his chin. "I did not."

"Why not?" Tom felt his anger rising.

"As I told you: it's against the rules."

"Did you tell them *why* I wanted to go back?"

"Didn't *you*? Wasn't that in your request?"

Tom looked icily at Jonathan. "You didn't even read it! Thanks a lot, *pal*," he spat and walked away, shoulders hunched and head down, like he was heading into a snowstorm.

Jonathan called out, "You can always appeal!"

Tom pushed his way through the crowd. The way he was walking, people made way. He didn't see anyone or anything; everything was darkness. It wasn't long before he was on the outskirts of the city. He figured he'd just head for the horizon and throw himself off the edge.

He plowed along, feeling stupid, dressed as he was in some kind of bathrobe and sandals. *You'd think they could come up with something a little more dignified.* Then he thought of Jonathan and his three-piece power suit and he got even angrier. *Of course they give the authority types the suits, a not-so-subtle way of telling the rest of us we're peons.*

He was walking along a path which wound between tall sycamores. The trimmed lawns had given way to mounds of bunch grass and bare earth. Here and there rocks jutted through. The land seemed drier. It was entirely comfortable, yet at the same time, entirely bothersome. Every plant and tree gave offense. The whole place was manicured—even this "ramshackle" area—designed to meet some perceived need for disorder, but never total disorder. Heaven forbid.

Heaven forbid. This is a place where they forbid everything. Boy, would I like to go back to Earth and tell them what Heaven isn't. It isn't peaceful and restful. It isn't a place where you are rewarded for a good life. It isn't home. It's just another station along their stupid "Continuum."

Tom was sure his thoughts were carrying for miles. He looked at the city rising grandly into the sky. He was finally alone. The garden had given way to stunted oaks and manzanita brush. The ground cover disappeared entirely. He decided to keep walking. Back on Earth, when he was upset he always went to the beach and stood on the cliffs, smelling the ocean. There was a place he knew where the winds had carved a narrow slit in the cliff, where you could lean over the hundred foot drop and not fall because the wind blew constantly, holding you up.

He didn't like the way he was feeling. On Earth his conscience always helped him avoid trouble. He was amazed that the very things that aided him on Earth were discounted here.

Besides, forget conscience. His request wasn't wicked or selfish. *Well, maybe a little selfish.* Although he would love to see April again, he needed to go back for *her* sake, not because he liked going against the grain. He had always had faith in the grace of God—he never figured it would somehow work against him.

"Besides," he said out loud as he trudged along, "I promised. Doesn't that mean anything?" As he crested a hill, a great vista opened up. A huge, red chasm cut diagonally across the view. He remembered seeing it from Jonathan's office. It was the first real boundary he'd seen and he was certain that those red walls plunged down forever.

He stopped short, his heart suddenly pounding. The idea that Paradise was some sort of pie tin in space with sharp edges falling off into nothing made him instantly queasy. He would have gone no closer to the chasm if not for the bridge.

It spanned the wide chasm like spun glass, glowing brilliantly, its ends arching down to meet the walls. The center of its span was fearfully thin. It couldn't be more than ten feet wide, a mere thread over a bottomless abyss. And it seemed to undulate as if it was alive.

The path wound down the hillside and crossed the bridge, then continued on the other side, disappearing into a forest, which was obscured by low clouds. They were the first clouds Tom had seen. With a shiver Tom suddenly knew that the land beyond the bridge was not Paradise. *Definitely* not Paradise.

Between Tom and the bridge the land was mostly empty, except for a few small forlorn stands of aspen. A shack faced the bridge terminus. As he walked up behind it, Tom made out a pair of white combat boots, crossed at the ankles, moving back and forth slowly.

He tried to keep his eyes off the chasm. The path paralleled the edge but kept its distance. Wind gusted up from the chasm, carrying the smell of darkness on it. He thought of the beach cliff. He would never trust this wind to hold him up. On the contrary, he was sure it would pull him into the abyss where he would fall forever.

The bridge was too bright to look at, but out of the corner of his eye he could tell that its brightness came from within. The topside was a narrow, smooth pathway, with a black cable running above it, three feet high, connected to nothing, just hanging there.

Tom approached quietly. He had almost arrived at the shack. The white combat boots moved rhythmically. As he neared, he heard humming. *Probably a hymn.* The humming stopped and the person began to sing, deep and low, "Honey, honey, yeah . . ." and then started humming again. Tom knew the song.

> *I heard it through the grape vine,*
> *Not much longer would you be mine, bay-bee . . .*

Tom couldn't help himself. He laughed. A chair leg scraped and the boots hit the ground. A huge man with a blonde crew cut and white fatigues rounded the corner. "Who are you?"

Tom looked up at the looming guard.

"I said, who are you?"

Tom could see the ropy muscles in the guard's neck. He had on a white helmet and held a white baton in one hand. "Nobody."

"Okay, Nobody, what're you doing here?"

"Taking a walk." Tom took a step back. "Looking around. I'm new."

"New Arrival, huh?" The guard shoved his baton back into its belt loop. "Shouldn't you be studying or something?"

"I saw this and wanted a closer look. What is it?"

"The Bridge. Haven't you been going to class?"

"Sure," said Tom. "But I've never seen it. It's amazing."

"It sure is," said the guard proudly. "That's for damn sure."

Tom gaped at the guard.

"Sorry. Twenty years in the Corps. Old habit."

"It's worth strong language."

"He built it, you know," said the guard, lifting his chin.

"What's on the other side?"

"Hell, of course. You better start taking notes in class, buddy. This is basic info."

"Hell," repeated Tom. *That's why it gave me the creeps.*

"I heard stories that'd make you wet yourself. That place is full of the worst there ever was on Earth. Quarantined."

"Then why is there a Bridge?" asked Tom, following the guard's inflection, emphasizing the word.

"Two reasons: one—and I got better things to do than tutor you so I'm only gonna say this once—one: it's so we can go over and teach those poor bastards—sorry—*slobs*, the truth, and two: so they can cross the Bridge once they believe and repent. Then they can live in Paradise. Got it?"

Tom felt like he should salute. "Yes, sir."

"Oh, and there's another reason."

"What's that?"

"Earth's that way."

"What?"

"No lie."

"I thought Earth was back there." He pointed toward Paradise City.

"That's coming *from* Earth. To go back, you cross the Bridge and turn right. Otherwise, you go straight . . ." He stopped, grinning.

Tom frowned, feeling like a straight man. "Straight where?"

"To Hell!" The guard guffawed at his joke.

Tom tried to laugh. "Does anybody ever go there . . . ?"

"Sure. Those that mess up here—"

"I mean, to *Earth*. Does anybody ever go back *there*?"

Tom could almost see the gears moving inside the guard's big square head. "That way's used by the Dark Spirits. People from the Upper Regions, guardian angels and such, leave from Heaven, where He lives."

"Well, thanks," Tom said, starting toward the Bridge.

The guard grabbed Tom's arm. "Where are *you* going?"

"For a walk, that's all."

"Well, you cross the Bridge and you might as well just keep going straight." He released Tom's arm. "Prime Directive: Nobody Does Nothin' With Out Permission."

"That's awful broad."

"Yeah, it creates a multitude of sins!" He laughed. Tom smiled thinly. *This guy's a dim bulb.* Suddenly, the guard stopped laughing. "I think you'd better get on back now," he said, putting his hand on the butt of his baton.

"Sorry. I didn't mean—"

"On your way," commanded the guard. "Go on."

Tom walked up the path. He could feel the guard's eyes boring into his back. *I knew this was a prison. Guard posts!* He clenched his fists. *The more I find out, the more I hate this—*

He stopped at the crest. Paradise City glinted on the horizon. Just off the path, twenty feet away, a man was lying on a large rock.

Not only that, he was lying there *naked.*

Tom laughed, but the man gave no indication he'd heard. He just lay there, arms stretched out, eyes closed, his tunic a pillow.

Tom couldn't help himself. "Uh . . . hello?"

The man opened one eye. "Hello," he said, and closed it again.

"Excuse me."

The man exhaled loudly. "You're excused."

"What are you doing?"

The man shook his head, his eyes still closed. "Isn't it obvious? I'm sunbathing."

Tom looked up. "But there's no sun."

"I don't see how that's any business of yours," said the man, raising himself up on one elbow and looking at Tom.

The guy really *was* naked. "You're right," said Tom, turning away. "I was just wondering."

The man uncoiled his tunic and put it on. "You can turn around now," he said, tying the belt. "I'm decent!"

The man was short and thin. He seemed to swim in his tunic. His short brown hair stuck out every which way and was mottled with gray. His ears protruded, making him look attentive, like a mouse. His eyes bulged and blinked often. His nose was large, with flaring nostrils. Tom walked over and extended his hand. "I'm Tom."

The little man frowned up at him, his arms folded across his chest. "That your Earth name or your pre-Earth name?"

"My Earth name."

"I'm Stan." He held out a large bony hand. "Hate those pre-Earth names. Pretentious." As they shook, Tom thought of twigs.

"I'm a New Arrival," said Tom.

"That a fact. I been here forever, seems like."

"You're the first one I've seen who wasn't rushing somewhere."

"What's wrong with that? What if you're in a hurry?"

"It's just that nobody takes time to . . . I don't know . . . *think*."

Stan furrowed his brow. "How do *you* know?"

"I don't. It just looks that way to me."

"Looks'll fool ya."

"But you haven't answered my question: why were you sunbathing, when there's no sun?"

"My answer is still the same: what business is it of yours?"

"None, I guess."

"Well," said Stan, "I don't tell nobody nothing I don't want. And if I *do* want, then I tell 'em *when* I want. Got it?"

Tom backed away. For some reason this Stan seemed awful hostile. "I was just asking." He turned to go.

"Now, if you'd asked me," said Stan, addressing Tom's back, "'What do you think about . . . *that*?' Well, I'd probably answer you straight up."

What an oddball, thought Tom, then regretted it. Tom turned, expecting a scowl, but Stan obviously hadn't heard a thing. He was just looking at Tom with his bulging gray eyes, his thin lips pursed.

"Okay. 'Hey, Stan, what do you think about . . . ?'"

"What?"

"Uh . . . sunbathing when there's no sun?"

"Ah!" said Stan, pushing off from the rock. "That's a very interesting question. Answer: I do it 'cause I like to."

"Oh."

"You expected something more . . . profound?" Stan had a tongue that moved too quickly. It made Tom think of snakes.

"No."

"Ask me another," said Stan, walking ahead. Tom fell in behind him, his usual position in Paradise.

"What do you think of Paradise?"

Stan stopped, put his hands on his hips and dropped his head, shaking it. "Don't tell me. You're one of *those*."

"I am not," said Tom reflexively.

Stan turned. His teeth were uneven. *This is not an attractive man*, thought Tom. He was pleased that he could think freely around someone who hadn't developed the ability to listen in.

"Are too," said Stan, sing-songing.

"Forget it." Tom walked toward the path.

Stan called out, "No more questions?"

"I don't like the answers."

"Ask better questions!" Stan walked back to the rock. He was loosening his robe, ready to shuck it.

"All right!" yelled Tom. "What do you do when you want to keep a promise, but nobody will let you?"

"Is this a trick question?"

"No!" yelled Tom, feeling instantly foolish.

"You keep it anyway!" yelled Stan, then turned away.

Tom yelled, "What if it means breaking a lot of rules?"

Stan had taken off his robe. As he lay down, he yelled, "Rules schmules!"

Tom shook his head. Rules schmules. This weird little guy was right. He remembered Jonathan saying something about an appeal. But he wouldn't do it Jonathan's way; he'd go straight to the top, to the Council itself. He felt a surge of energy. "Rules schmules!" he yelled, waving.

Stan's eyes were closed. He yawned. "Whatever."

17

They were still settling into their new home and everything was in boxes. Josh was perturbed. April told him he could be Batman for Halloween, but her sewing machine was still packed away. Josh sat in the Nissan, sulking. "You said I could."

She made a turn onto Genessee, avoiding a boy on a bike who looked like he was going to fall. Josh watched the boy and turned to April. "You said you'd help me on my bike, too."

"I will. But I'm busy now. You'll have to hold your horses."

"I hate horses," sneered Josh.

April sighed. This was the worst time of year to move. Josh had already started school. But the lease was up on the house in Solana Beach, and with Tom gone there was no reason to live that far north. Kearny Mesa was just ten minutes from downtown. That meant she had another two hours a day to spend with Josh, who clearly needed the attention. "We'll get started on your costume tonight."

"It's too late," he said.

"We've got three days."

"I want the one at the store."

"We can't afford it. They want fifty bucks."

"It's worth it," countered Josh.

"It'll have to do, Josh-man."

"Don't call me that."

"But you like being called Josh-man."

He scowled at her, his arms folded. "Not any more." He was implacable, his arms folded across his chest, his face dark with anger.

It wasn't until they pulled into the driveway that he quit pouting, jumping out and running inside. "Ted! Here boy!" Ted bounded out of the living room with something red in his mouth.

"Ted!" yelled April, prying a silk scarf from his mouth. "It's ruined! Bad dog! Bad *dog*!"

Josh, glad to see someone else get yelled at, pointed his finger at Ted. "Bad dog! Bad *dog*!" Ted accepted the compliment, barking and wagging his tail.

April threw the scarf in the trash. The kitchen was full of boxes. She was so tired from the move that they were still sleeping on mattresses on the floor. She looked at the kitchen. *I can't do this.* Josh walked around, kicking cardboard boxes. He stopped in front of her and said, "My costume!"

"I told you: I don't know where the sewing machine is. We'll have to find it."

"I'm hungry."

"Well, which is it? The costume or dinner?"

"Both," said Josh, kicking a box as walked out.

"Don't do that!"

In the hallway, he kicked another box. She started after him. The doorbell rang. She looked through the peep hole. "Oh no."

It was Dan. He was standing on the porch holding a flat cardboard box in one hand, a plastic sack in the other. He was looking around at the overgrown yard.

Josh ran back into the entry. "Who is it?" Ted was barking.

April looked at herself in the entry mirror. She was still in her work clothes, so that wasn't too bad. But her hair! She smoothed it down in one place and fluffed it in another. The bell rang again.

Josh yelled, "Open it!"

April did. There was Dan, wearing jeans and a black polo shirt. "Pizza man!"

"All right!" yelled Josh.

"Hi, Dan," said April. "I'm afraid you've caught us . . . in a mess here."

Dan hefted the plastic sack. "Then I'm glad I bought dinner."

"All right!" yelled Josh.

Ted barked his approval.

"Shh!" April waved Dan in. He put the pizza on the counter and began clearing away boxes. April helped. "We're in such a mess. I'm so embarrassed."

"You offended me, you know, by not asking for help."

"I didn't ask anyone."

"I know, and we all hate you for it." He opened the pizza box. Josh pulled off a pepperoni and tossed it to Ted.

April started rinsing glasses. "You didn't have to."

Dan opened a Coke. "That's why I wanted to." He turned to Josh, who was eyeing the pizza. "So, you're Josh."

"Uh-huh."

"I'm Dan. I'd like to be your friend."

"Okay," said Josh warily.

"Here's how it works. If I ask you to do something, you do it. And if you ask me to do something, I do it. Deal?" He stuck out his hand.

"Okay," said Josh, shaking it.

"Now here's what I'd like you to do. Are you listening?"

Josh nodded.

"Would you please clear the table so we can eat?"

"Yessir!" said Josh, getting right to his task.

April dried a glass. Dan found a knife and cut the pizza. Josh was indeed clearing the table. *Yessir. This is more like it.*

Tom walked briskly toward the Council building. He paid no attention to the people passing through the glass doors, each with a Record under their arm, eyes focused ahead.

Inside, he paid no attention to the marble floor which was polished to such a gloss that an exact reflection of himself walked in perfect cadence on the soles of his feet.

In the elevator, Tom *did* pay attention to his own heartbeat, which bumped along feverishly as the car sped upward. When their speed equalized, he took a breath and looked around. He was met by noncommittal smiles. *If they knew what I was about to do, they wouldn't be smiling.*

The door opened several times on the way up and people exited and entered, but well before the one hundred fiftieth floor Tom was alone, looking at his reflection in the stainless steel doors. He was split from head to toe by the seam where the doors met. He noted how appropriate the image was.

The message board above the button console said, "Trust in the Lord with all thine heart; and lean not unto thine own understanding. Proverbs 3:5." He frowned. *That's the trick, isn't it? You've got to choose between your head and your heart. My head tells me one thing and my heart says another.* He watched the final numbers flick by: 197, 198, 199 . . . . Then the car stopped and the doors slid open.

He stepped into a plush reception area. An empty desk stood in front of two heavy oak doors. The walls were papered in foiled patterns above a dark mahogany wainscot. Pools of light bathed ornate couches and chairs. Windows formed one wall. Tom was drawn to the view. From this height, he could see the arc of the horizon. His eyes searched for the chasm. There it was, slicing across the distance.

"May I help you?" A middle-aged woman with silver hair stood before him, her fleshy arms folded across her chest.

"I'm here to see the Council."

She walked to her desk and sat. Tom followed her. "Out of the question. If you had an appointment"—she tapped her Record as evidence—"*then* you would be received."

"I made a formal request of the Council, but it was denied."

"Well," she said conclusively.

"And I thought that maybe I didn't explain what I needed very well, because, you know, it isn't much I was asking for after all, just a small thing, and a very important thing—for me, not for them. I mean, for them, it's just a snap of the fingers."

She closed her Record, her eyes hard. "I'm sorry."

You're not sorry at all. "But—"

Just then the elevator doors opened and Jonathan stepped out.

"Jonathan!"

"Thomas?"

"Nuts," said the receptionist.

"What brings you here?" asked Jonathan, arriving at the receptionist's desk. She invented a tight smile for him. "Good day," he said. She nodded, then went back to her Record.

"Jonathan, it's about my Policy Change Request."

"Thomas, what, pray tell, are you doing here?"

Tom took Jonathan's arm and pulled him over by the windows. Jonathan glanced down at Tom's hand, frowning. Tom let go. "I came to see the Council."

"You *what?*" sputtered Jonathan. "Now listen here—"

"The answer . . ." Tom took a breath. ". . . I can't accept it."

Jonathan looked at him like he had two heads. "Your request was denied, Thomas—by the Council. They do not reverse themselves. You simply must accept their decision."

"But I can't!" He raised his arms, placed them against the window, and rested his forehead on the cool glass. "It's not fair."

"Well, perhaps not—by *your* lights—but I assure you that it is quite fair. Prime Directives always are, in the long run."

"The real problem is this: I've been talking with a guy who said I shouldn't just accept the Council's decision."

"Indeed. And who was this malcontent?"

A strange feeling surfaced in Tom's chest. "Just some guy."

"What was his name?" pressed Jonathan.

"I'd rather not say."

"Thomas, do you hear yourself? When you arrived, you were pleasant enough—perhaps a bit flummoxed—but on the whole you exerted acceptable effort to get acclimated. But now, you're withholding information and getting advice from the wrong sorts of people—"

"I thought only good people made it here."

"People are people. They have their pride, which is the worst sin of all. A prideful person often winds up being both wrong *and* disobedient."

"I'm tired of hearing about obedience."

"It's the first law of heaven, Thomas."

"I made a *promise*. On Earth, that means something."

"It's very commendable."

"Except when it conflicts with *your* agenda."

"It's not *my* agenda, and I'd appreciate it if you wouldn't make this personal. I am not your enemy—I am your Guide. I have nothing but empathy for your position, but the Council made its decision, and I tend to agree."

Tom looked at him hard. "Did you love anyone on Earth?"

"Of course."

"Who?"

"That's none of your business." Seeing Tom's face, he softened. "My wife. I loved her very much."

"How much?"

"I don't know what this has to do—"

"How much?"

Jonathan stared out the window, his jaw set, a small vein pulsing at his temple. "More than my own soul," he said quietly.

"Is she here? Is she with you?"

"Yes, she is."

"Then you're lucky. You're together."

"I suppose that's true."

"Which is true? That you're together or that you're lucky?"

"Both, I suppose."

"Well, I may not be so lucky because April doesn't believe in any of this. In my Eternal Choices class they said everyone on Earth gets one chance to believe—one good, solid chance. Right?"

"Yes."

"So what did I do? I spend the last six years trying to give April her chance! I tried to set an example: I invited her to church; I prayed for her. But she couldn't bring herself to believe; it doesn't make sense to her. And if she doesn't believe, she won't be allowed in Paradise, isn't that right?"

Jonathan didn't answer.

"And I'm to blame! I think *I* was her chance!"

"What? You?"

"Her chance wasn't just when I was with her, during my life. It's going on right *now*! This second! When I was dying, it took a lot for her to ask me to return. But she did and I said I would. *I promised!* Now, if I *don't* return, she'll *know* there's nothing more. Don't you see? *I'm* her chance. *I'm* the one who's supposed to give her the sign she needs to believe! And you won't let me!"

"Tom—"

"She'll be sent across the chasm." He pointed toward the horizon. "To Hell . . . and I'll never see her again!"

"Thomas—"

"And to make matters worse, I learned that when people are reunited with their loved ones, the memories of their mortal life will be restored."

"That's true, but—"

"Those that are *reunited*! But how about those who aren't? What about those who are separated by the chasm—do *they* get their memories back?"

Jonathan sighed. "It would only bring them pain."

Tom slammed his fist against the window. A web of cracks radiated outward. "As if losing her isn't enough! I have to lose my *memory* of her as well?!" He smashed his fist against the glass again. Another starburst of cracks appeared, some intersecting with the first.

Tom looked at Jonathan miserably. "I said I'd return because I want her to believe, but if I don't go back, she won't ever know the truth. *And I'll destroy the one person I love more than my own soul!*" He leaned against the glass, burying his head in his arms.

For a long moment Jonathan looked at Tom. Then quietly, he said, "Her 'chance,' as you put it, isn't over yet. You don't know what God has in store—"

Tom let out a derisive laugh, his breath fogging the glass. "God! Is this the same guy who ruined *both* our lives?"

"You mustn't talk like that—"

A hand fell on Jonathan's shoulder. A giant man with dark curly hair and deep-set dark eyes stood behind him, his brow furrowed. "What is this blasphemy?" he boomed, looking at the broken window.

"Chairman Anatoli!" said Jonathan.

Anatoli scowled at Tom. "Vandalism is punishable."

"I'm sorry."

"I'm very sorry," said Jonathan, "we were just talking—"

"Your *talking* interrupted the Council."

"I'm very sorry, sir," repeated Jonathan.

Anatoli's eyes bored into Tom. "So why are you breaking windows and blaspheming the Lord?"

"Well, he—"

"I was addressing him." Anatoli nodded at Tom.

Tom looked up at his inquisitor. "It's about my request."

"Yes?"

"It was denied, and—"

Anatoli walked away. "I'm sure there was a good reason."

Tom followed him. "No, there wasn't."

Anatoli stopped, turned, and pointed at Jonathan. "Is this man in your charge? Who are you?"

"Jonathan."

"Well? Is he?"

Jonathan nodded. Tom had never seen him speechless before.

"Have you acquainted him with our policies?"

Tom thought Jonathan's head would bend off his neck.

"Well?"

Jonathan started to speak, but Tom cut him off. "It's not his fault."

Anatoli grunted, his eyes searing a hole into Tom.

Tom managed to squeak, "I have some questions and wanted to talk to . . ."

"To whom?" boomed Anatoli.

Tom steeled himself and met Anatoli's eyes. "You, I guess."

Anatoli glared at Jonathan, then headed for the Council chambers. The receptionist opened the door for him, giving Tom a withering look. "Come on, then," groused Anatoli as he passed through the doorway. The receptionist's mouth fell open.

Jonathan nodded toward the doorway and whispered to Tom, "Watch your tongue. The Chairman is not a man to be trifled with." Tom walked through the doorway, followed by Jonathan.

It was dark inside. The light from the doorway revealed a conference table surrounded by eleven high-backed chairs, five on a side and one at the far end where Anatoli was settling himself. Each chair was occupied by someone wearing a white suit, but Tom couldn't make out any faces. He could see an occasional reflection of light on spectacles, or a pair of hands folded in a lap, but beyond this, he had no idea who these people were.

The door closed and the room grew even darker. Tom stood at the foot of the table. Anatoli leaned forward, his face entering the light which illuminated his place. He knocked on the surface. "You asked for an audience. You have one." He leaned back.

"Make it short," Jonathan whispered.

Ten chairs swivelled toward Tom. The table was empty except
for a white book in front of each person. Each book was illuminated
by a light from high above. Each had gold lettering on the cover.

"My name is Tom Waring—"

"We know who you are," said someone from the darkness.

"Oh. I'm here to, ah . . ." He searched for the word.

"Appeal!" hissed Jonathan.

"Appeal the decision of the Council concerning my—"

"We also know why you are here," said someone from the other
side of the table. An Asian man leaned forward, his face entering the
light. He was not smiling.

"We know who you are and why you are here," said Anatoli,
tapping the volume in front of him as evidence.

Tom could make out shapes nodding, but their faces remained in
darkness. "Oh. Okay. Then what I'd like to ask is this—"

"Mr. Waring?" A man leaned into the light. His face was
heavily scarred and his nose was beak-like. He had a tall forehead, no
hair except for a white fringe, and wore wire-rimmed glasses. Tom
couldn't see his eyes through the opaque lenses.

"Yes?"

"Mr. Waring," continued the councilman, "I have just one
question for you that I believe will help the Council understand why
you are appealing our decision. It is this: do you know the mind of
God?"

Tom shook his head slowly.

"Do you understand His plan?"

He shook his head again.

"Then how is it that you know more than we on this matter?"

Tom raised his hands. "I don't know the mind of God. It's just
that . . . well, I'm just not sure that . . ." *Don't make me say it.*

"We're waiting."

Tom gulped. "Are you *sure* this is God's will?"

There was complete silence. Behind him, Jonathan moaned.
Slowly, each man at the table leaned forward until his face was visible.

They were of all ages and nationalities, but they all wore the same expression: incredulity.

Anatoli lumbered to his feet and pointed at Tom. "You dare to question *us*?" he roared. "We know who *you* are, Thomas Philip Waring, but do you know who *we* are?"

He moved behind the chair next to his and grasped the top with both hands. A man with deep vertical wrinkles running from his eyes to his chin stared serenely at Tom. "This is Yung Wei, who lived three thousand years ago in central China. There was a great drought. His village was starving. He prayed with such faith that God finally sent rain, saving his people."

He moved to the next chair, where a dark man with black hair sat. "This is Alberto de Moranis, who lived in fourth century Spain. He was an ascetic who suffered death rather than renounce God."

He moved to the next chair. "This is Mirawanu Lazzi, born in the Yucatan peninsula, who walked sixty straight days to rescue the daughter of an enemy who had been kidnapped by marauding tribes."

"I didn't mean—"

"Quiet!" bellowed Anatoli. "You have questioned us, now we will question you. Do you believe that we do not know what it means to keep a promise? Many of us were tortured to death rather than renounce our faith!"

Tom felt the floor shake as Anatoli walked toward him. He stopped a pace away and leaned forward until his mouth was an inch from Tom's ear. Tom shook with fear. Anatoli's voice was low. "My Earth name was Stepan Anatoli. I lived in the fourteenth century on the Eurasian steppes during a time of feudal war, where tens of thousands were slaughtered. My family was murdered because my wife had a trinket valued by a warlord. I was thrust into prison and blinded so that I could not identify the man who butchered my family.

"For forty years I rotted in a dungeon, where my hatred grew. Because of what I had seen, I *believed* there was no God. After I was blinded, I *knew* there was no God. I tried take my own life. But there was a man there, also a prisoner, who knew the true God. Over many years, he taught me about faith. He changed my heart and took my hate from me. I forgave my tormentors. It was God's Law that saved my soul."

He walked back to his seat.   The others leaned back, disappearing. From the darkness came Anatoli's voice. "Know the truth, and the truth shall make you free."

The silence stretched out. Finally, Tom said quietly, "I didn't mean to offend you. But if you know me as I believe you do, then you know that I am a Believer. I have tried to live my life in accordance with God's grace.

A voice said, "This is true."

"But I do not understand this decision."

"What don't you understand?" asked another.

"I promised my wife I'd return and tell her that there is a God, because she doesn't believe. I can't bear the thought of not being with her."

"Why are you concerned? She is in God's hands."

"My reason for returning has nothing to do with Him. It has to do with her, and *me*. I promised. She knows I would never lie. So if I don't return, she will *know* that there is nothing after death. And so she will never believe, and we will not be together in Heaven because she had her chance and rejected the truth."

Anatoli said, "If, as you say, she has received her chance and has rejected it, she will be given other chances in the future. If she eventually accepts the truth, she will be rewarded, although she will not accompany you on the Continuum. Her actions will have held her back."

He opened his book and turned pages, finally stopping. He read: "Only like-minded people travel the Continuum together. A different arrangement would mean misery: those who reject the light would be unhappy among people who were more evolved, who in turn would be saddened to be the source of unhappiness for their loved ones. So people of similar natures dwell together. This is just. Our happiness is God's highest purpose. The highest houses are reserved for those who have lived the highest law." He closed the book.

Tom looked around the table. "All the more reason why I *must* return. She doesn't have the gift of faith."

Jonathan stepped forward. "Not everyone receives the gift of faith at birth. But it is a gift freely given to all those who ask."

"She doesn't ask because she *can't*! It's contrary to everything she's seen in the world: the misery and the cruelty. She doesn't believe because she *can't*. How can someone ask in faith *for* faith? You have to already have it to get it!"

Anatoli said, "Would it make any difference if we told you that you may be released from your promise?"

Tom shook his head.

"Suppose a man made a promise," continued Anatoli, turning pages rapidly as he spoke. "A promise is a contract, of which there are two kinds: unilateral and bilateral." He was reading now. The other books were opened and pages quickly found. Faces appeared, reading along as the Chairman continued. "A unilateral contract is one in which one party makes an express engagement or undertakes a performance without receiving in return any express engagement or promise of performance from the other. A *bilateral agreement*, on the other hand, is one by which the parties expressly enter into mutual engagements." He looked up from the book. "Did your wife make any promise in return for yours?"

Tom remembered the hospital. April knelt by his side, her hands holding his. *Finally, her hands are warmer than mine.* He looked into her flooded eyes. "Promise me," she said. "Promise you'll come back."

"She asked me to come back because she knew her lack of belief meant that she didn't merit heaven."

"Did she promise you anything in return for your promise?" repeated a councilman.

Tom shook his head.

"She never promised to do anything, with or without your return, did she?" asked Anatoli.

"It was clear to me: if I returned, she would believe."

"What is clear is that it was a unilateral contract. And according to the Law," said a black-skinned man, reading from his book, "there is only one way a unilateral contract may be made binding on the promisor—you."

"What's that?" asked Tom, feeling this man was on his side.

"If the non-promising party later executes a form of consideration, then the promising party is bound to the original promise."

"What does that mean?"

"It means," said the black man, "that if your wife gains faith herself, then you may be bound to your promise and we may have to reconsider and let you return to Earth."

"It won't happen," said Tom miserably.

"Is anything too hard for the Lord?" asked Anatoli gently.

Several councilmen exchanged looks. One rifled through his book. He coughed to get attention. He was an albino and the whites of his eyes were yellow, surrounding pale green irises. "The discussion as to whether he entered into a unilateral or bilateral agreement is academic. There is another problem. Gentlemen, please consult page five hundred four." Jonathan leaned over a councilman's chair, reading along.

"It is this," said the albino. "Regardless of the form of contract, if a party, by his action or inaction, repudiates the premise of the agreement, then the contract is rescinded and the non-breaching party is released from his performance."

Anatoli said, "It means that if, by her actions, your beloved shows that she no longer wishes you to keep your promise, then you are released."

"From the contract," amended the albino councilman.

Anatoli nodded.

"I don't understand," said Tom.

Jonathan said, "Just as you are slowly forgetting Earth and your relationships, mortals are also forgetting."

"Not her."

Anatoli closed his book. As if on cue, all the other books were closed and removed from the table. As the lights dimmed, Anatoli said, "You are a man of great passion, Thomas. You are about to receive a marvelous gift. See to it that you are not ungrateful."

From the darkness, eleven voices spoke in unison: "Open your heart and mind and they shall be filled."

A tiny white light coalesced above the center of the table. Swirling colors circled an invisible center. Growing in brightness, they formed shapes and a shimmering vision appeared, which soon solidified. Block-like shapes arranged themselves in two rows. A black strip appeared between them. It was a residential street, lined with clapboard homes and elm trees. The leaves were yellow and gold. Some wafted to the ground. A red sun perched on the horizon. Tom's attention was pulled to the foreground, where a white house stood, surrounded by trees and a leaf-covered lawn. He smelled wood smoke. The front door opened and Josh burst out, flying down the steps to the driveway where he picked up a bicycle and hauled it toward the front door.

Tom's heart leapt. Joshua! Then April appeared in the doorway. She wore gray Levis and a maroon sweater. Her hair was short. She was radiant. She gave Josh a smile that melted Tom's heart. *How can she be happy?* He felt guilty for being selfish. *No one can mourn all the time.*

Josh was scooting around on the bike, the middle bar forcing him to his tiptoes, his face ruddy in the crisp air.

A man appeared in the doorway behind April. He was tall and had black hair and wore a black polo shirt. He touched her on the shoulder as he passed. She smiled. Tom knew instantly that this man was no stranger to April—he was very close to her. You could see it in the way they looked at each other when he passed. Tom's mind reeled. The rest of the scene seemed to fade away; only the man seemed real. He moved in crisp detail toward Josh.

As he watched the man lift Josh onto the seat, Tom's heart cracked. *Don't touch him, he's* my *son!* Josh bore down on the pedals and the man held the seat, trotting behind. They disappeared beyond the hedge that separated her house—*or is it* their *house?*—from the neighbors. Tom focused on April. Her smile didn't mask any grief. It was an easy smile as she watched Josh being helped by a total stranger . . . no . . . someone she let touch her—*don't think about that!*—and her son—*my son!*—in such a personal way.

Josh reappeared, pedaling furiously. The man let go and Josh rode, handlebars weaving, then stabilizing, and Tom heard his delighted squeal as Josh learned something that only Tom could teach him, not this stranger who had taken over his life.

Josh made a wide turn and headed back toward the house, wobbling. The man trotted behind. There they were, in some kind of slo-mo Norman Rockwell moment, the sun going down, the porch lights coming on, as Tom's heart split open, emptying out everything he ever cared about.

The vision faded, and the scene became more vague until the autumn colors, so beautiful just moments ago, were black and gray, the colors of death. Tom leaned against the table as the last of it broke apart, leaving everything in darkness. The lights came up. Anatoli stood, his head bowed. "I'm sorry."

"No," said Tom in a hollow voice, "I should not have questioned your judgment. Forgive me." He walked stiffly from the room.

"I think he's getting it," yelled Dan, running behind Josh, who was concentrating on the handlebars.

April held her breath. "Stay on the sidewalk, honey!" He was moving slowly enough that a spill right now wouldn't do too much damage. Still, she feared the worst.

"All right, Josh!" said Dan, steadying the seat. Josh regained his balance and Dan let go. Josh raised a hand to wave; Dan caught the bike just before it tumbled. "Careful!" he said, pulling Josh to a stop. Josh jumped off and flew toward April. "Did you see? I rode it! I stayed up! All by myself!"

"Yes, you did great!"

"Can I call Adam and tell him I did it? Please?" Not waiting for an answer, he disappeared indoors.

Dan stood before her. "Not bad."

"Not bad yourself."

"Is that really his first time?"

"He's been working on it by himself. I haven't had time to help him."

"It's all over now," said Dan. "He's got a need for speed. It's a guy thing."

"Is that right?"

"Next thing you know, he'll be driving a car, roaring around town like a maniac."

"Thanks for that delightful image, Dan. Let's not get ahead of ourselves. He hasn't sustained his first skinned knee yet. That might slow him down a bit."

"Or you."

"Or me."

Dan smiled, saying nothing. April hugged herself, rubbing her upper arms. "Cooling off, isn't it?"

The sky was turning purple. Dan said, "So. How do *you* cope with skinned knees?"

"With a band-aid."

"You know what I mean."

"Oh. *That* kind of skinned knee. Not too well, I guess."

Dan watched the sunset. Suddenly there wasn't enough distance between them. April knew what was coming. Before she could say anything, he blurted out, "How about dinner?"

"We just had dinner. And thank you."

"You know what I mean: dinner *out*."

"I don't know."

"How about this? Dinner with all of us. You and Josh and me and my two girls. A real family kind of thing."

"You're subtle."

"I'm trying to be anything but. I'm trying to ask you out."

"And I'm trying not to appear ungrateful. But the dynamic, as well as the timing, are difficult. You *are* my boss."

"I'll quit."

She laughed. "You can't."

"Then I'll fire you." April grimaced but Dan was smiling. "And what about the timing?"

"It's too soon."

Dan looked through the open doorway. Josh was sitting on the couch talking on the phone, his feet bouncing, embellishing his feat to Jeremy. "He needs a dad."

"Cheap shot."

"I'm not saying you should run out and get married. I'm just saying you should consider *his* needs when you consider how much time *you* need."

"I do," said April, feeling cornered.

Dan saw it. "I'm sorry. I know you do. That's why I'm asking you out. You have so much of what I'm looking for. I just wish you'd take a look at *me* to see if I have anything *you're* looking for."

April fidgeted. Dan waited. He had backed down another step; for once she didn't have to look up at him. He had kind eyes. He always spoke to her with patience and interest. He never raised his voice at work. He was a fine therapist. He was attractive, successful, intelligent, and kind. What was her problem?

"I don't think I'm looking for anything yet," was all she said.

After Dan left and April was cleaning up, Josh got on a stool and leaned on the counter. "Mom?"

"What is it?"

"Do you like that man?"

"You mean Dan?"

He nodded.

"Sure. He's nice."

"He's your boss."

"That's right. We work together."

"Is he a shrink, too?"

"Yes, honey. He helps people be happy."

Josh nodded. "He helped me!"

"So you're gonna ride the two-wheeler from now on?"

"Yeah!"

"But remember: stay on the sidewalk, okay?"

"Aw, Mom."

"I mean it."

"Mom, do you like him?"

Once he gets a train of thought, he takes it to the end of the line.
"I said I did."

"I mean *really* like him."

"Sure. He's nice."

"I mean, do you like him like a *daddy*?"

She didn't know what to say. It seemed all men, big or small, had a way of putting her on the spot. "We're friends—the way you and Adam are friends."

"Good," said Josh. "Because I don't want another daddy—I already got one."

"Well, no matter what happens, your daddy will always be your daddy, even if I ever . . . get married again."

Josh looked at her, eyes wide. "You would?"

April picked up a box, set it on the counter, and began pulling out kitchen utensils. "I'm just saying that maybe someday I might, but Daddy will still be your daddy and nothing will ever change that."

"I don't want you to."

"Me neither. But right now, you need a bath. Scoot."

Josh walked toward the doorway, then stopped, turning. "I guess it's okay for you to call me Josh-man. If you want . . . ."

———

Tom didn't remember leaving the Council chambers or walking to the elevator or taking it down two hundred floors. He didn't remember passing the fountain. If he had, he would have seen himself staring at the ground in total despair.

The first thing he remembered was walking into his room. He closed the drapes, but not before placing his phone on the balcony and shutting the glass door. He lay down on the bed, staring at the ceiling, thinking about April and the promise she had forgotten so quickly.

18

Tom dragged himself out of bed, relieved he couldn't remember any dreams. When he got out of the shower his phone was ringing on the balcony. He considered ignoring it but it rang and didn't stop. He finally retrieved it, punching SEND.

Jonathan appeared. "How are you?"

Tom shrugged.

Jonathan said, "Drapes: open," and the curtains opened.

Tom walked over and closed them. "I like it dark."

"Fine. How do you feel?" Jonathan tugged at a shirt sleeve.

"Just peachy. I wish I was dead."

"You are dead," said Jonathan, attempting a joke.

"Not dead enough—I can still feel something. Bring on the mega-death." He laughed bitterly. "That's a heavy metal band."

"A what?"

"Forget it."

"Thomas, I'm sorry it was so painful. But you insisted."

"And you think I deserved it, right?"

Jonathan shrugged. "We all learn. One way or another."

Tom tossed the towel aside and got back into the bed.

"What are you doing?"

"Going back to bed." He switched off the bedside lamp.

Jonathan snapped his fingers. The lamp came back on. "You cannot remain in bed, Thomas."

"Watch me." He pulled the covers over his head.

"The best thing is to stay active. You mustn't dwell on this. And I have just the ticket. This morning, you will take a Personality Profile which will determine your aptitudes. Then you will receive a work assignment that will enhance your self-worth."

"I'm enhanced to death," said Tom from under the covers.

"And after yesterday, I believe you should reconsider the Naming Ritual. I think it would help you gain . . . perspective."

Tom stuck his head out. "I've had about all the perspective I can take, thank you."

Jonathan exhaled sharply. "You seem to forget that I am trying to help."

Tom glared at him. "You know what I think? I think I'm some kind of chore on your 'To Do' list."

"That is not true."

"I'm gonna tell you something you want to hear."

"That would be nice."

"I quit."

Jonathan frowned. "Meaning?"

"I give up. No more griping, no more complaining, no more Policy Change Requests, no more appeals. You win."

"*I* don't win."

Tom smiled. "Yes, you do! You get to get back to your orderly life. You can fill in the box marked 'Tom Waring' with a big checkmark. I'll be obedient; a good little sheep. There. Feel better?"

Jonathan opened his mouth, but Tom said, "End!" and the image disappeared. "If I'd known it was that easy, I'd've read the manual before." He pulled the covers back over his head.

For two more cycles, Tom stayed in his room. Since he didn't *have* to eat, he didn't need to go out. He lay there, thinking about April and the stranger and feeling sorry for himself.

Jonathan must've gotten the hint because he didn't bother Tom. In fact, by evening of the second cycle, Tom was beginning to wonder if anyone in Paradise had noticed his disappearance. He opened his Record. No letters glowed, no icons pulsated. It was like they'd taken him off-line.

The feeling that he was being allowed to be alone made him even angrier. It was as if he was falling into another one of their categories—"Broken Hearts"—and they were giving him his 3.2 cycles of grieving time. He had no doubt that if he stayed in his room beyond a predetermined time limit, someone would show up to pester him. He decided not to give them the pleasure.

Besides, after all the thinking, it had finally started to sink in. Things had changed. April had moved on, Josh had a new dad, and Tom seemed to be the only one who wasn't getting on with his life. When he looked at it that way—and it took some effort because at first he couldn't even bear to think along those lines—it seemed like he *was* acting childish.

He knew he'd never be happy without April, but at least he could be useful. He got out of bed the morning of the seventh cycle and opened his Record. The page fell open and the words PERSONALITY PROFILE blinked. He tasted gall as he thought how accurately they'd estimated his down time. *I guess you can't fight city hall. Not when God's the mayor.*

Tom followed the map through the busy streets. His destination was a featureless cube of a building, ten stories high. Inside, he was faced with a lengthy counter, behind which people worked on a raised platform, so they could look down on you. *Typical*, he thought.

A clerk scanned Tom's Record and pointed to a doorway on the left. Tom fell into step behind another guy his age—*What? Is everybody here my age?!* It occurred to him how little fun a basketball game would be, with everybody in their prime. Everyone would have a beautiful jump shot; everyone would be sinking three-pointers; every game would end in a tie. He pondered the end of competitive sports as he walked into a large room where a hundred carrels stood, each a chalky white color. Tom took a seat, rotating inward. As he did, the screen on the desktop displayed the check-mark-in-a-square logo, accompanied by some bombastic music, the kind they play when someone wins an Olympic medal.

He touched the screen when commanded and spoke slowly and enunciated carefully when commanded.

After more than two hours, he was tired and irritable. It was one of those tests where they give you a choice between two unrelated things, like 'What would yóu rather do: go to a party full of interesting people or watch a football game?' The answer was obvious but that option was not available: It depends! Sometimes a party is fun, and sometimes a game is too. He couldn't see how such distinctions were helpful in determining what he was suited for. Why didn't they just ask him? It's not like he hadn't lived for thirty-four years without finding out what he was good at.

Back at the front counter, Tom handed the clerk his Record for another scan. He would probably end up as a street sweeper or something. That *was* an accurate measurement of his abilities.

The clerk handed him an envelope. He opened it. "Thomas Philip Waring, son of Donald and . . ." After a long paragraph about the scientific nature of the test and the mechanisms for appeal if you disagree with their findings (Tom nearly laughed out loud at that one), in bold, capital letters, were the words: DEPARTMENT OF PUBLIC WORKS.

"I knew it," he said, picturing himself pushing a broom along an alabaster sidewalk. The letter continued with another paragraph of congratulations and ended with the location of the Public Works Building and the time he was to report there.

His Record beeped. The appointment had already been entered and the map icon was blinking. He had twenty minutes to get there.

As he made his way along the busy streets, he tried not to think about April. He was both angry and hurt by her actions. Who was the guy? Tom had never seen him before. He couldn't believe she'd hook up with someone so soon. He must've totally misunderstood their relationship. So many times he'd watched her sleeping, wondering what he would do if she ever left. He never considered that it might be *him* who would leave, even against his will.

As he walked, head down, a man with very dark, almost blue-black skin fell into step beside him. He had long, white hair and blue eyes. He was thin and muscular. "You know me," he said, almost smiling. It was not a question.

"I don't think so." Tom kept walking, shoulders hunched.

"You're Thomas Waring."

One of Jonathan's spies.

"I am not. I don't even know this Jonathan."

"So how do you know me?" He walked faster, irritated.

The man chuckled. "You are in a hurry. I will walk with you, if that is acceptable."

"Suit yourself," said Tom, but something within him shifted.

"You've been here, what, one, maybe two cycles, right?"

"Seven. This is my seventh cycle."

The man stopped and faced Tom. "You do not recognize me? These," he said, pointing to his eyes, "do not stir any memories?"

The man was singular, of that there was no doubt. Almost alien in the odd juxtaposition of black skin and blue eyes. And the flowing white hair. He was memorable, but not to Tom. "Sorry, I can't place you."

"The veil has not yet lifted. I can see that now. But I recognized your walk. The way you lead with your chest, confident and full of purpose."

"Oh, I'm full of something, all right," said Tom ruefully. But something bothered him. "You seem to know me, but who are *you*?"

"Suffice it to say that in our pre-mortal life, you and I were friends. We shared a passion for music. *You* were a great musician. You had a different name then, as did I." He suddenly gave Tom a powerful hug. "I have missed you, my dear friend." He pulled back.

Tom returned his look blankly. "Me? A musician?"

"And I was your poor student. I am Amisthar. You will soon remember me. Unfortunately, you will also remember the practical jokes I used to play on you."

"Amisthar?" No bells rang.

"You have not undergone the Naming Ritual?"

Tom shook his head.

"The Veil varies with each person, but seven cycles is a long time. What prevents you? This is not like you at all."

Tom looked at the stranger who claimed to be his life-long friend—or was it *lives*-long? He felt his core of loneliness expanding, even though he was in the presence of someone he had probably known forever. "It's a long story."

"I am most interested to hear it."

"I don't think so. But when I do the naming thing I'll invite you, if you want."

Amisthar's face lit up. "Nothing—and I do mean nothing— would be more joyful for me! I am so glad," he said, hugging Tom again, "that you have remained true and faithful, Bela . . ." He stopped short.

"Bela . . . ?"

"I am sorry. I misspoke."

"Is that my real name?"

"Your real name, *Thomas*, is the one you choose each day; your real name is nothing more or less than what you *do*. And you have always been a great inspiration to me. I am honored that you would invite me to your Naming Ritual." He grasped Tom's hand firmly. "I look forward to your call." He moved quickly away through the crowd.

"Wait! I have a question!"

Amisthar waved back, calling out over the heads of the passers-by, "You always *did*!"

"Who am I?" Tom asked himself.

By the time he arrived at the Public Works building, Tom was genuinely angry that he'd let Amisthar get away without answering some questions. He felt a sincere caring from him that buoyed his spirits. It was the opposite of the judgment he got from Jonathan. He reconsidered the Naming Ritual. Perhaps, if it would help him remember a person like Amisthar, it wasn't such a bad idea.

He entered the building, handed his card to the woman behind a counter and stood back, waiting to be issued his broom and dustpan.

Presently a young woman with pale skin came out to greet him. "I'm Berenda."

They shook hands. He introduced himself and was aware that he was beginning to be embarrassed by his own name. It couldn't be as impressive as his other name was. "Is Berenda your chosen name?"

"Of course not."

"Do you remember your chosen name?"

"Yes." She looked quizzically at him.

"How come you don't use it?"

"I do, but only with people who have chosen *their* name. You obviously have not."

"How can you tell?"

"I just can. I knew when you came in, so with you, I use my Earth name."

"What is your chosen name?"

"I cannot reveal it to you."

"Why not?"

"You are not ready."

"I'm sorry. I'm having a hard time getting acclimated here."

"I understand you were a carpenter."

He nodded. His life was looking smaller and smaller.

"Wonderful!" she exclaimed. "We are lucky to get you!"

"No kidding," said Tom without emotion.

"The Planning Commission needs someone with your skills. We're up to our necks in architects with no practical building experience."

"Why is that?"

"I guess it's because on Earth such people lead pretty staid lives, very conservative, you know: building codes, plans. Architects fit into the personality type that predominates here. But carpenters, free-wheeling, seat-of-their-pants, *carpenters* are harder to come by."

"Why is that?"

"Wild living, I suppose. There just aren't many that make it."

He glared at her. "I recall someone pretty important who was a carpenter."

Berenda blushed. "Well, of course. I didn't mean that . . . ." She dropped her eyes. "Sorry."

Tom didn't feel like turning the knife. "Maybe you're right."

"I was generalizing, but that isn't fair to you. You were a person of quality, or else—"

"I wouldn't be here. Right."

"Right." She paused. "Are you going to hate me?"

"I thought we weren't supposed to hate anybody."

Berenda smiled uncertainly. "You don't seem convinced of that."

"Sure I am. I don't hate you. What have you got for me?

"We need a supervisor for one of our big public works jobs."

Tom said, "I thought you just snapped your fingers."

She laughed. "I wish that were true, but it's a Prime Directive that we labor, and many of us love the trades. You do, don't you?"

"Sure. Why wouldn't I? I mean, do I get a choice?"

She was genuinely perplexed. "Of course! Nothing is constrained here. We are here because we choose to be."

"Right," he said flatly.

"You don't agree?"

"Sure," said Tom. "Whatever you say."

She brightened. "If you'll follow me, I'll show you around."

"That would be terrific," said Tom without enthusiasm.

She showed him the planning rooms, the library, the immense stacks of plans and accumulated architectural knowledge. She showed him the architects' rooms, where dozens of people sat at tables covered with blueprints.

Throughout the tour, Tom tried to be positive. He could hardly expect others to give him a break if he wasn't willing to do the same for them. Berenda showed him a scale model of a magnificent stadium—*why? To watch a whole court of Michael Jordans flying through the air, effortlessly slam-dunking? What was the thrill in that?*—an even more impressive future Council Building, and an expansion of Paradise Station. Tom tried to remain blasé, but he couldn't mask the fact that he *was* impressed. The projects were challenges and would use techniques and materials he'd never heard of. And he was going to be a supervisor, in charge of building one of these impressive structures.

But in a way he was also disappointed. All his life, Tom felt like fate was in control. His father worked in the trades, installing air-conditioners, so it seemed natural—fated—that Tom should do the same. He never took school very seriously because he knew he would be a tradesman like his father. But now he was in Paradise, a place of supposed unlimited potential, and fate was still running things. His loftiest talent was still swinging a hammer. This place was so much like Earth. If he was still a carpenter here, even a glorified one, what was this nonsense about his "limitless" potential?

He thought about this on his walk home. In a place of such infinite vistas, Tom's worldview had been severely stunted. He felt crushed by his own limitations. He remembered the time his family went to the Grand Canyon. When they looked out across the expanse, he had felt small, but not unimportant. His whole future lay before him then. But this was the end of the trail. His whole life he'd felt like something was heading his way. *Something was headed my way, all right. And it's about to run me over.*

For the next two cycles Tom made a conscious effort to stay busy, as Jonathan had advised. He went to classes, took notes, wrote in his Record and went to work. Berenda took him to the construction sites and introduced him around. The people were, without exception, cordial. But they also seemed distant, probably because he was distant himself. He shied away from personal questions, preferring to turn the question back upon the questioner. It deflected a lot of probing.

He found himself thinking of Helen, the librarian. After work on his eighth cycle, he went to the Library to talk to her but she wasn't there. He went and found his book, thumbing through it. He knew he should start editing it, but the idea was distasteful. He figured that editing his book was an admission that his life was really over.

Maybe it was. The thought made him feel empty. He decided that from now on, he would speak when spoken to, do his work, go to class, mind his business, and hope that someday his depression would pass. But this was eternity—and as everyone kept telling him, eternity went on forever.

19

O n his tenth cycle, Tom went for a walk after work. He had no destination in mind. He just wanted to be moving, hoping he could somehow leave his worries behind.

The day was as they all were, clear, warm, and cloudless. He had ceased to notice the auras around everything; he didn't even see his own anymore. The lush, groomed gardens gave him no pleasure. There were too many people. He felt like a pretender, faking interest in others. He was afraid of the dark thoughts he harbored, but most people gave no indication they could hear them, or else they ignored them. Tom figured it was because they were too involved in their own lives. For his part, that was fine. He had no interest in others' inner voices, either. *I don't even want to hear my own.*

So he walked, seeking isolation. It was no surprise when he found himself near the borders of the garden, walking up the rise toward the crest of the hill, beyond which lay the Bridge.

It came into view, blinding him. He felt exposed and stepped off the path, moving toward a stand of aspens. The Bridge shone, white, transcendent, and grand.

"What do you see?"

Tom whirled around, nearly falling in the process. He grabbed a tree for balance. It was Stan, his arms crossed over his skinny chest.

"Don't *do* that!" hissed Tom, feeling his heart race.

"Careful," said Stan, wagging a finger. "Loose lips . . ."

"What are you doing here? And why are you sneaking up on me?"

"I thought you heard me. Why are you skulking around, staking out the Bridge? You a suicide bomber?"

"Of course not!"

Stan winked. "But you're up to something . . . Tom, right?"

"I'm not up to anything. Just going for a walk."

Stan let out a tinny laugh. "I'm not the Spirit Police. I don't care what you do." He winked again. "So . . . what *are* you up to?"

"Nothing! Drop it!"

Stan looked at Tom with something approaching humor, but didn't say anything.

Tom glanced at the Bridge. "If you must know—"

"I couldn't care less," said Stan, walking away.

"Rules schmules."

Stan let out a squeaky laugh and stopped.

"I did what you said," said Tom.

Stan turned and squinted at him.

"I had it out with the Council. Even the Chairman himself."

Stan raised his eyebrows. "No kidding."

"Yeah. Bulled my way in there and gave 'em what for."

"And what happened?"

Tom spit on the ground. "Turned me down flat."

"What a surprise."

"It's probably for the best. That's what I keep telling myself."

"You're not sure?"

"I don't know. You know my situation, right?"

"I remember you were asking me a *hypothetical* about a guy who made a promise and he couldn't keep it and I said, why not? and you said because they wouldn't let him."

"That guy was me."

Stan laid a palm against his cheek. "No!"

"When I was dying, my wife made me promise that if there is a God, I'd come back to Earth and tell her."

Stan burst out in a long, nasal, coughing laugh. He doubled over. His large bony hands were splayed across his stomach. Tears squirted out of the corners of his eyes.

Tom's anger rose. "I'm glad you think it's so funny."

Stan was crimson. Between gasps he said, "Funniest thing . . . I ever heard! Come back . . . and tell her . . . if there is . . . a God!" He collapsed into gales of laughter again.

Tom remembered that this bony little idiot couldn't read his thoughts and so he hurled a nasty one at him: *It won't be so funny when my hands are around your scrawny throat, pipsqueak!*

Stan had fallen down on the dry grass. He stopped laughing for a second, looked up at Tom with wet eyes, then burst into laughter again. Tom took a step, making fists. "So . . . is there?" asked Stan.

"Is there what?" barked Tom.

"A God!" howled Stan, wiping his face with his sleeve.

Tom looked away. "Haven't met Him . . . yet."

This set Stan off again. He reared back, mouth open in a huge, scornful laugh. "Well, let me know when you do," he said, nearly choking. "I got a couple of questions for the old boy!"

"You'll be first on my list," said Tom bitterly.

Stan dried his eyes on his sleeve. "Oh, lighten up. It's pretty funny, if you ask me."

"Nobody asked you."

"So why are you giving up? Am I missing something?"

Just a personality. "They showed me my wife's life. She's forgotten about me."

"How do you know?"

"I saw it myself."

"And that convinced you?"

"Sure. Why wouldn't it?"

Stan whistled. "Boy, you sure give up easy."

"I know the truth when I see it."

Stan grimaced. "You are so full of it."

"You don't even know me."

"I know enough. And I'm smart, did I tell you? *Really* smart." He tapped his forehead. "I know things."

"Oh, yeah? What things?"

"Well, for instance: I know you're a quitter."

"Wow, you must be a psychic." *Or a psycho.*

"Not really," said Stan, completely missing the sarcasm. "It's pretty obvious."

"Well, when the game's over you quit."

"You think you know what the truth is, do you?"

Tom shrugged. "I know when it's time to cut my losses, if that's what you mean." He tore at a patch of grass.

"Your wife, what's she look like?"

Tom tossed the grass into the air. The wind carried it away. "She's attractive."

Stan's eyes narrowed to slits. "Beautiful?" He jabbed an elbow in Tom's ribs.

Tom edged away, giving him an angry look. "Knock it off."

"I'm just asking. What's she look like?"

"No cracks, all right?"

Stan crossed his heart.

"She's got auburn hair, about shoulder length. No. She just cut it. She's got a great figure, tiny waist, and delicate hands. And great legs." He looked at Stan, who was smiling. Tom didn't like that smile, but at least he wasn't drooling. "Anyway, she's got full lips and her eyes . . ."

Stan lay back in the grass, eyes closed, still smiling stupidly. After Tom didn't continue, he said, "Go ahead. I'm not going to say anything."

Tom was racking his brain. *What color were her eyes? Blue? Gray? Green? Or were they brown?* He felt the earth shifting below him. He put his hands on the ground to steady himself. He looked at Stan. "I can't remember her eyes."

"It's not important—"

"It is to me! They're . . . they're . . . !" He jumped to his feet. "They're . . . blue. No! Not blue, because mine are blue and—"

"I like blue eyes," said Stan dreamily.

"What color are they?! THIS ISN'T HAPPENING!"

Stan opened one eye. Tom stood with his back to him, his hands on his hips, his head bowed in concentration, his shoulders hunched. Stan said, "Hey, no big deal—"

Tom whirled around. "Those rotten, conniving . . . they're taking my memories! In another day, I won't remember the color of her hair. In a week, I'll forget her name!"

"Them's the rules."

Tom's eyes burned with anger. "Oh, yeah? We'll just see." He started down the hillside.

Stan jumped to his feet. "Where you going?"

"To Earth," said Tom, picking up speed.

"But you said she forgot about your promise." He walked after Tom.

"Doesn't matter. In the end, it's not about her, it's about me. I'm the one who made the promise, and I'm the one who's gotta keep it. She can do what she wants with the information."

Stan bounced up alongside him. "You'll get in trouble," he said. "*Big* trouble." His eyes were bright with mischief.

Tom shrugged. "Nobody—and I mean *nobody*—is gonna take my memories away without a fight."

Stan grinned. "Oh, boy," he said, rubbing his bony hands together. "I love a good fight!"

Jonathan dialed Tom one more time before getting on the elevator. The phone rang. The beacon indicated the phone was in Tom's apartment, but it gave no indication where Tom was. Likewise, the central computer said it had been transmitting updates to Tom's Record, which was also in his apartment. *Probably sleeping*, thought Jonathan as the elevator doors closed.

When there was no answer at Tom's door, he opened it. The room was dark. On the balcony, he found the Record and the phone. Inside the Record a half dozen entries blinked red. He put it down and leaned on the railing, looking out over the city. *Where are you, Thomas Waring?*

The Bridge was a quarter mile away. It swayed in the crosswind like something alive. Stan followed a couple of steps back. "What're you doing?" asked Tom.

"Just tagging along."

"I'm gonna cross and I don't want to get caught. So shut up."

"Quiet as a mouse," said Stan. "But I hope you know that if they *do* catch you, they'll send you . . . over *there*." He pointed.

Tom slowed, looking across the chasm. "So why are *you* here?"

Stan shrugged. "Something to do."

They kept trees between them and the guard shack. They still hadn't seen the guard anywhere. In a small copse of aspens thirty yards from the Bridge, they stopped. "Look!" whispered Stan.

A pair of white boots appeared. The blonde guard from before leaned forward, rubbed his hands together, and yawned. Then he leaned back, disappearing.

"This place is so strange," said Tom. "Creepy, you know?"

"Look around—you'll see why."

Tom looked around. "I don't know what you mean."

"Shh . . . listen."

"I don't hear anything."

"No. *Listen*."

Stan pointed up. Above, yellow and gold aspen leaves twirled on the gentle breeze, rubbing against each other, making a noise like distant waves. Tom shook his head. Stan blew out a breath. "What color are the leaves?"

"Yellow. Why?"

"Think about it."

Suddenly it dawned. "It's autumn here, but it's spring everywhere else, right?"

A breeze moved past, raising goose bumps. Stan's eyes were slits. "Paradise is starting to wind down. And it's starting here."

"Why?"

"The Bridge is a conduit to Earth. And Earth is nearing the end—it's winter there, the last days. We feel it here as well."

Tom noticed a gray slab of cloud hovering on the horizon. "Look," he said, pointing.

Stan nodded. "Big storm coming."

"How am I gonna get across?"

"I look forward to seeing that myself," said Stan, sitting down.

"Any ideas?"

"None whatsoever." Stan closed his eyes, his face tilted upward. He appeared to be listening. Or sleeping.

Sounds came to them on the cool wind. A fog had arisen on the far side of the chasm, shrouding the Bridge there. Tom heard it again; voices. The guard walked to the Bridge and stood at attention.

The fog moved across the Bridge, curling around the glass spans, dulling their reflection so that for the first time Tom could actually see the Bridge. Where the fog eddied across the top, he saw a walkway, looking perilously slippery and narrow. The black cable hung tautly above it, connected to nothing. He heard a voice, and in another moment he saw a blonde man in a gray cloak emerge from the fog, making his way hand over hand along the cable. "Stan!"

Stan opened an eye. "You got a plan?"

"Look!"

By now three people had emerged from the fog, moving in single file along the cable. The fog moved forward with them, obscuring the Bridge. Behind the man came a woman with dark hair, also wearing a gray robe. "We're almost there!" she shouted.

"I'd say now's as good a time as any," said Stan, slapping Tom's back.

"What?"

"The fog—perfect cover. But I'll bet it won't last long."

Tom gulped back fear and trotted toward the Bridge, keeping the guard shack between him and the guard. He made it to the shack and peered around the corner. Five people had emerged from the fog, progressing along the cable.

Stan joined him at the shack. He nodded at the people. "Souls crossing over from Hell."

The blonde man arrived at solid ground and let go of the cable. The guard stood before him at parade rest, his face impassive. The man approached the guard and gave him a hug. The guard withstood it stiffly, then waved the man on. Next came the woman. She kissed the guard's hand, then fainted into his arms. The blonde man returned and helped the guard carry her off the path.

Tom ducked and ran to a scrubby bush near the edge of the abyss. He could feel the cold air ascending and felt the hackles on his neck rise. He was close to where the Bridge met the chasm wall. On the Bridge, the pilgrims edged along, their attention forward. The guard and the blonde man had placed the woman on the chair in the shack. They were trying to revive her, their backs to the Bridge.

When the last of the pilgrims had passed, Tom felt it was time to move, but his feet wouldn't respond. His hands were sweating. Up close, the fog was impenetrable. All he could see of the Bridge was a pulsating whiteness in a gray casing. He imagined the surface slick with moisture. The cable would be wet too. It was too dangerous. He looked into the chasm. The light from the Bridge gave way to darkness. He knew with absolute certainty that if he fell, he would never stop falling.

By now all the people stood around the guard, who had his Record opened and was checking off names.

Tom was about to turn back when Stan ran past him, loping along easily. He leapt up onto the Bridge, grabbed the cable, and disappeared into the mist.

Tom's mouth dropped open. *The guy's a regular monkey!*

Seeing Stan do it gave him heart. He bolted for the Bridge but didn't leap up. Instead, he pressed himself against it, keeping his head low. Fingers of mist curled over the edge.

The guard looked over and Tom ducked. When he ventured a look again, the guard was writing in his Record.

Now or never. Tom hoisted himself up onto the Bridge. The surface was warm and wet. He fumbled for the cable, pulling himself to his feet. He faced the fog, took a deep breath, and plunged in.

Inside the wet grayness, he took a few steps and looked behind him. The guard and the pilgrims were barely visible. No one was looking in his direction. The Bridge was barely six feet wide. He slid his hands along the wet cable, his lead hand pushing water before it. He didn't dare let go to wipe his hand off. Under foot, the Bridge undulated. He focused on the unmoving black line disappearing into the fog before him and moved forward with a slow, shuffling step.

Beneath him, the walkway seemed to flow, a river of colors in slender transparent tubes, like fiber optics. He imagined a million conversations taking place; people talking about box scores or gossiping, without a clue that he was hanging onto a black thread which at any moment could snap, loose coils spiraling out of the mist, sending him over the edge.

He willed the image away and focused on his hands. They wouldn't move. Nor would his feet, which were silhouettes against the brilliant pathway. A thought surfaced, laced with inevitability. *Let go,* it whispered. *Let go.*

Tom shook his head, fighting the impulse. He shut his eyes and held on. He could feel the darkness growing. When he finally opened his eyes he had forgotten which direction he was going. Had the cable been on his right side or his left? He sunk to his knees, the cable pinned under his arm.

Let go, came the soothing voice. *Relax and let go.*

Tom was breathing rapidly. *I'm hyperventilating. I'm going to pass out.* He closed his eyes and darkness enveloped him. He quickly opened them again, terrified at the emptiness behind his eyelids. He needed to wipe his hands off—they were streaming perspiration—but he couldn't let go of the cable.

Let go! said the voice insistently.

An image shimmered out of the fog. It was April. She walked toward him, one hand lightly grazing the cable. She stopped fifteen feet away and waved him onward, speaking. He couldn't hear her. He was about to call out when her words arrived. "Come to me."

The sound of her voice calmed him, a tiny thread of warmth encircling his heart. The suicidal voice screeched, *LET GO!* He shook his head, concentrating on the growing warmth, keeping his eyes on April, who beckoned him. He moved one hand along the cable, then the other. She was just a few feet away, her forearm resting casually on the cable. Her eyes were inviting. "Tom, come to me."

Tom reached toward her. "April." He almost touched her when the mist drew in and she disappeared.

He struggled on. "April! April!"

Then the fog thinned and there was Stan, his back to Tom, the end of the cable stopping at his side. Beyond him the path disappeared into the trees. Stan turned and asked, "What took you so long?"

Tom stumbled the last few steps to solid ground. "Shut up." He fell to his hands and knees, trembling.

"Afraid of heights, are we?"

Tom got slowly to his feet.

Stan grinned. "The fog was delicious! If I'd known it was that easy, I would have crossed over a long time ago."

The wind began clearing the fog. Tom could make out the far canyon wall. *I can't believe I actually came across that.* He looked at Stan. "I don't want any company."

"I know the way."

"How do *you* know the way?"

"I've been around."

"All right. Just don't get in my way."

"I won't," said Stan. "But we'd better get moving or they'll see us." He trotted into the woods.

At the edge of the woods Tom turned and watched last shreds of fog carried away on the wind. The Bridge shone brightly again. On the far side, the pilgrims were moving toward Paradise City.

From the opposite direction, a group of people crested the hill. A woman ran ahead of them. One of the male pilgrims broke into a run. They fell into each other's arms.

Tom turned and walked into the forest.

The guard watched the reunion on the path for a moment, then turned back to his post. Something caught his eye on the other side of the chasm. He squinted, wondering if he had seen someone step into the dark woods there.

20

Tom followed Stan through the dense forest. Stan strode along like he knew the way, which gave Tom pause. If he had been aching to get out of Paradise for so long—which was a question in itself—and hadn't, how would he know the way? Something about him was wrong.

Trees pressed in, their branches joining in a dark canopy. They were unlike any trees he'd ever seen: thick black trunks and shiny greenish-black leaves. The smell of decay rose. The light was weak.

The path itself was clean and smooth, constructed of some black seamless material. It disappeared around a tree a few feet ahead.

When Stan glanced back, Tom read a new expression on his face: fear. Tom felt his spine tingle as he processed Stan's look. He drew along side Stan, who was moving with impressive alacrity. "What's your hurry?"

Stan looked at him as if it were obvious.

"Is there any danger?"

"Only if we get caught."

Talking to this guy was like having a conversation with a four-year old. "Do *you* think we'll get caught?"

Stan stopped. "What is it with you? You chafe against the rules in Paradise. So you decide to break a couple—a Prime Directive in fact—and now you wonder if you're in trouble? Give me a break. If we get caught, *yes*, we're in trouble. What you need to do is to come up with a good explanation—you'll probably need it."

"I don't care."

"Nobody ever does." He walked on ahead.

"I still don't know why you're here."

"I got my own reasons and they don't concern you."

Tom started to speak but Stan stopped. A few feet ahead, the forest gave out and the path continued across a meadow of tall grass. "Look," whispered Stan.

At the other end of the meadow stood two pillars with an iron arch overhead and black gates below. The gates had to be a hundred feet tall. The massive pillars were made of rough-hewn stone, with walls disappearing into the forest on each side. The words GATES OF HELL were formed in the arch by twisted iron. Men in dark robes patrolled the top of the wall. Tom felt an impulse to run.

"Reminds me of that concentration camp," said Tom.

"Auschwitz: 'Arbeit Macht Frei'—Freedom Through Work. It was designed to lull them into a hope of getting out one day."

Tom shivered.

"If they catch us, they'll just keep us there."

Stan moved furtively, not looking back to see if Tom was following. As they drew near the Gates, Stan stopped behind a tree. Tom crouched beside him. "What is it?"

"Don't you want a look inside?"

Through the Gates Tom saw a wide road running to the horizon, where it met an impressive city skyline, full of tall, beautiful buildings.

"*That's* Hell?"

Stan nodded gravely.

"It looks like Paradise, only . . ."

"Bigger and more impressive."

He seems proud of it.

"You expected fire and brimstone?"

Suddenly, a sentry turned toward them. Tom hit the deck. Stan didn't move. "Get down!" hissed Tom.

Stan didn't budge. The sentry turned away. "So?"

Tom got up on his hands and knees. "I guess. You know, burning and suffering."

"Oh, there's suffering, all right, if that's what you like." His voice was rising. "Millions of people suffering, simply because they can't get in line with the precious Plan, the glorious Continuum—"

"Keep it down! What's wrong with you?"

Stan shrugged.

"How come you answer every question with a shrug?"

Stan shrugged, then smiled. Tom felt an urge to hit him.

"And you wanna know the kicker?" mused Stan. "They're in there because they *want* to be! They could march right out and cross over if they wanted to! But no, they're lazy!"

Tom stood, understanding. "You've been there."

Stan turned slowly, his jaw set. "What if I have?"

Standing like this, facing each other, they were in full view of the sentries. "I was just wondering," Tom said mildly.

"It's none of your business, so why don't *you* just shut up?"

"Okay. Don't come unglued."

"I'm not unglued. I'm sick of your superiority. Just 'cause you're bigger doesn't mean you can take me. Looks can fool you. You wanna get into it with me, just say the word."

"All right," said Tom, crouching. Stan stood there, hands on his hips, leaning forward angrily.

"And another thing," he said, "I'm not here because of your virtuous quest. As far as I'm concerned, you're precious integrity is nothing." He pointed at the Gates of Hell. "That place is full of people with integrity. They had integrity when they murdered for king or country. They had integrity when they lied for a 'greater good.' They had integrity when they oppressed the weak in the name of progress. So I don't want to hear any more about integrity. I'm going to Earth. I have business there. If you want to tag along with *me*, fine. But you'd better understand that *I'm* in charge now. So *shut* up."

"Okay," Tom heard himself say.

Stan stomped away into the trees.

Tom looked over his shoulder. The sentries hadn't moved.

Out of sight of the Gates, Stan stepped back onto the path. They walked on for several minutes in silence. Ahead was a large green sign with an arrow: EARTH. Underneath, someone had scratched the words, "Abandon hope all who enter here."

Stan laughed. He hadn't said two words to Tom since the Gates of Hell, but that was okay. It would be best to get to Earth and part ways. Tom didn't want to have anything to do with Stan's "business," whatever it was. Just the thought made his skin crawl.

The forest thinned and a brown plain stretched out before them. The ground was cracked and devoid of vegetation. The pathway disappeared. "The Portal," said Stan.

"Where is it?"

"Out there. You think about where you want to go and boom! you're there."

"I was hoping for the star field, like when I came to Paradise."

"That's for the tourists. For those who want to arrive, not travel, this is the way. Instantaneous. Go ahead."

"Aren't you going?"

"Sure. After you."

"Maybe you should show me."

Stan laughed. "You're afraid! Boy, are you a lousy hero! How are you going to rescue the fair maiden if you're chicken?"

"Go to Hell," barked Tom, walking past Stan.

"See you there."

Tom kept walking. "I'm not going to Hell, I'm going to Earth."

"What's the difference?" laughed Stan.

Tom ignored him and thought about April and Josh and where they might be. He had no idea what day it was on Earth. He'd been gone about ten days but that didn't help much. *I'll go home. That's where they'll be.*

He thought about their little house in Solana Beach with the gravel driveway and the hardwood floors. He imagined April's Maxima in the drive. He pictured Josh's bike on the lawn and Josh playing with Ted. He saw April, calling them to dinner.

Tom felt a pulling at his sternum. There was blackness before him, as well as behind. The Plain was gone. He could see nothing, no stars, constellations, no colorful warp streaks. Just blackness.

Then he felt something against the soles of his feet. The darkness dissipated. Shapes appeared, then colors within a large ring. The edges burned with white light. He saw his house, the juniper trees, and the scabby lawn shimmering within the ring—*No, it's called a Portal.*

Tom stepped through and found himself standing in the street in front of his house. He turned and saw a black Chrysler minivan bearing down on him. He started to move, but it was too late. The van roared right through him. He felt his molecules distend, jiggle about, then reform. The taillights glowed as the van turned the corner. Tom felt himself; he was in one piece.

Of course. I'm a spirit. He was glad to be here, glad to be away from Stan, and glad to be so close to seeing April again.

It was a beautiful day. The sun wasn't bright; he could look directly at it. There were many brighter things in Paradise: the Archangel Gabriel, for example, as well as the Portal he'd just walked through. But the sun was pleasant and he luxuriated in it. He suddenly missed the beach.

Another car came down the street. Tom sauntered to the curb, noticing that although it barely missed him, the driver gave no indication he'd seen him.

The house looked the same, except the flowerbed needed weeding. *April must've been really distracted to not get out here. But I just died. Reason enough.*

There were no cars in the drive. The kitchen blinds were drawn, and a Big Wheel lay on the lawn. The paint was peeling on the front door. *Strange, I just painted that door last fall.* Green hills rose in the east, meaning no more than a few days had passed. Spring lasted about three weeks in southern California, then the brown took over again.

He reached to knock and fell through the door. He turned back and gingerly stuck his hand through one of the diamond-shaped glass panes. It tingled where it intersected with the glass. It wasn't unpleasant but it wasn't *right*, either. It felt like he was interfering with the molecules and they didn't like it.

The house was a mess, strewn with fast food wrappers. A big screen TV dominated the living room, fronted by a ratty couch. The dining set was oak, not white pine. A strange feeling took hold. In Josh's room, instead of his twin bed, a bunkbed filled the room. Posters of sullen rock bands hung on the walls.

Their brass bed was gone from the master bedroom, a waterbed in its place. Tom stepped into the bathroom and looked at himself in the mirror. *At least I'm not a vampire.*

He was pretty sure April had moved but he had to make sure. He pushed himself through the garage door. The garage was dark and full of moving boxes, old lamps, and bulging plastic garbage bags. It smelled of animal urine. "Ted?" he said hopefully.

There was a low growl.

"Ted, boy? Is that you?"

On a dirty blanket behind a pile of cardboard boxes sat a German shepherd, staring right at him, even though he knew it was impossible. The dog eyed him malevolently, growling as Tom backed up the stairs.

Suddenly the shepherd lunged. Tom fell back and heard a thump as the dog hit the door. A soft mewl of pain, then the growling continued as the dog padded to its blanket.

Tom's heart raced. In the kitchen, letters lay under a black purse, their addresses obscured. He tried moving the purse but couldn't. A calendar hung on a wall. It was May. *Okay, it hasn't been too long.* From the looks of the place, the new tenants had just moved in.

But something on the calendar wasn't right. The year: 1998.

She's not here because I've been dead for over a year.

How could a week in Paradise turn out to be a whole year on Earth? Now, his whole plan was in danger. Suddenly he was both happy and angry; happy because it wasn't so horrible for April to be married after a year; angry because she might *be* married after a year.

He left the house with no idea how to find her. Not only that, he didn't know what he would do if he did. He decided a look at the ocean would clear his mind.

Tom stepped from the Portal to 14th street, the dead end street on the cliff above the best shore break in the county. It was night; a half moon was out. But something was wrong. There were no houses, no street lights, no streets—no sign of civilization at all. The arc of coastline was black and featureless as far as he could see.

There was nothing on the cliff except sagebrush and dry grass. On the beach, breakers crashed, the foam white in the moonlight.

I finally get the beach to myself and I can't even surf. I could walk out there and not even get wet. Besides, surfboards had not even been invented yet—it had to be a thousand years ago. *Or a thousand years in the future—after the radioactive clouds dissipate. Humanity destroys itself, and the Earth recovers silently on its own.*

A great loneliness settled over him. The thought of living in an empty world wasn't so bad—the idea had a certain antisocial appeal—but being here without April was too much.

If she was here they would travel together across empty deserts and climb mountains, going days at a time without speaking, just touching each other and pointing out some remarkable sight. They would sleep at night under strange, unknown constellations. They would eat ripe fruit, juice running down their chins, the sun browning their bodies.

"I'll be damned if I'm gonna miss *that*," he said, turning away from the sea. "Gimme the Portal."

As he walked across the plaza, Jonathan dialed Tom's Quantum Mechanics instructor. He said Tom had missed class two cycles in a row. Jonathan thanked him and hung up.

At Public Works, Tom's supervisor said he had been there the previous cycle and that although he was quiet, he seemed like a nice man. She asked if anything was wrong. Jonathan said no and left.

As he entered the Great Library, he was feeling quite put out. *I have better things to do than chase this man down.* He inquired at the reference desk. The librarian studied the photo of Tom. "I've seen him before."

"Has he been here this cycle?"

"No. I only met him once. He came in looking lonely. I tried to cheer him up by showing him his book."

"Show it to me," commanded Jonathan.

"Ask me nicely."

Jonathan exhaled sharply. "All right. *Please.*"

"I'd be delighted," she said, a triumphant smile on her face.

She took him upstairs. Jonathan examined Tom's book, ignoring the pudgy librarian. After a minute, she said, "Do you need anything else?" Jonathan shook his head and waved her off. He heard her mutter something as she walked away.

He skimmed the book, searching for something that would illuminate Tom's behavior. After just a few pages, he found it, the story of Tom's conversion, which he read carefully.

When he finished the account, he put the book back on the shelf and walked to the end of the row and leaned on the balustrade, thinking. *I may have underestimated Thomas Waring. He's a True Believer, someone for whom grace isn't just wishful thinking. He believes he is guided by the Spirit and such people are often unpredictable.*

This is worse than I thought.

21

Tom stepped into the United Family Services reception area. The receptionist chomped gum, reading a magazine, oblivious to him. He couldn't get over how mortals couldn't see the Portal's brilliant display.

He headed down the hall, looking for April's office. The clinic was quiet; everyone seemed to have left. He saw her nameplate on an open door. She wasn't there, but the desk looked worked-in. On the desk was a photo of Tom, April and Josh, taken Christmas 1996. She still had a picture of him on display! *I wonder what he thinks about that.*

On the window sill sat the conch shell he bought April on their honeymoon. She had wanted to "liberate" it back into the ocean. Tom told her she wasn't 'liberating' it as long as they were married.

She's still got it. Maybe this quest wasn't hopeless after all.

"I don't care," said a woman from the hallway. "Tell her I'm booked." A woman in a gold knit dress walked by. Tom tried to remember her name—she looked familiar.

She turned into the office across the hall. The nameplate on her door read MICHELLE DEWITT. She picked up the phone, punching the keypad.

Tom remembered. They met a few months before he died, when he came downtown to take April to lunch. April and Michelle emerged from the building, laughing in that conspiratorial way women do. Michelle looked at Tom like she was casting a film, probably wondering how he could be the guy April was always talking about. They shook hands and Tom was overwhelmed by her perfume. Later, he wondered aloud what kind of a therapist Michelle was. "Sexual dysfunction," said April. He nodded. Perfect.

Michelle had the phone on her shoulder, her acrylic nails clicking on the desk. She was looking in his direction. He met her eyes. "Michelle."

Not a flicker.

"Michelle," he said more forcefully.

Her eyes suddenly brightened. "Hell-o, Janice! What's up?" She leaned back, her eyes focusing on the empty doorway.

Tom moved into her eye line. *Windows to the soul.*

Michelle listened, then laughed. "He didn't!"

Tom leaned in. "MICHELLE!" She swivelled her chair and looked out the window, saying, "Uh huh. No kidding?"

Tom tried grasping the chair, but his hands passed through it. He walked through the desk and whispered. "Where's April?"

Michelle said goodbye, put the phone down, and leaned back, looking out the window dreamily.

Tom said, "April. April. APRIL!"

She popped the phone off the hook. A phone rang elsewhere in the office and a woman's voice said, "This is Trish."

"Where's April today?"

Tom cheered. He leaned forward, eager to hear everything. His hand passed through the phone. "Oww!" It was red hot. He jerked his hand back, wringing it, looking for scald marks.

"She didn't come in?" Michelle was saying.

Tom scowled at the phone.

"How come *I* don't get a personal day?" asked Michelle.

Tom touched the phone and felt another powerful shock, but resisted pulling back. After a moment, the tingling subsided. It wasn't really painful—it was just *busy*. Somehow he knew what was going on: the electrons were pushing each other along the phone line. Their activity caused the burning.

Michelle said, "Well, tell Dan I'm taking a day off next week. I got a life too." She hit the FLASH button and punched some numbers.

Tom held his hand in place and hoped. The phone rang three times before the machine picked up.

"I'm sorry, but we're unable to come to the phone . . ."

It was April! But he didn't have her number; Michelle had punched it in too quickly for him to catch it. *It doesn't matter. I can't use a phone anyway.*

". . . If you'd like to leave your name and number . . ."

Michelle drummed her nails.

". . . after the tone, we'll . . ."

Tom could tell by the way Michelle was holding the phone that she was going to hang up. He only had a couple of seconds. She took the phone away from her ear.

". . . call you back as soon . . ."

Suddenly, Tom's mind caught fire. "Portal!" he yelled. The wheel of light appeared instantly. He kept his hand immersed in the phone, feeling the hot electrons slamming into each other.

"Follow the line!"

As Michelle hung up, darkness surrounded him. He felt something warm in his hand. It was a phone line, pulsing red and orange. Beyond him the wire disappeared into darkness. Behind him the tail ran for ten feet, then stopped in a burst of sparks, like a lit fuse. It was growing shorter; the broken connection was chasing him.

He willed himself to go faster and watched as the tail extended out behind him. Ahead, a white circle of light appeared and grew, becoming the Portal ring. Shimmering inside was a kitchen counter with a black box atop it. The connection ended there.

The answering machine. Tom was about to step through when the broken connection zipped through his fingers and winked out at the answering machine. A red message indicator blinked.

Tom stepped into the kitchen. It was dark and cool. The dining set was pushed against the wall, too large for the room. Their sofa sat in front of the television in the living room. A pizza box lay on the coffee table, along with an empty liter of Diet Coke.

Somewhere water shut off and things suddenly got quiet. Someone was in the bath. Tom headed down the hall, passing a bedroom. There was his roll-top desk. Across the hall was a bedroom with Josh's bed. His clothes were scattered across the floor.

At the end of the hall was a closed door, a slice of light leaking out the bottom. Without giving himself time to think, he walked through it.

The room was full of steam. April stood before the mirror in a terry bathrobe, her hair wrapped in a towel.

Tom watched her in the mirror as she rubbed moisturizer onto her face, his heart singing. "Your eyes are *brown*, full of gold flecks." He felt relieved; the memory was safely back.

She was as beautiful as ever. He ached to put his arms around her waist and feel her wet hair against his cheek. He reached out but his hand passed through her. He felt just the slightest tingle.

She shook her hair free and began combing it, looking blankly in the mirror.

"April," said Tom. "April, honey, it's me."

She combed out a tangle, grimacing. Tom moved to one side, taking in the upturned nose with freckles across the bridge, the large, liquid eyes, the full lips. He felt weak being this close to her.

"April, can you hear me?"

She kept on combing.

"I've come back."

April surprised him by looking at him, but her eyes showed no recognition. She reached out and her hand passed through him, grasping the doorknob, opening it. Tom backed out into the hall. She came out and turned toward the kitchen.

She got a pint of ice cream from the freezer and retrieved a spoon from the sink. She went into the living room, sat down on the couch, and clicked the remote. On the TV, Oprah was discussing a book. April pushed the pizza box off the coffee table with her foot.

Tom kneeled before her. "Can't you even *feel* me?" April laconically took another bite of ice cream. He could count the times April ate ice cream on one hand—especially *chocolate* ice cream. She simply didn't like it.

He left the room, his mind in a whirl. He'd never imagined he'd get back and find she couldn't even *hear* him. He felt betrayed by his own stupidity.

The clock in Josh's room read 12:43. *Josh is at school. He's in first grade now.*

The thought made him tired. On the dresser was a framed picture of Josh with a Mickey Mouse hat on, his name stitched on it in gold thread. He was holding April's hand. She wore shorts and a tee shirt, her eyes invisible behind sunglasses. Holding Josh's other hand was the stranger. He also had on sunglasses. Tom wished he could turn the picture face down. Instead, he trudged back to the living room.

April sat listlessly on the couch, the ice cream container on her lap. Oprah was taking questions from the audience.

Tom shook his head. He thought he'd bottomed out when he saw the stranger helping Josh ride his bike in the vision. But it was nothing compared to this. Something was wrong with *April*—she had changed. She had simply . . .

"You've moved on. You don't even remember me."

April hit the channel button. A woman and a hunk were in a clutch. She flipped channels again.

Tom moved closer. "I thought I was coming back to tell you about Heaven, but now I know why I really came back: to tell you how much I miss you. How much I love you."

April punched the channel button again.

Tom knelt before her. "I only want you to be happy. If you are, then that's enough for me." He put his hand against her cheek. He couldn't feel a thing.

On the television, a reporter was talking about a traffic accident. April flipped the channel. After a long time, Tom stood and walked toward the door.

Outside, he paused on the stoop. It was the neighborhood he'd seen in the vision. A bicycle lay on the lawn. Tom didn't recognize it. Josh's step dad had probably bought it for him for Christmas.

He walked to the sidewalk. *You did your part. You delivered the message. What else can you do?*

"Gang way!" A bicycle roared by, narrowly missing him. The rider wobbled down the sidewalk, barely in control.

"Stan?"

Stan rode the old beach cruiser off the curb so hard Tom felt his own teeth rattle. Out in the street, he made a shaky U-turn.

"Hey, you're riding a bike!"

Stan picked up speed and hit a curb, flying off the bike and into the air. He hit the ground hard. Tom ran to him. Stan jumped up. "Not a scratch!" He spread his arms grandly as proof.

Tom stared. "Is that a *real* bike?"

Stan straightened his tunic. "Real as a skinned knee!"

Tom pinched him. "Ouch!" said Stan. "What's that for?"

"You're just like me—a spirit."

Stan rubbed his arm and looked at Tom with hooded eyes. "How'd you like to see a spirit get a bloody nose?" He held his bony fist up in Tom's face.

"You rode the bike. How?"

"It's a secret."

"Tell me."

"No."

The bike lay on the grass, the rear wheel still ticking around. Tom put out his foot to stop it but it kept on spinning. "How?"

Stan put his bare foot out and stopped the wheel. He grinned. "Nifty, huh?"

"Are you gonna tell me how you did that?"

"Probably not. But I *will* tell you this: anyone can do it."

"Will you show me?"

"Figure it out yourself. It'll mean more to ya."

"*You* probably don't even know how you do it."

"Nice try," winked Stan.

"Forget it," said Tom. "I'm too tired to fight."

"So," said Stan, nodding at the house. "How'd it go? You give her The Message?" He chuckled.

Tom felt a stab of anger. "What're *you* doing here?"

"I was heading out. Wondered what you were gonna do."

"You came by to laugh at me."

"Why? You do something funny?"

Tom felt his anger rise. "Look, if you want to take off, don't let me stop you."

"Couldn't if you tried."

"Are you always like this?"

"Like what?"

"An insufferable jerk."

"What?" asked Stan, offended.

It made Tom happy. He nodded.

Stan made a face. "*You're* the jerk."

"Here we go again," Tom said. "I'm outta here." He started walking away. Stan kept pace with him, just out of range. Tom thought about calling for the Portal, just to get away.

"You came all this way to talk to her. What did she say?"

Tom gauged his sincerity. "Nothing."

"What?"

"I don't think she heard me."

Stan smiled. "Oh! So she isn't a *Listener!*"

"What's that?"

"You oughta know—you were one. A Listener is someone who is tuned-in to spiritual things. They get premonitions, inspirations, feelings—you know."

"Well she doesn't get those things." Tom threw his hands up. "This is just like my meeting with the Council. They told me that in order to get faith, you've got to have it already. And now you're telling me that unless she's a Listener, she can't *hear* what I'm saying. Talk about circular reasoning."

Stan's grin grew larger. "That's about right."

"Well, it's a load of crap."

Stan shrugged. "Could be."

"Hey," said Tom suddenly. "*You* could make her hear."

"Me?"

"Yeah," said Tom, warming to it. "You know, rattle the blinds, move the furniture around or something."

"Good idea," laughed Stan. "That'd put her in the right mood. 'Oh, hey, by the way, while I'm scaring the wits out of you, there's a God and everything's A-OK!'"

"You could find a way."

"But I won't."

"Why not?" growled Tom.

"This is *your* hero's journey, not mine. I've already done more than I should have."

"Like what?"

"I got you across the Bridge."

"I got myself across!"

"You wouldn't have gone if I hadn't gone first. You were about to give up. And what about the Portal? If it wasn't for me, you'd've never found it. You'd still be wandering around on the Plain, looking for a big door marked EARTH!"

Tom almost popped him, but then a dawning awareness settled on him. He began to feel giddy. He slapped his knee and laughed. Stan watched him the way one watches a dangerous lunatic.

"Only a Listener can hear, right?" asked Tom.

Stan said nothing.

Tom shouted, "I want the Portal!" An instant later, he stepped through the ring of white fire.

Sitting on the couch, blindly watching TV, April thought of Tom. She closed her eyes, pretending he was pressing his palm against her cheek, looking at her, smiling. As the feeling lingered, she felt tears building and kept very still, trying to push them away. They spilled out anyway and tracked down her cheeks. *Oh, Tom, where are you?*

She felt a draft and looked around. The front door was closed. Like her heart. She tasted tears—salty, like the ocean.

She saw Tom coming in from the waves, his board under his arm, water dripping off him. And a smile that said, *What a day!* and *I love you!* at the same time.

Then, just as he was about to touch her, he vanished. All that was left was the taste of salt at the corners of her mouth.

The TV droned on. April buried her face in her hands.

22

Tom stepped into Chuck's living room. The drapes were shut; the place was musty. The carpet was littered with newspapers. The pile of new age books stood by the recliner.

He went to the front door and poked his head through. Chuck's green Ford sat in the drive, the front tire flat and the windshield layered with dust. Tom pulled his head back inside just in time to see the white flash of the Portal disappear. Stan remained, eating a popsicle.

"What do you want?" complained Tom.

"You want some?"

"Show-off."

"Mmm," said Stan, smacking his lips. "I love sherbet."

"Food's for unevolved people."

"Call me a missing link, then," said Stan, biting off a big chunk. "It's dee-licious!" He held it out.

Tom was tempted but wouldn't give Stan the satisfaction. Besides, he doubted he could manage even a lick off it. Instead, he walked toward the kitchen. "Chuck?"

Stan looked around. "So this guy's a crackpot, huh?"

"He's just got an open mind."

Stan gestured at the Ouija board on the coffee table. "An open mind's great." He picked up *Tolkin's Spirit Guide*, flipping pages. "But this guy's mind is so open his brain must've fallen out."

Tom reached out but his hand moved right through the book. "How do you *do* that?"

Stan smirked. "Don't say I never did anything for you." He held the book out. "It's easy. You ask the molecules in the book if they will let you move *them* instead of you moving *around* them. Since their highest objective is to serve, they will usually comply. Usually." He put the book down. "You try."

Tom bent over the book. It was probably too big for his first try but he wasn't going to squander a learning opportunity. In a low voice, he said, "May I pick you up?"

Stan sputtered.

"What?"

"Do it silently: let it know that you really need to move it; that it would serve a good purpose if you could. Then just pick it up."

Tom concentrated. *Please, I need your help. I need to be able to move physical objects. Will you help me?*

Nothing happened.

"Wait," said Stan.

The book slowly rose into the air. The leather cover opened and the pages began to turn, lifted by an invisible finger.

Stan smiled. "Pretty cool, huh?"

The book hovered in front of Tom. Pages turned slowly until they reached a place marked by a red ribbon.

"You didn't even touch it," said Stan. "Now who's showing off?"

Tom placed his hands under the book and it settled onto his palms. He could feel its weight. He blew on a page. It popped up and turned gracefully.

"Thank you," said Tom to the book. He felt a gentle buzz of electricity on his fingers. "It's thanking me!"

"It exists to serve."

Behind him, someone said, "Oh my Lord!"

Tom turned. Chuck stood in his pajamas and bathrobe, his eyes popping, watching the *Spirit Guide* floating in mid-air.

"Chuck!" said Tom, closing the book. Chuck raised his hands, terror in his eyes.

"You're scaring him," said Stan.

"Chuck, it's me! Tom!" He put the book under his arm, extending his free hand. Chuck stepped back, his mouth open.

"Put the book down before you give him a heart attack."

Tom put the *Guide* on the stack of books. "I thought a Listener can hear spirits," whispered Tom.

"Not unless you . . . YELL!"

Chuck stared at the *Spirit Guide.*

Stan whispered in Chuck's ear. "We're from the library! These books are overdue! We've come to take them baaaack!"

"Cut it out!" yelled Tom.

Stan turned to Tom. "I said a Listener gets *impressions*—he doesn't hear actual words. He'd have to be as dead as we are . . ." He stopped. "On the other hand," he amended, "he looks near dead already."

Chuck was sitting on the ratty couch, still staring at the book. He pulled a string of beads from his bathrobe and began mumbling. Chuck's whiteness wasn't fear, it was the translucence of old age. His skin hung loosely under his chin. His eyes were sunken, and one was cloudy with cataracts.

"He's sick," realized Tom.

"He's dying," said Stan matter-of-factly.

Tom kneeled in front of Chuck, who was looking through him, focused on the book. He finished the rosary and started again. "Chuck, can you hear me?" asked Tom in a low voice.

Chuck was breathing in short, hitching draws. He fingered the beads with bony fingers. Tom reached to touch his knee but pulled back. "Will he feel anything if I touch him?"

Stan was examining a crucifix above the mantle, his brow furrowed. "I doubt it. His molecules serve *him*, not you. Besides, touching is included in *The* Prime Directive: 'Never Interfere With Another's Mortality'."

"I just want to touch him."

"It's still interfering."

"Why is it such a bad thing?"

"Simple touching is no big deal, but any mortal sensation is addictive and you'll want more—remember how great it was to have a physical body?—and you'll be tempted to use a person's body for your own purposes. That's a classic violation."

"But a simple touch . . ."

"Suit yourself," shrugged Stan.

Tom hadn't counted on Chuck being so frail, but he really needed to talk to him. He reached out to touch Chuck's knee, but his hand passed through, unimpeded. "It doesn't work!"

"Hmm," mused Stan. "It works when I do it."

"Then do it."

Stan shook his head emphatically.

Tom turned to Chuck. "Chuck, can you hear me?"

Chuck put the rosary away. He got to his feet and hobbled to his lounger. He picked up the *Spirit Guide*, opening it where the ribbon marked the place. He put on a pair of glasses and bent over the book.

Stan went into the kitchen. Tom hoped he wouldn't make any noise. Chuck looked like he'd have a seizure any second. Chuck's lips silently formed words as he read.

Tom whispered, "Chuck, it's me, Tom."

Chuck lifted his head. "Mom?"

Tom blinked, pleased. "No, it's me, *Tom!*"

"See Mom," echoed Chuck, his eyes glazed.

"No! TOM!"

"Keep it down in there," came Stan's voice from the kitchen.

"See Mom tomorrow," murmured Chuck.

Tom went into the kitchen. Stan was poking around in the freezer. After a moment, he emerged, holding a foil covered disk. "Ding Dongs!"

Tom pushed against the fridge door without thinking and felt the smooth plastic surface. He stared at it as it closed.

Stan unwrapped the Ding Dong. "You think he'll miss one of these?"

"He can hear me, but he gets what I say confused."

Stan bit into the Ding Dong, his eyes closed. "I love these things!" He held it out to Tom.

Tom shook his head. "What am I gonna do?"

"About what?" said Stan, taking a big bite.

"He can't understand. He's too old."

Stan took another bite. "It happens."

"I was counting on him."

Stan wadded the tin foil into a ball and tossed it at the trashcan. It missed cleanly. "Losing it," he said, walking over and picking it up.

"Stan!"

"What?"

"He can't hear me! I need him to hear me!"

Stan returned, turned back, and arced the foil ball high overhead. It fell into the basket. "That's two!"

"Stan!"

Stan frowned at Tom. "Let me see if I understand the objective here. You want old one-foot-in-the-grave out there to be your messenger boy. Is that about right?"

Tom nodded.

"Dream on."

"He's a Listener if there ever was one," affirmed Tom.

"He's too old. And even if you do get through to him, he probably can't take the excitement." He drew a finger across his neck.

"What was that?"

Stan made the cutting motion again.

"You said I was making Chuck my messenger boy . . ."

"So?"

"And then you said. . ." Tom brightened. "'Dream on.'"

Stan shrugged.

Tom slapped him on the shoulder. "You're a genius, man." He walked into the livingroom.

Stan opened the fridge and grabbed another Ding Dong. "Tell me something I don't know."

The streets were empty as Jonathan walked back from the Library. Normally, during the dark half of a cycle, he meditated or studied. But tonight he was searching for Tom, feeling very put out. As he walked across the Council Building plaza, he considered the possibility that he might have to seek help from Upstairs. He looked up to the topmost floor. It would look bad on his record. He had underestimated the trouble Thomas was getting to be. His eyes moved down the tall building. It gave him great pleasure to know that his office was only fifty-two floors below the Council chambers. When he arrived here just over a fifty cycles ago, he made quite a splash. They called him a rising star and friends and jealous competitors alike were amazed at the speed with which he grasped the intricacies of what he privately called "People Processing." Not that he thought of people as objects. But his upbringing in Victorian England, combined with the achievement ethic of Paradise, had made him a formidable administrator. Up until now.

Jonathan had underestimated Thomas's will. *What kind of a person doesn't feel gratitude at being rewarded with a place in Paradise?* And to make matters worse, Thomas didn't respect Jonathan's place here either. That was the most galling thing of all!

Jonathan opened his Record, finding the page chronicling his search, with small boxes containing check marks for items he'd accomplished. He'd looked everywhere: Thomas's apartment, his classes, the Library, his job. Only the last box was blank, the words MISSING PERSONS beside it. That would mean informing his superior, the thoroughly disagreeable Beverly Parker. He felt his skin crawl. She would love to see him fail, but he would not give her the satisfaction. Thomas Waring would reappear and no one would be the wiser, except Thomas, for whom Jonathan would devise an exquisite punishment.

As he walked toward the building, he passed the fountain. He never really liked it. It was too *modern*, with those jarring geometrics and water curtains. It lacked the *majesty* that should befit a fountain in this location.

He saw his reflection in the water and remembered a conversation with Thomas on this very spot. Thomas had seen himself in the fountain, looking up at a beautiful woman in a window.

In Thomas's book was a description of his wife, April. She had dark hair and was described as pretty. Jonathan's exhaustive psychological training (accomplished in one afternoon) had prepared him to evaluate dreams. The woman in the elevated window (elevated = lofty aspirations; window = a short time frame for action) was April (Thomas's aspiration), waving (encouraging action) to Thomas's reflection, who was laughing (fearless and heroic, as Thomas wished he was), and when the real Thomas looked up at her, she was gone (the psychic distance between Thomas's aspirations and his reality).

Jonathan congratulated himself on his unimpeachable analysis. But there was something more. He focused on the wall of water and recreated the dream. Of course, it was not *his* vision, but Thomas had related the story himself. He would have included all important elements. Jonathan imagined Thomas standing in the desert, looking up at the woman in the window. *No, the word he used was "plain."* Standing on a *plain*.

Jonathan suddenly felt as if he had arrived at a party to find that everyone had already gone home. *Could Thomas have unwittingly conjured the Plain of Portals in his vision?*

"Thomas Waring," he said as he walked briskly away, "you may be in a world of trouble." Opening a glass door, he thought secretly, *You and I both.*

Tom trotted into the living room. Chuck was hunched over the *Spirit Guide*, reading, his hands trembling faintly.

Stan followed. "What's up?"

"I'm going into his dreams."

Stan took the last bite of Ding Dong. "How?"

"I hope it's the same principle as moving the book: since his conscious mind is old, I'll ask his subconscious to help me. It's his spirit; it's ageless, isn't it?"

Stan shook his head. "Where did you get such a goofy idea?"

"It won't work?"

"I didn't say that. I just wondered where you got the idea."

Tom pointed to his head. "Because . . . I'm *smart*. I just wish I didn't have to wait for him to go to bed."

Stan gave Tom a sidelong look. "Your I.Q. just took a nose dive. Time and space are variable."

"What?"

Stan snapped his fingers and the Portal appeared. "Why wait?" He nodded at the dark interior. Forms began to take shape. In a moment there was Chuck's living room, exactly as it was now, except the lounger was empty. "He's in bed."

"Amazing," grinned Tom.

"After you," Stan said, bowing.

Tom stepped through, feeling odd to be entering the same place he was leaving. The wall clock said 2:35. Stan stepped out of the Portal and it winked out. They walked to Chuck's bedroom and passed through the door. Chuck was asleep on one side of the bed. The other side was unmussed. A picture of Carolyn, taken during World War Two, stood on the nightstand. Her lips were as red as her curly hair. Tom placed his hand on Chuck's hand, trying to feel his papery skin. After a minute of trying, he gave up.

Stan sat on the bed. "What now?"

"I'm going in," said Tom.

"I'll cover you!" said Stan, cocking an invisible rifle and training it on the door.

Tom put his hand on Chuck's brow. *Chuck, it's Tom. I need to talk to you—the real you, your spirit.*

He felt a gentle warmth under his hand. Stan was poking around in the closet. He turned, holding a bolo tie under his chin. "What do you think?"

Tom tried again. *Chuck, I need your help. Let me in your dream. Please.*

He felt a pulling sensation. He opened his eyes and saw his hand deep inside Chuck's skull. He tried to pull it out but couldn't. Soon his arm was inside Chuck's head up to his elbow. The old guy lay there quietly, his breath gently wheezing in and out. Tom looked at Stan, alarmed. Stan had his back to him, looking at another tie in the mirror. "Stan! Help!"

Stan turned, saw what was happening, and said, "You asked for it." He turned back to the mirror, trying to decide between a bolo with a ruby and one with a tiny Aztec calendar.

Suddenly, Tom felt himself falling through darkness, twisting and turning. He fell a great distance, listening to a distant droning sound rising and falling.

Breathing, he thought, plunging into a gray cloud. He hit the ground face first, his head bouncing off the floor, sparks flying before his eyes. He heard steel striking steel and sat up weakly. Before him was a tremendous stairway, stretching up into the darkness. A man was bent over, swinging a hammer. He set another nail and drove it in in two great swings. Tom got to his feet groggily. "Howdy."

"Howdy yourself," said the man, driving another nail home.

"What you building?"

"Pretty obvious, ain't it?" said the man, turning. He smiled suddenly. "Why, howdy, Tom."

"Chuck? That you?" This was a Chuck Tom had never met. He was young with thick black hair. He wore jeans and a tool belt but had no moustache. But Tom could see his friend inside the eyes.

Chuck was looking around for something. "It was here a minute ago . . ." He went to a box and started pulling tools out.

"What are you looking for?"

"My hammer."

"It's in your belt."

Chuck's hand went to his tool belt like a gunfighter. He withdrew the hammer. "Where you been?" he asked the hammer, walking back to the stairway.

"Chuck, you remember me, don't you?"

"Ayup," said Chuck, marking a length of wood with a pencil. "Especially around pay day. Which reminds me, you owe me back pay." He took the wood to a table saw Tom hadn't noticed before and flipped on the saw, made the cut, and walked back to the stairway.

"Back pay?"

"You left me hanging, boss."

"Sorry."

Chuck put the piece of wood in place as a riser. "Never mind. You had a good excuse, being dead and all." He pulled out a finish nail and reached for his hammer. It wasn't in his belt loop.

"So you know I'm dead?"

"Say, where is it now? The hammer?"

Tom looked over at the table saw. The hammer wasn't there.

"I'm gettin' bored with this," said Chuck. "Can't make no headway if my tools keep growin' legs and walking off."

"You had it a moment ago." The hammer was suddenly lying on the ground by Chuck's foot. "There it is."

Chuck picked up the hammer and shook it. "I'm gonna tie this thing to my wrist!" He reached into his pouch. "What? I had a whole pocket of nails a second ago." He dropped the hammer onto the floor, daring it to walk off again.

"Chuck," said Tom gently. "This is a *dream*, a frustration dream, you know, where nothing works? The car won't start, you can't sink the nine ball, you miss the turn off?"

Chuck looked around, squinting. "Dream, huh?"

"Yep," said Tom, sitting next to him. "Look." He pointed.

"Well, I'll be!" said Chuck. The hammer had disappeared.

"I've had dreams like this. I think I'm *living* one these days."

"Well, it don't feel like a dream, except for you: you're dead, you know," stated Chuck.

"Yeah. And I've come back to ask you a big favor."

"If I can."

"I need you to deliver a message to April for me."

"Why don't you deliver it?"

"I tried, but you know April, she's not open to promptings. She can't hear me like you can."

"Hey, look!" said Chuck. Atop a pile of lumber that Tom *knew* wasn't there a moment ago was the hammer. Chuck laughed. "Thing gets around, don't it?"

"So you know what I mean?"

"What makes you think she'll hear me?"

"You can talk to her. You're still alive."

"Just barely. You tried talking to me earlier but I got it all wrong." He looked down, embarrassed.

"You heard me?"

"I couldn't understand you. Most the time, when I'm awake, I feel like I got the flu *and* a cold. I'm in bad shape."

"You're fine."

"I'm dying." He looked at Tom evenly. "Know how I know?"

Tom shook his head.

Chuck held out a chiseled forearm and made a fist. "It's an old man's dream, being young again."

Tom didn't know what to say.

"So what's your message?" asked Chuck.

"I promised April I'd return and tell her if there was a God."

"That's quite a promise. You must've ruffled a few feathers keeping that one!"

"How'd you know?"

"Judging by the number of people who die and the number who come back, I'd say it was against the rules."

Tom nodded.

"Must've cost you."

"I think I'm in pretty big trouble."

Chuck considered this. "This ain't like you, going against the grain. Why don't you just trust God to take care of things?"

"Heaven's not like you think, Chuck. I didn't want to break any rules—but I had to! And I'm not proud of what I'm doing."

"So what's wrong with the way they run heaven?"

"It's like one big positive mental attitude seminar. Everybody's busy as bees, running around like ants, doing what they're told—like a bunch of sheep."

"Sounds like a real barnyard," mused Chuck. "No offense," he continued, "but I recall a Tom Waring who would've been happy just to be there. What changed?"

"Me, I guess." He hung his head. "I never had any conflict before; I just believed and let God do the rest."

"Sounds like good advice."

"But God wasn't doing anything."

"You got impatient, too," said Chuck. "But all right. I'll deliver your message on one condition. You gotta tell me something."

"Anything."

"How's my Carolyn? Is she all right?"

Tom felt like a traitor. "I haven't seen her."

"What's that supposed to mean?"

"I haven't seen her. It's a big place, Chuck."

"Well, did you even *try* to find her?"

Tom looked at him weakly.

"You're a piece of work, Tom," said Chuck, standing. "A real piece of work." He turned his back, his hands on his hips. After a moment he walked to the woodpile, picked up the hammer and dropped it into its loop on his belt. He walked back to Tom.

"I'm sorry, Chuck."

"Forget it. Ain't none of us perfect, from what I seen lookin' in the mirror. I'll deliver your message, but when this is all over, and you go back, you find Carolyn and tell her I asked about her. Deal?"

"I'll tell her."

"And when you leave this dream, pinch me. I'm tired of fighting this contrary staircase."

"Okay. And thanks."

"On your way," said Chuck, turning to his work.

Tom walked a few steps, then turned. Chuck was looking for something again.

23

B y the time Chuck woke up, the sun was shining through the bedroom window. He rolled onto his side, his head aching.

He didn't get migraines very often, but when he did, they shut him down for days. He pulled the pillow over his face to block the light. He knew he should close the drapes but dying would be easier than getting up just now. His head pounded and the light drilled through his eyelids. He found it hard to breathe. The dizziness hit him and he felt like his head would burst. *I'm dying . . . .*

After a long time, the spinning slowed. Keeping his eyes closed, he reached for the nightstand and found a plastic bottle. He thumbed the lid off and swallowed two tablets. He lay back on the bed and put the pillow over his face, waiting for the Vicodin to go to work.

Lying there, the dream came back, fuzzy behind the wall of pain. He was working on a staircase when Tom Waring walked up. He said he had come back from heaven to tell April there was a God after all. But she couldn't hear him and so he had come to Chuck for help.

The pain was letting up a little. Chuck didn't dare open his eyes but at least the throbbing subsided to something like being beaten over the head with an ax handle. He knew he would pay later for taking the Vicodin, which never completely killed the migraine. Instead, it forced the pain into the background, where it hung on twice as long as it would if he just rode it out without medication.

In the dream they talked about Carolyn. Tom had made no effort to locate her in heaven. *He didn't even know if she was there!*

It suddenly hit him that he was mad because of something Tom said in a *dream*. It seemed real, but Tom and Carolyn were in heaven and he was here in Migraine Hell. He pulled the covers over his head.

Tom and Stan stepped through the Portal. Tom looked at the lump under the covers and glanced at the clock. Ten thirty seven. "Still sleeping? I'm gonna wake him—I'm not coming back a third time."

"I'm hungry," said Stan, leaving the room.

Tom tried to pull the covers back but his hand passed through them. He rebelled at the arbitrariness of it all. Sometimes you could effect physical things and sometimes you couldn't. It didn't really matter if your cause was good or not. It was pure luck. He sat and rested his chin in his hands, resigned to wait.

He hadn't waited a full minute before Chuck got groggily up and went into the bathroom. When he came out a few minutes later, Tom saw how different the real Chuck was from his dream counterpart. He was gaunt and moved slowly. Tom left while he dressed.

Tom was trying to open the *Spirit Guide* when Chuck came in, wearing a blue checked shirt and brown slacks which seemed too large. He walked with one hand slightly forward, as if to fend things off. He went to the kitchen and drank a glass of water, then closed the blinds and sat at the kitchen table, resting his head in his hands.

"Chuck," said Tom.

After a long time Chuck pulled the phone off the counter and placed it in front of him. Tom's heart pounded. Chuck dialed Tom's old number. Tom dipped a forefinger into the phone. It rang twice, then a recorded voice came on, saying the number had been disconnected and no further information existed. Chuck hung up and stared at the phone.

"It's not gonna be that easy," said Tom gently.

Chuck opened a drawer and took out the white pages, scanning the "W's".

"She's got a new last name," said Tom.

Chuck rubbed his temples.

"Don't give up," whispered Tom, kicking himself for not telling Chuck more in his dream, when he was clear and lucid.

"Her work!" he said suddenly. "United Family Services," he enunciated slowly. "Call her at work!"

Chuck still rubbed his temples slowly.

"United Family Services," said Tom. Nothing. "Stan!"

"What?"

"Come here!"

"You come *here.*"

Tom hated the guy, but he went into the living room anyway. Stan was watching TV from Chuck's lounger, the sound off. "Anything good on?" asked Tom.

"Naw." He hit the OFF button and the set went dead.

"We've got a problem. He remembers his dream, but he can't locate her."

"Who?"

"April, you idiot!"

Stan smiled broadly.

He wins again!

"So tell him where she lives." Stan picked up a magazine and thumbed through it.

"He can't hear me! Besides, *I* don't even know her address!"

Stan flipped a page. "Sure you do."

"No. I just followed the phone line."

"Just remember what you saw." He picked up a copy of the *Watch Tower.*

"I never saw anything!"

"Sure you did."

"But I don't—"

Stan threw the magazine down. Tom heard a chair leg scrape in the kitchen. Chuck appeared, looking around warily.

"You know where she lives," continued Stan, ignoring Chuck.

"I said I didn't see!"

"You were there."

"So were you! Tell me!"

Stan looked away. "No."

Tom almost punched him.

"If you want, you can remember," repeated Stan. "Your spirit mind—where the *real* thinking goes on—isn't saddled with a mortal brain. Everything you've ever seen, thought, felt, or experienced is in there. You just have to recall it."

"No way."

"Would I lie to you?"

Only if there was a laugh in it. Tom had no choice. Chuck was staring at the *Watch Tower*, waiting for it to move. Tom sighed. "Okay." He concentrated.

The scene slowly emerged in his mind's eye. There was the residential street. The leaves were gold, the street lights had just come on, a couple of kids ran down the sidewalk. Tom felt a heaviness, a fear that he was about to see the horrible scene he'd witnessed before: the stranger teaching Josh to ride the bike. But so far, the street was nearly deserted.

April's house was on the left. The stoop was gray concrete (he hadn't noticed that before) and the front door was green. Brass numerals on the casing said 6735. "6735," said Tom.

"Mmm?" Stan was watching Chuck, who was watching the magazine on the floor. "Go ahead, pick it up," whispered Stan. "It won't bite."

Sure enough, Chuck picked up the *Watch Tower*. "Now you are in my power!" cackled Stan.

Tom concentrated again. April's street shimmered in front of him. *Another angle*, he thought, trying to will himself to back up. The perspective changed and a blue sedan inched into view. *More.* He drew further back. Finally, on the right was a pole topped by a green metal street sign. "Corrado."

"Bingo!" said Stan.

"She lives on 6735 Corrado Street."

"Avenue," corrected Stan. "There's a Corrado *Street* in Coronado. Corrado, Coronado. She sells sea shells by the sea shore!"

Chuck stared at the magazine on his lap. He closed his eyes. "Please," he said quietly.

"He's praying," said Tom.

"That's peachy," mocked Stan.

"Chuck, she lives at 6735 Corrado."

Chuck's lips moved silently.

"Corrado," said Tom, enunciating it as clearly as he could.

"Means 'running,' did you know that?" remarked Stan.

"Corrado," whispered Tom, placing a hand on Chuck's shoulder. Tom looked up, surprised. "I can feel his shoulder!"

Stan yawned, closing his eyes. Tom could feel the warmth of Chuck's skin, the blood flowing in the veins, the marbling of the muscles. He squeezed gently and whispered, "Corrado."

In a distant voice, Chuck echoed, "Coronado."

Stan laughed. "Told you. Guy knows his way around!"

"Corrado," said Tom.

"Corrado," repeated Chuck.

"All right!"

"Coronado."

"No! Corrado *Avenue*. Kearny Mesa."

"Coronado."

"No!" howled Tom, squeezing Chuck's shoulder. Chuck winced and pulled away. Tom reacted. "Oh! Sorry. Corrado Avenue. Chuck, please hear me."

"Why don't you just lend him your memory?" asked Stan, leaning back in the lounger. Tom looked at Chuck, hoping he hadn't seen the chair move. His eyes were closed. *Just keep 'em closed, old boy.* "What do you mean 'lend him my memory'?"

Stan opened one eye. "You just do." He closed it again.

Tom placed his hand on Chuck's brow. It was hot and sheened with sweat. He recalled the image of April's street and willed it into Chuck's mind. He saw the street sign and centered on it for a long moment, then moved toward April's house, finally centering on the brass numbers. 6735.

"April's house," said Tom. "You've got to go there." He withdrew his hand. Chuck opened his eyes and looked around the room, stopping at his lounger.

Tom followed his look. The lounger was upright again. Stan was gone.

"Sixty seven thirty five Corrado Avenue," said Chuck slowly. "April's house."

Tom almost hugged him.

Chuck slowly got to his feet. Tom guided him to the front door. Chuck was reaching for the knob when Tom remembered the flat tire. He steered Chuck back toward the kitchen. "Taxi."

Chuck sat down at the dinette, breathing raggedly. He rubbed his temple. His eyes were bloodshot.

"Taxi," said Tom again.

"Tom," came Stan's voice. He was leaning against the jamb, arms folded.

When he didn't say anything, Tom said, "Taxi," again, then turned to Stan. "What is it?"

Stan's eyes were dark with anger. He turned away. "Nothing."

Chuck opened his eyes and reached for the phone. "Operator," he croaked, "would you connect me to Yellow Cab?"

Tom cheered.

Jonathan crested the hill at twilight. In the distance was the Bridge. As he passed the guard shack, the guard jumped to his feet. "Who goes there?"

Jonathan ignored him, continuing to the Bridge. The guard followed but didn't stop him. He would recognize an administrator's suit and would wait until addressed. Finally, Jonathan turned and said, "I'm looking for someone."

"Who?"

Jonathan showed the guard a picture. "Have you seen him?"

"I'm not sure."

"Are you certain?"

"He was here?"

"He *may* have been here." Jonathan nodded at the Bridge. "He may have crossed over."

"I doubt it, sir. Without permission, no one crosses over."

Jonathan looked away, preparing to enter the guard's mind. His eyes drifted across the canyon, settling on the far side, where the path disappeared into the woods. He entered the guard's mind easily. Advanced souls could detect probing and would resist, setting up a mental block or asking the person to stop. An intelligent being would attempt the former; a properly trained military man would never presume to demand the latter. The guard was neither.

Beyond a curtain of admirable rigidity, Jonathan accessed the guard's memories, reviewing each face he had seen during the last ten cycles. He found Tom several cycles ago but he did not reappear in the guard's memory recently.

The whole thing took just five seconds.

Jonathan slipped out of the guard's mind and turned to face him. The guard was searching the far cliffs, trying to see what Jonathan was looking at over there. "You don't remember?" asked Jonathan.

"Not him," said the guard, "but there's something else that's been bothering me. Yesterday, after a group of pilgrims crossed over, I thought I saw someone walk into the forest over there.

"He certainly could not have come from *this* side. You told me no one crosses over without your permission."

The guard nodded forcefully.

"So I am safe to assume that whomever you believe you saw, *belonged* over there, am I not?"

"I saw someone, sir."

"And I appreciate it, my good man." Jonathan looked at the woods on the far side. "Thank you." He walked past the guard, back toward the city.

At the crest of the hill, Jonathan turned back. Thomas had no way of knowing about the Plain. Only fallen spirits used the Portals. Messengers from the Upper Realms used more efficient methods of travel. Besides, even if Thomas found the Plain, there was no way he could know about the Portals, much less how to use them. He was surprised when an unbidden thought bubbled into his mind:

You are wrong.

24

Chuck battled the migraine. His sunglasses did little to improve things. He kept his eyes closed. The taxi smelled of stale sweat. The two-way radio crackled now and then, punctuating his throbbing head. As they left the freeway, he pulled out his wallet. He had twenty two dollars—he hoped it was enough.

The only good thing about today was the fact that he wasn't crazy. The dream was strange, but it proved to be inspired. He had never heard of Corrado Avenue before this morning but the driver found it in the Thomas Bros. guide, asking if he wanted the one in Kearny Mesa or Coronado. Chuck said Kearny Mesa, remembering the distinction from a prompting he had this morning. Tom must be with him, even now. "Great to hear from you, Tom."

"What's that?" said the driver, turning around.

"Nothing." Chuck closed his eyes against the pounding sunlight. He didn't open them again until the taxi stopped in front of 6735 Corrado. He got out, wincing at the pain from the bright morning, grateful that rain clouds were gathering.

The driver said, "That'll be twenty two bucks. Even."

Chuck couldn't believe his luck. *Not luck*, he amended silently. He handed the bills to the driver.

"No tip?"

"That's all I have. If you want, I can mail you a tip."

"Right," said the driver, slamming the car into gear.

"I'm sorry," said Chuck at the departing cab.

He felt a tug at his trouser pocket. Josh smiled up at him. "I knew you were coming."

"Didn't know myself," said Chuck, squinting at the gray sky. He felt a raindrop on his neck. He made his eyes slits, following Josh toward the house like a blind man.

"I dreamed about you last night," affirmed Josh. "You said you were coming to visit us today."

"That a fact?" said Chuck, walking carefully up the steps. Josh opened the door. Inside, it was cool and dark, the curtains drawn.

"Chuck's here!" yelled Josh, running down the hall. "Mom!"

Chuck groped his way to the couch, removing his sunglasses.

"Chuck?" April appeared, wearing cut-offs and a tank top.

"Hi, April," he said.

"Told you," said Josh.

April looked confused. "Josh had a dream. Said we'd see you today."

"Imagine that," said Chuck, holding his head in his hands.

"Are you okay?"

"Headache."

"Have you taken anything?"

"It's a migraine. Nothing much helps."

"You poor thing," said April, sitting. "Josh, go get Chuck a glass of water."

Josh ran out of the room. The footfalls hurt Chuck's head.

"Lie down," said April, lifting his legs and pivoting him around. He lay back. She put a pillow under his head. "Is that better?" Josh arrived with a cup of water. Chuck took a sip. April sat on the coffee table. "Chuck, is everything all right?"

"Came a-visitin'," he said. "Hope your husband don't mind."

"We don't mind. But remember? Tom passed away."

Chuck nodded. "Over a year ago."

"In May," added Josh.

"I meant your new husband."

"I'm not married."

"Do you hear that?!" yelled Tom. He slapped Stan on the back. "She's not married!" He hunkered down, eager to see what would come next.

"Tom said you were married," said Chuck.

April stole a look at Josh. "I'm not married, Chuck." She put her hand on his forehead. "You're burning up."

"I'll be okay."

"No, you won't," said Stan.

"Yes, he will," said Tom.

"I had a dream last night, too," said Chuck. "I wanted to call you but I didn't have your new number."

"What about the dream?"

"Tom was in it. He's why I'm here."

"Oh," said April, feeling a thickness at the back of her throat.

"Tom told me to come see you. Your address came to me in a vision this morning."

April helped him take another sip of water. He settled back. She wanted to look at Josh to see how he was taking this, but for some reason, she was afraid to.

"Tell her, Chuck," said Tom.

"Tom said he'd been to heaven. I asked him if he'd seen Carolyn there."

"Cool," said Josh, leaning forward, his chin in his hands, fascinated.

April looked at Josh, a frown on her face. "Go on."

"He said he hadn't seen her; hadn't even looked."

Tom put his hand over his eyes. "Oh boy."

"Guilty as charged," said Stan.

"He was probably busy," said April uneasily.

"Yeah," mumbled Tom.

"Maybe, but there was something different about him," said Chuck, sitting up with some difficulty.

"You should lie down," cautioned April.

"I gotta see you while I say this." He cleared his throat, looking at her with bloodshot eyes. One was cloudy with cataracts. He looked very old. "I know what you're thinking, April, but it's true."

"I know you *think* it is, but—"

"Oh no," moaned Tom.

"What did my daddy say?" pressed Josh.

"Yeah!" said Stan eagerly, sitting down next to Josh and draping his arm around his shoulders. Tom looked daggers at him. Stan stuck his tongue out.

Guy's an idiot, thought Tom.

You're an idiot, he heard Stan think. Tom looked up. Stan was glaring at him.

"What did my *daddy* say?" pushed Josh.

"Josh!" said April. "Stop it!"

He stuck his tongue out at her.

Tom scowled at Stan.

"That'll be enough, young man," said April firmly.

Chuck cleared his throat. "Tom looked like he'd been through a lot." He was oblivious to the looks April and Josh were exchanging. "He wanted me to tell you something."

"Did he have wings?" asked Josh.

"Josh!" said April, fixing him with a hard look.

"Did he have wings?"

"That's it," said April. "Go to your room."

"No!"

"I said—"

"April," said Chuck.

She ignored him. "Go to your room. Now."

Josh folded his arms defiantly. April wagged a finger at him. "Don't even think about it."

"I wasn't." But his tongue was restless in his mouth.

"Yes, you were."

"April," interrupted Chuck.

Josh and April glowered at each other. Chuck opened his mouth to speak. "Excuse us," she said, grabbing Josh's arm.

"That hurts!" wailed Josh as she dragged him from the room. Chuck closed his mouth. Tom felt embarrassed. From the kitchen came the sharp report of a spank and Josh's excessive wails. Chuck lay back on the couch and closed his eyes, grimacing.

"What a mess," lamented Tom, going into the kitchen.

Josh sat on the dining table, whimpering. April was whispering fiercely to him. "Now you listen to me," she hissed. "When I ask you to do something, you do it! Chuck doesn't need to see you pitch a fit!"

"I wanna know about my daddy," said Josh, hiccuping tears.

"It was just a dream, it wasn't real."

"No!" said Tom.

"He said it was real," countered Josh.

"Dreams seem very real, but they're not. They're pretend."

"But I dreamed about Chuck and he's here."

"That's a coincidence, honey."

"Daddy told him where we lived—"

"Josh." April placed a finger under his chin and lifted it. She said quietly, "Honey, Mr. Blankenship is old. He can't remember things. I gave him our address when we moved. He just forgot about it until today."

"Oh, no," groaned Tom.

"He misses your daddy, like we do. He had a dream about him, like we do sometimes."

Josh nodded, eyes downcast. "Can I go now?"

"Sure, go see how Chuck's doing." Josh left and she turned to the sink. *Poor old Chuck. He's lonely and sick. He looks like he'd come apart in a good stiff wind.*

Tom took his hand off her shoulder; he had heard every thought. April looked out the window. It was sprinkling. He put his arms around her and nuzzled her neck, although he couldn't feel her.

"Mom?"

She turned. Josh's face was white. "What is it, honey?"

"You better come."

April ran into the living room. Chuck had fallen off the couch. April rolled him over. His face was pallid and his breathing was erratic. "Call 911! Hurry!"

"Oh, no," moaned Tom. Stan was shaking his head, a hard look in his small eyes. "Do something!" yelled Tom.

"Like what?"

"Can't you help him?"

"Nothing I can do. No interference: The Prime Directive."

April began pumping Chuck's chest. Tom put a hand on Chuck's head and closed his eyes. "Please don't take him."

Stan dropped to his knees, clasped his hands and looked piously heavenward. "Not until we're through using him!"

"Shut up!" wailed Tom. He looked upward and whispered, "Please, God, don't let him die!"

April trotted to keep up with the two attendants as they whisked the gurney through the Emergency Room doors. Inside, the air was warm and mediciny. They passed a man at the registration desk who was holding a bloody compress to his head.

The gurney turned into an examination room. April followed, watching as they pulled Chuck onto a table. One attendant was ventilating Chuck with the respirator as he had in the ambulance. The other began removing his clothing. A young doctor swept past her, looking at his clipboard. "What've we got here?"

"Myocardial infarction," said the attendant squeezing the ventilator.

"Vitals?" He was washing his hands at the sink. April backed against a wall, feeling like an intruder. The other attendant tossed Chuck's clothes onto the floor and opened a blanket over him.

The first attendant said, "Pulse sporadic and weak."

"We might have to crack his chest," said the doctor, pulling on his gloves. "See if Allen is—" He stopped, noticing April for the first time. "Can I help you?"

"I'm with him. His name is Chuck."

"Chuck. Okay," said the doctor, nodding at the second attendant.

The attendant came over. "I'm sorry, but you'll have to leave."

"Sorry," said April, backing into the hallway.

"We'll take care of him," he said, closing the door.

April walked to the lobby and called Myra Snowden, her next door neighbor, who was watching Josh. She had given him some Tylenol and wrapped him in a big blanket. He was watching TV, a glazed look on his face, but he wasn't crying. Before April could ask, Myra offered to keep him overnight. When April expressed reservations, Myra reminded her that she was a grandma seven times. "He'll be here when you get back," she said, her voice warm.

April hung up, relieved. When she moved to Kearney Mesa three months ago, Myra Snowden came over the first evening to welcome her and invite her over for coffee. There, she noticed a Bible on the sofa. Red pencil underlined several passages. April had relaxed then. It was her experience that people who actually *studied* the scriptures often actually *lived* them. April knew Josh was safe at Myra's house.

Sitting in the ER waiting room for the next two hours, April saw a constant stream of people coming and going, intent upon their own disasters. So many children with cuts and broken legs. One had arrived, held in his father's arms, badly burned after tipping a skillet off the stove onto himself. The nurse took the child and calmed the father, who was beside himself with guilt. She said the boy would be all right. "If they're screaming, they'll live." He looked at her hopefully, then came and sat near April. Her heart went out to him, but she didn't speak because she couldn't handle another tragedy—one was her limit.

A black orderly came over, his shaved head glistening. "You're here for Chuck Blankenship?"

April nodded.

"He's in ICU. I'll take you there."

"Thank you," she said. His name tag said LUCKY. He led the way across the polished floor, his sneakers squeaking. He stopped at the elevator. "You look familiar," she said.

He smiled, revealing a gold front tooth. "I'm Lucky."

April looked up into his face. "I hope so."

Lucky opened the door. The room was dark except for a flourescent light above the bed. Chuck lay under a thin blanket, an oxygen tube in his nose and an I.V. needle in the back of his hand. The oxygen machine purred. His eyes were closed and his skin was gray. His chest barely moved.

Lucky said, "I'll be at the station if you need me." He flashed his gold tooth and left.

April pulled up a plastic chair and sat down. The last time she'd been in a hospital was when Tom was in one, a year ago.

"I wonder what she's thinking," said Tom, standing on the other side of the bed. She was looking right through him.

"She's wondering if it's gonna rain some more," said Stan, leaning against the window sill.

Tom raked his fingers through his hair. "If I'd known this was gonna hurt him, I'd of—"

"Come off it!" barked Stan. "You didn't care what happened to him, as long as he delivered your message!"

Ton's jaw dropped. "How was I supposed to know he was sick? He could have told me! He could have said 'No'!"

"Would you listen to yourself? He wouldn't say 'No'! He thought you were an *angel,* for crying out loud!"

"He did not."

"Can't you see?" said Stan. "He'd have done anything for you. And look how it turned out: you practically killed him and for what? Your precious message is still undelivered."

Tom looked at Chuck, feeling horrible. *I never meant for you to get hurt. Why didn't you tell me you were so sick?* He shook his head. "We've come so far. . ." He stared hard at Chuck, gears turning.

Stan frowned and pointed at Tom. "Don't you dare."

Tom looked intently at Chuck, his lips pursed.

"Don't do it!"

Tom looked up. "I have to."

"You'll kill him. Is that what you want?"

Tom placed his hand on Chuck's forehead. "I'm not going to hurt him. I'll just ask him how he's doing. If he's up to it, then okay. But it'll be *his* decision."

Stan threw his hands up and turned away.

Tom concentrated. He felt great cold. Chuck's spirit had retreated into the darkness. He called Chuck's name. On the bed, Chuck stirred. Tom heard a voice in the distance. "Tommy?"

Chuck, are you okay?

"I'm tired. I wanna sleep."

Why didn't you tell me you were so sick?

"It was a migraine. I didn't know my heart was gonna give out. I tried to tell her your message."

That's okay. Are you feeling better?

"Really tired."

Tom still couldn't see Chuck. He was just a muffled voice in the darkness. *Chuck, I'm sorry for pushing you.*

"I wanted to help. I still do. When I get better . . ."

Tom couldn't help himself. *Chuck, she's right here, right next to you. You could just open your eyes and tell her.*

"Can I sleep afterwards?"

You bet. Anything you want.

"Okay. I'll try."

Tom removed his hand from Chuck's forehead. After a minute, Chuck opened his eyes and smiled weakly at April.

"Hi," she said.

"Hey, sweetie," he croaked. "Hospital, huh?"

She nodded.

"Chest hurts."

"You had a heart attack."

"Figures. Try to do a good deed . . ."

She looked at him, perplexed.

"Well," he rasped. "Gotta go sometime. I almost made it . . ."

"You're gonna make it," confirmed April.

Chuck smiled. "I was headed somewhere else, hon."

"Oh, Chuck."

Chuck, Chuck . . . tell her, please.

Chuck's eyes took on a glazed sheen. "Gotta tell you something."

April took his hand in hers.

"Message from Tom."

April hung her head. *It's too much.*

"Open your heart, child." He sandwiched her hand between his hands, water springing to his eyes with the effort.

April nodded.

Chuck opened his mouth to speak. Then his eyes rolled back in his head. A loud continuous tone shrilled.

"Chuck, no!" said Tom.

April cried out, "No! Chuck!"

Lucky burst into the room, followed by a nurse. April stood back, her hands over her mouth. "Call the code!" yelled Lucky. The nurse ran from the room.

"This isn't happening!" said Tom. "It's not *fair!*"

"I'll say it isn't. Look!" said Stan.

Chuck was growing fuzzy around the edges. Whispering filled the room. Tiny particles of light gathered around his body, then moved to one side, where they took on form and color. In a moment, Chuck's spirit stood by them in his hospital gown, translucent.

"I can't believe it! He's dead!" said Tom.

Chuck's eyes were open wide in surprise. "What's going on?"

Lucky was pumping on Chuck's chest. April was crying.

"Dead, am I?" said Chuck.

"Chuck, I'm sorry," said Tom.

The doctor, a small Asian woman, ran into the room, followed by the nurse, who was pushing the defrib cart. She plugged it in and handed the corded paddles to the doctor. Chuck watched the commotion with grim fascination. "Never mind, Tom. It's okay."

The doctor yelled, "Clear!" and placed the paddles on Chuck's chest. His back arched violently.

"Ohh," moaned Chuck's spirit, as hundreds of streaks of light arced toward him. He staggered back. Tom caught him.

"Anything?" yelled the doctor. The nurse held a stethoscope to Chuck's chest. His mouth was agape and his eyes stared blindly.

"Nothing!" yelled the nurse.

"I don't want to go back," said Chuck.

"Charging!" said Lucky. The machine cycled up.

Stan leaned against the window sill, his arms folded, his eyes slits. Tom noticed that he hadn't said a thing.

The doctor rubbed the paddles together and Chuck grimaced, placing a hand on his chest. "I don't wanna go back."

Tom turned Chuck toward him. "Then don't!"

"Now wait a minute," said Stan. "He *has* to go back. See the sparks?" Thousands of tiny blue sparks jumped between Chuck's spirit and his body on the bed, a neon connection that fizzled and snapped. "It isn't his time yet!" said Stan.

Tom stepped between Chuck and the sparks, breaking the connection. The sparks howled, swirling in the air, crackling against the wall, the bed frame, anything. Chuck's spirit slumped against the wall. The doctor yelled, "Clear!" and shocked Chuck's body, which hitched upward with a loud crack!

April cried, "You're hurting him!"

Lucky grabbed her. The doctor forced a long needle between Chuck's ribs. April sobbed into Lucky's white coat.

The sparks danced in the air, crackling and humming. Tom stepped closer. One spark found him, then another. In a moment, hundreds of tiny blue lightning bolts were hitting him. He stood still, his fists clenched, shuddering at the pain. Stan approached, keeping his distance from the sparks. "Don't do this!"

Tom was looking at April. "Why not?" Thousands of sparks were growing together, forming a conduit that linked Tom's chest with Chuck's body.

"The Prime!" yelled Stan. "You're risking annihilation!"

Tom was focused on April.

Stan reached through the swirling sparks and grabbed Tom's shoulder, grimacing as shocks coursed up his arm. Slowly, Tom turned his head toward Stan. "Look at her," he said, his voice hoarse.

April had broken free of Lucky. She was crying in the corner. "She's lost so many people. Can you imagine how she feels—believing there's no purpose to all this?" He gestured at the flurry of activity as the doctor and nurse worked feverishly on Chuck's body.

"You'll be damned if you do this," asserted Stan.

"I'll be damned if I don't." Tom shook Stan's hand off his shoulder and stepped through the nurse's body. He placed his hand over Chuck's heart, concentrating.

"Last time!" yelled the doctor, rubbing the paddles together. The blue conduit disconnected from Chuck's body and lashed about, striking the metal bedstead with carbon-arc intensity. It walked across the headboard and jumped out at the doctor, alighting on the defrib paddles, giving them an eerie neon glow.

Tom felt himself loosen inside. He looked at his hand, which shifted and doubled over Chuck's chest. He heard a whispering sound. The last thing he saw was a ring of fire.

"Clear!" yelled the doctor, the paddles poised.

"Wait!" yelled the nurse, raising her hand. "I've got a pulse!"

"Thank heaven," said the doctor.

April took Chuck's hand as the nurse pulled the gown over his bruised chest. Lucky looked upward, mouthing the words, "Thank you."

"Come on, Chuck," said April.

"Pulse is solid," said the nurse.

Chuck opened his eyes. "April."

April kissed his forehead.

"Still here," he said.

"Don't talk."

"Oh, April, it's wonderful to see you."

"You're gonna be okay."

"April." His lips barely moved.

"Shh."

"Can you see me?"

"See you?"

The doctor and the nurse exchanged a look.

"Can you *really* see me?" he croaked.

"Yes, Chuck, I can see you."

He took a breath. "Look deeper."

"Deeper?"

"I keep my promises, sweetheart . . ."

"Oh, Chuck—"

Tom struggled inside Chuck's weakened body. Darkness was a great, descending blanket. He only had a few moments. "You asked me if He exists. He does. He loves you, and so do I." He slowly pointed to his head, his heart, then to her, their secret code.

April's heart was in her throat as she took Chuck's face in her shaking hands. "Tom? Is it really you?" Her tears fell onto his face.

Tom raised a strange, gnarled hand and caressed her cheek. "I love you."

"Me too you," cried April, kissing him over and over.

"I can't stay," he whispered.

"Don't go!"

"I'll be waiting for you. I love you."

Suddenly the EKG alarm screamed.

"Tom! Tom!"

The doctor put a hand on her shoulder but April just held Chuck, crying softly. After a long time she pulled back, wiped her eyes, and studied Chuck's face intently. The hand she held a moment ago lay quietly on the covers. She pointed to her head, her heart, and to Chuck, mouthing the words "I love you."

Lucky steered the defrib cart out the door. The doctor pulled off her gloves and threw them into a trashcan. The nurse stood facing April, her face flushed.

Tom found himself on the floor. Stan and Chuck pulled him to his feet. "What happened?"

"Boy, that was quite a show," said Chuck in wonder.

"Here comes Act Two," said Stan, nodding at a corner where the walls and ceiling came together. A tiny white light burned. The whispering started again.

"It's for me," said Chuck. He walked toward the light as it grew, passing through his body on the bed. As he passed April he touched her shoulder.

The light is right next to her, and she can't even see it. "April, look up," pleaded Tom.

Chuck turned back to Tom. "It's going to be all right."

"I hope so," Tom said.

The light surrounded Chuck with a brilliance that exceeded even the Portal. Every corner of the room was overexposed, the color bleached away. A feeling of warmth flowed from the light. The voices were no longer whispers; they resolved into a soaring chorus.

"Say hello to Uncle Harold," said Tom.

"Who?" asked Chuck, a perplexed look on his face. He turned back as the light swallowed him. It pulled into itself until it was a tiny blinding spot in the corner, then it winked out.

"Amazing," said Tom.

Stan was glaring at him.

"What's the matter?"

"You'll see."

April positioned Chuck's hands across his chest and smoothed his hair. The door closed, leaving her alone. Tom leaned across the bed, putting his hand over hers. "He's going to be fine."

Her eyes were searching Chuck's face.

"I'd give anything to know what you're thinking," said Tom.

"Anything? You have nothing left."

Tom whirled around. Jonathan stood in the doorway, flanked by two large men in white suits. They stared ahead, their faces passive, their hands clasped behind their backs. "Thomas Waring," stated Jonathan with finality.

Tom could only stare.

"You have violated The Prime Directive."

"I did what I had to do."

"For all the good it has done."

April pulled the cover over Chuck. "Goodbye."

Jonathan said to Tom, "You accomplished nothing."

"Says you . . ." came a voice.

Jonathan peered into the darkened corner. "You, there! Step forward!"

Stan walked out of the shadows. His eyes were hard and his lips were drawn up into a smirk.

"Who are you?" demanded Jonathan.

"Who are *you*?"

"I asked you first!" sputtered Jonathan.

"But I asked you LOUDER!" yelled Stan.

"Forget it," said Tom. "You'll never get a straight answer out of him."

"We'll just see about this!" said Jonathan, producing his Record. "What is your name?" He held his pen poised above the page.

Stan yawned.

"Well?"

"Deep subject," said Stan.

Tom put his head in his hands. "Here we go."

"Now you listen here, whoever you are! I demand to know your name and your business here!"

Stan stuck his tongue out.

Jonathan recoiled. "Seize him!" The two guards grabbed Stan by his arms, lifting him off the ground. He made comical running motions in the air, laughing.

"We'll soon find out what's funny," said Jonathan, once more in control. He turned to Tom. "You are in very big trouble. I debated about following you, but your trail was so clear, if I hadn't, I would have been guilty of dereliction of duty."

"You're just doing your job," said Tom. "It's okay."

"Of course it's okay! It's *you* who are in trouble! Your very soul is in jeopardy! I hope it was worth it!"

Tom looked at April, who was sitting quietly, looking out the window, thinking. "It was."

"We shall see."

"May I say goodbye?" asked Tom.

Jonathan scanned his Record. "According to this, she's not a Listener. I can't see what good it will do."

"Or what harm," said Stan, still suspended by his arms.

Jonathan turned away. "Make it quick."

April's eyes were dry now, her tears spent. Tom kneeled before her and put his palm against her cheek. "I love you, sweetheart. More than my own soul."

April stared at the dark window beyond him.

"That will do," said Jonathan. He nodded at the guards, who marched Stan toward him. Jonathan sneered. "I have no idea who you are or what you are doing here, but I have a feeling—a very *strong* feeling—that you are quite a catch, my rude little friend." His voice dropped to a whisper and he leaned closer. "I am also sure that your crimes are legion. I shall enjoy watching your judgment from a comfortable front-row seat."

The merriness went out of Stan's face. He pointed at Tom. "It was all his idea."

Jonathan waved him away. "So much for honor among thieves."

The guards hauled Stan away, passing through the door. Jonathan turned to Tom, who still knelt by April.

"Thomas? Come, the Council awaits."

"Oh, sweetheart, what will become of you?" Tom asked April.

Jonathan hauled him to his feet. "Her fate is undecided. Unfortunately, yours is now sealed." He pulled Tom out the door.

25

No sooner had they stepped through the door than they were in the Council chambers. No flaming Portal, no brilliant display, just one step and there they were.

Stan was sandwiched between the two Spirit Policemen. *He doesn't look so carefree now*, thought Tom, thoroughly disgusted with himself for getting involved with Stan in the first place. Stan looked at him but Tom avoided his eyes. He had no doubt that Jonathan was right: Stan had probably committed a bunch of crimes and Tom's involvement with him could only hurt his own situation.

The receptionist snapped her Record closed and looked up, her eyes boring holes into him. One cop left Stan and came over and stood by Tom. He knew if he moved, those big hands would be on him in an instant.

Jonathan walked toward the heavy doors and knocked. They swung silently outward. Darkness lay beyond. Jonathan nodded at the policemen. Tom was nudged forward. Stan watched him silently. *Guy finally ran out of smart-aleck remarks*, thought Tom. *Please let it stay that way.*

Tom walked into the dark room. The lights over the table came up, illuminating the books. Here and there a chair moved or a hand was visible on the table. At the far end was the Chairman, his head rising above the seat back. Tom could feel eleven sets of eyes on him.

Jonathan stationed himself to his left, the cop shoved Stan to his right. A light came on over Tom. The cops took their positions on either side of the doors behind him.

Before long, Anatoli stood, his face illuminated from above, shadows concealing his deep-set eyes. "Thomas Philip Waring," he said gravely.

Tom nodded.

Jonathan whispered. "Out loud!"

"Yes, sir," said Tom.

"You have been brought before the Council for violations of numerous laws, rules, and regulations pertaining to the Order of Heaven. Who accuses you?"

Jonathan stepped forward. "I do."

"Of what crimes do you accuse the defendant?"

Jonathan opened his Record. "I have transmitted the complaint. You will find it in your Proceedings section."

The Councilmen opened the white books. Pages turned and faces came into the light.

Jonathan held his Record like a hymnal. "Aside from various misdemeanors such as sloth and laziness, disobedience, questioning authority, and a general bad attitude, the defendant has committed numerous felonies, including violations of several Prime Directives." He paused for effect.

Tom had a sinking feeling. *I wish I had a lawyer.*

"You don't need a lawyer, Mr. Waring," snapped Anatoli. "What you need is contrition!"

Jonathan cleared his throat. "The defendant is charged with disruption of classes, ignoring schedules, missing work, failure to undergo the Naming Ritual—"

"You said I didn't have to do that!" interrupted Tom.

"You didn't, for a *reasonable* amount of time, but your refusal went beyond the allotted three cycles."

"But no one told me!"

"We are more interested in the violations of the Primes," came a voice from the darkness. The others murmured assent. "Since violation of a Prime Directive merits expulsion from Paradise," continued the Councilman in an Oriental accent, "all lesser crimes are of merely academic interest."

"Get on with it," Anatoli commanded. Jonathan blanched.

He doesn't like Jonathan either, thought Tom.

Jonathan read from his Record. "This is the five count indictment for violations of Prime Directives. Count One: the defendant did, with evil intent and through subterfuge, leave Paradise without permission."

"It wasn't subterfuge," said Tom. "I just walked across the Bridge."

"Mr. Waring!" said Anatoli. "You will get your chance to respond to the charges!"

Tom looked at the floor.

"Count Two: The defendant made unauthorized use of the Portals."

A number of Council members conversed in low tones.

"Count Three: The defendant manipulated a mortal being into performing actions against his will—"

"That's not true!" said Tom, slamming his hands on the table.

Stan laughed. Tom looked at him. He was beaming like a proud father.

"Is it?" said Anatoli, looking at Stan.

Stan pointed to himself. "You talking to me?"

"Yes."

Stan's small eyes were bright with . . . what? "Absolutely true," he trumpeted, slapping Tom on the back.

"Don't help me, okay?" said Tom through gritted teeth.

Stan shrugged and stepped out of the light.

"Count Four: The defendant, with malice aforethought, did unlawfully enter into the mortality of one Charles Blankenship, and did take possession of Mr. Blankenship's mortal body for his own selfish purposes."

Jonathan looked at Tom for a rebuttal. Tom said nothing.

"And Count Five, the most serious crime of all: The defendant, though the misuse of said body, did effectively cause Mr. Blankenship's death." He closed his Record.

There was a great intake of breath as the Council processed the gravity of the charge.

"Then Charles Blankenship has passed over?" asked someone.

"Yes," said Jonathan crisply. "He is dead."

Tom bowed his head.

"Before his assigned time?" asked someone else.

Tom nodded slowly. Jonathan dug an elbow into his ribs. "Yes," said Tom.

Slowly, each book was closed.

"Your defense, Mr. Waring?" came Anatoli's voice.

Tom stared at the table.

"Mr. Waring? You wish to defend yourself?"

Tom shook his head slowly.

He felt another elbow in his ribs, this time from his right. Stan was frowning. "Say something!"

Drop dead.

Anatoli stood and leaned on the table. "Well?"

Stan spoke. "Deep sub—"

"I have no defense," said Tom, giving Stan an angry look. "I made a promise I had to keep. That's all."

Anatoli snorted. "This is your defense? A promise?"

Tom nodded.

Anatoli looked at his fellow Council members. Each one nodded gravely. Anatoli fixed Tom with his iron gaze. "Thomas Philip Waring, you have been found guilty of violation of The Preeminent Prime Directive. To destroy another's mortality is the most serious crime of all. It exceeds that of mere possession. You caused the death of an innocent mortal. You robbed him of his life, for no greater purpose than your own selfish desires."

Out of the corner of his eye, Tom saw Stan fold his arms and turn away.

Anatoli took no notice. "Your actions prove that you are unfit to dwell in Paradise. You are hereby remanded to Hell, where you shall remain, worlds without end. It is so ordered."

"Amen," came a chorus of voices from around the table.

"I have something to say," said Tom. "You call this place Paradise, but for me, to be here with no hope of seeing my wife again, it was Hell. I did what I had to do . . . I guess I'd do it again." He met Anatoli's look directly.

Anatoli shook his head and sat down. "So be it." He looked around the table, receiving a nod from each of the councilmen. Then he looked back at Tom. "No contrition?" he asked quietly.

Tom was perplexed. "What do you mean?"

Anatoli sighed. "None at all?"

Tom shook his head and lowered his eyes. "I'm sorry . . . no."

The room became very quiet. Everyone seemed to be studying their hands, thinking. Finally, Anatoli looked up, and in a small voice, said, "Master?"

Tom turned, following Anatoli's gaze.

He was looking at *Stan*.

Stan stood with his back to them, his arms folded, his head bowed. He lifted his head and began to turn, and as he did, he began to change. He grew a foot taller and his shoulders broadened. By the time he completed his turn, in the place of a small, wretched, balding, hook-nosed outcast, there was a tall, regal being with flowing white hair and a full white beard. His eyes were like crystal fire and his countenance was blinding. Tom shielded his face, his heart pounding.

To his left he heard movement. Out of the corner of his eye, he saw Jonathan sinking to his knees, his eyes bright with fear and awe, his mouth working but nothing coming out.

Tom looked back at the magnificent being, who was clothed in exquisite whiteness. Light burst from him like the sun itself. His eyes were the deepest blue and they were looking directly at him with an intensity that made Tom shiver. He felt like running, but his feet wouldn't move.

Tom felt his knees give way. He sunk to the ground, bowing his head. "Lord," was all he could think of to say.

"Thomas," said God.

Tom looked up, hope instantly washing over him. Hearing God speak his name filled Tom with a joy beyond comprehension. He no longer had the desire to run, but his apprehension remained.

God reached out and touched his shoulder lightly, raising him to his feet. From the touch, Tom felt an overpowering feeling of love radiate throughout his being, a warmth that drowned all fear, sadness, pain, and guilt. He felt the marrow in his bones melting in the warmth of that love.

God waved his hand and room became brighter. The councilmen sat silently, their faces glowing. Tom noticed they were smiling . . . every one of them.

"Well done," said God gravely, nodding at the Council. "Well done indeed."

The Councilmen nodded as one. Anatoli stood. Tom noticed something different about the man. For the first time, he was smiling. "It was our pleasure, Lord. Thomas was splendid."

The others nodded, then began to clap. The room rang with their applause. The councilmen exchanged handshakes. The Oriental councilman caught Tom's eye and winked.

Anatoli looked at Tom. "After we opened the window onto Earth and you left so disheartened," he said softly, "I feared you would give up. I feared you would abandon your quest."

Anatoli rounded the table and strode toward Tom, taking his hand warmly in both of his. "But your love proved stronger than the chains of death." There were tears in Anatoli's eyes.

God touched Anatoli's arm and said, "Thank you, my friend."

Anatoli turned and placed his hand on God's shoulder. The two looked at each other intently for a moment as old friends do, then Anatoli turned and walked back to his seat.

God turned to Jonathan, who was still on his knees. He beckoned him to stand. "This was your test, too, Jonathan. We will talk about it soon, but in the meantime, please consider why you did what you did."

Jonathan nodded, afraid to look up.

"Until then," God said, laying a hand on Tom's shoulder. It felt warm where He touched him. Tom looked up into His refulgent face. "Now, we must go. There is something important we must do."

He led Tom from the room.

26

They rode the elevator down two hundred floors to the lobby. During their descent, several people got in and out of the elevator, but no one noticed God, who stood relaxing against the back elevator wall, arms folded, eyes on the counter, whistling quietly to himself. Tom stood next to Him, unable to do anything but stare at His marvelous face. But God just rocked back and forth on his heels, moving slightly to the tune He whistled.

As the door opened on the ground floor, God said, "After you," and Tom stepped out. As they walked across the lobby, a woman with owlish eyes and cropped black hair stopped and stared, her mouth open. "Oh," she said. "It's you!"

God smiled and placed his palm against her cheek. She leaned against it, closing her eyes. "I am so glad to see you, Rachel," He said.

She looked at Him through falling tears. "You know me?"

"Yes. Never doubt."

She shook her head. "No. Never."

"Goodbye." He held her hand briefly, then turned and headed toward the doors. Rachel stood frozen, her face confused and bright.

Tom wanted to speak, but the words wouldn't come. God pushed his way through the glass door and said, "You have a question?"

Tom nodded.

"Just ask."

"How . . . how come nobody recognizes you?"

"I wouldn't say *nobody*."

"But how come that woman knew you but others don't?"

"How come *you* didn't, Tom?"

They walked past the fountain. Sheets of water fell in silver curtains. Tom saw his companion's reflection: Stan plodded beside him, his shoulders stooped, his neck stretched forward, his hawk-like nose cutting the air, his hands and feet out of sync as he walked.

Tom looked at the marvelous being directly. "I wasn't looking, I guess."

God gestured around. "When I look at my children, do you know what I see?"

Tom shook his head.

"What Rachel saw: divinity." He laughed, a sparkling, effusive laugh that filled Tom's heart with joy. "The Continuum is an incredible gift. We are fortunate beyond words!" He shook his head in wonder.

Tom looked around as they walked. Something was different. The buildings and the streets were the same clean, urban steel, marble and concrete, but something had changed. Instead of a frenzied rush-hour press, people were strolling along, chatting, or sitting in pairs and threes, quietly conversing. They all seemed peaceful and happy, not stressed and harried. But there was something more.

"Listen," murmured Tom.

Music. Music of the sort he hadn't heard since his orientation with the Archangel Gabriel. It came on the soft, warm breeze, light, beautiful, and soaring, music of a thousand voices, singing words he didn't understand, but he nevertheless knew they were words of praise . . . praise for the wonder of life itself.

Tom stopped. "Everything's different."

God cocked his head, listening. "What's different?" he said, a smile playing about his lips.

"The people. I feel like I know them; like I could talk to them. And there's music. It's so beautiful! It makes me so happy I could . . . you know . . . " He shook his head, embarrassed.

God looked at Tom intently. "The music has always been here, Tom. It exists in every moment, in every place, in every *thing*. It is everlasting joy given melody. It is the light of the eternal worlds—it is everywhere and in everything."

"But why didn't I hear it before?" asked Tom, still marveling.

"Because *you* were different. You came here with certain expectations, desires, and needs. You created a reality that was rather . . . tone deaf. But the music was always playing."

"You mean, it wasn't like that for everyone? Cold, lonely . . . depressing?"

God shook his head. "Of course not. You *make* Heaven, Tom. *You* make it—every day of your life."

Tom shook his head, trying to take it all in.

God laughed. "You always thought of life as a test, didn't you?"

Tom nodded.

"Well, did you think your test was over simply because you left Earth? You haven't forgotten about the Continuum, haven't you?"

"No."

"Well, I guess you could call the Continuum a test, but I prefer to think of it as a string of *experiences*, one after another, until we learn all there is to know about love. And as such, it never ends."

Tom furrowed his brow, surprised. "Not even for you?"

God clapped Tom on the back and led him toward the sidewalk. "Love is a journey that never ends, Tom," he said, shaking his head. "Not even for me."

They turned down a narrow side street and God opened a gray metal fire door. They entered a tiled hallway that smelled of ammonia. Tom suddenly noticed that his feet were bare and he was wearing a hospital gown. He reflexively reached back and held it closed. "Where are we?"

They started walking. A woman in a pink and white striped smock pushed an old man in a wheelchair toward them. As they passed, God touched the man's shoulder. A smile appeared on the old man's wrinkled face.

"What's happening?" asked Tom. "More testing?"

"More *experiences*," said God. "I'm giving you another chance."

"Another chance?"

"To live."

"You mean I get to go back to my family? Like before?"

"Not like before. Someone is entirely different."

Tom smiled, pleased. "Me?"

God shrugged. "Could be."

"And you can *do* that?"

God smiled. "I can do anything I want!" Tom saw a bit of Stan in that smile.

"But I thought it was against the rules to go back to Earth once you've died."

"That's generally true."

"So . . . why *me?*"

"Well, it's been a long time since I heard a prayer of such remarkable faith. I had to answer it."

Tom could feel his face turn red. He heard his voice, small and distant. "But I never even thought of praying . . . ."

They stopped in front of a tan door. God reached past Tom and pushed it open. He shook his head. "I wasn't talking about you."

It was a hospital room. Tom's unmoving body lay in the bed. Near the doorway stood Dr. Gardener, talking to the nurse. April knelt by the bed, her head buried in her hands, sobbing, "Please don't take him, God, please . . ."

Tom turned back, speechless.

"It's true," said God.

"I don't know what to say."

"Say thank you."

"Thank you." Tom's spine tingled.

"No. Thank *her*. It was her prayer I heard."

Tom looked longingly at April as she prayed quietly by his body.

God touched Tom's arm. "One thing: your memory of Paradise is fading, even now. Your memories of Earth have been restored. You are mortal once again. You will have only your heart to guide you."

"Will it be enough?"

"It always has been." He looked at April, who was crying by the bed. God's face was full of compassion. "I'm counting on you to bring her home."

"How do I do that?"

"Love her."

"I always have." A shadow crossed Tom's face. "I'm sorry about Chuck."

"I know."

"Would you tell him for me? That I'm sorry?"

"Tell him yourself. He's as alive as you are—or will be."

"What?"

"You passed away almost two years before Chuck. We're back in that time. Chuck is alive. He's on his way over here with your son right now. Now, you do *me* a favor."

"Anything."

"Tell him I'm watching over Carolyn until he comes home."

With that, God took Tom into his arms and held him close, the way a father hugs a long-lost son. "Come back to me, Tom," He whispered. "And bring your family with you."

Tom blinked back tears. "I will."

"Good boy." God turned him around and gently pushed him into the room.

Tom looked over his shoulder. "See ya, Stan."

God smiled.

Tom walked into the room and the door closed behind him. April was praying. "Oh, God, if you're there, please don't take him. Please."

Tom put his hand on her shoulder. A blue spark arced from his hand, alighting on the body in the bed. April opened her eyes.

Another spark jumped off Tom and onto his body. In a moment, the bright blue conduit between his spirit and body pulsated. The room grew bright. In the rain-streaked window Tom watched himself disincorporate, his molecules dissolving into pinpoints of light, flowing toward his body. Then a burst of white light engulfed him.

April looked at Dr. Gardner. "I felt something!" Dr. Gardener came forward and pressed two fingers against Tom's neck. He flipped on the EKG machine. It cycled up, the green line jumping regularly. "I don't believe it," he said, placing his stethoscope on Tom's chest.

After a long moment, Tom opened his eyes.

April took his hands in hers. "Oh, Tom!"

He smiled weakly.

"I thought I'd lost you," she said, wiping her tears away, but to no avail; they were followed by fresh ones. A tear fell on Tom's cheek. She kissed his cheek, then his forehead.

"Never," he said weakly.

Dr. Gardener shook his head. "Unbelievable! I'll be! His signs are spectacular."

April held Tom's face in her hands. "Your hear that? You're spectacular."

"No," he said, touching her cheek. "You are."

"Oh, Tom, I love you so much."

"Me too you."

Epilogue

Chuck felt fine. The Light came for him one evening during a peaceful dream about Carolyn. It lifted him into the air and he was on his way, passing stars and galaxies.

Then he felt pressure on the soles of his feet. He found himself on a stairway which disappeared into the brightness above. Below him, the staircase disappeared into whiteness as well.

My whole life is staircases. The stairs were wide, but his legs felt strong, and something important awaited him. He climbed a few steps, then stopped, feeling a presence. Trotting up from below, taking the stairs two at a time, was a skinny little man. His arms were pumping inside the loose sleeves of an oversized white tunic. He was barefoot. Chuck was in his pajamas. *We look like we're going to a slumber party.*

"Hey!" called the man. "Wait up!" He had a sharp nose and gray eyes. He took the last stair and stopped, breathing heavily, his hand at his side. His face was red.

"Howdy," ventured Chuck.

"Howdy yourself," said the man, sticking a hand out. "I'm Stan," he wheezed.

"Name's Chuck." He took Stan's bony hand and squeezed it, too hard, because Stan looked up, pain on his face.

"Sorry," said Chuck, releasing him. "Just excited, I guess."

Stan massaged his hand. "Me, too! Quite a day for me!"

"Ayup," said Chuck, looking up the stairs. "I'm hoping to see my sweetheart. I'm hoping she's waiting on me."

"Mind if I tag along?"

"Not at all, friend. I'd like the company."

"Thanks," said Stan. They began climbing, taking the steps in tandem.

Chuck kept stealing glances at Stan. Finally, he said, "You ever seen me before? 'Cause I feel like I know you."

"We probably know some of the same people."

"Yeah. Maybe."

"Hey, look," said Stan, pointing. "We're almost there."

Above them, the stairs ended. Chuck ran up the last ten steps and found himself on a round platform of glistening white stone, surrounded by sheer curtains whose tops disappeared into a blue sky. A breeze stirred the curtains, revealing a lush garden beyond. In the middle of the platform stood a small group of people in white robes. And in the center was Carolyn, her eyes open wide with hope.

"Carolyn!" He bounded to her, sweeping her into his arms, kissing her.

The others applauded and clapped him on the back.

From the stairs, Stan watched the reunion. A short, round man tapped Chuck's shoulder and said "Hello, Charles, remember me? I'm your Uncle Harold!" He shook Chuck's hand furiously, glancing over at Stan. He winked. Stan winked back.

"Pardon me," came a voice.

Stan turned. Jonathan was there, staring at the ground, embarrassed.

"Hello, Jonathan," said Stan quietly. "How are you?"

Jonathan looked up warily.

"I don't bite."

"Yes, you do," said Jonathan carefully.

Stan laughed. "I suppose that's true."

"I wanted to say I'm sorry for getting in Thomas's way . . . ."

Stan nodded at him encouragingly.

"I was just trying to do my job . . . ."

Stan frowned. "You were doing so well—don't blow it."

Jonathan met Stan's eyes. "I'm sorry. I'll do better."

"You already are." He touched Jonathan on the shoulder and Jonathan felt a warmth fill him, opening his mind and banishing his pride. Jonathan suddenly comprehended that there was nothing, *nothing in the universe* that this Person would not do for him, nothing He would not bear on his behalf, nothing He would not help him accomplish, and *nothing* He would not understand. Jonathan's knees felt weak.

"I love you, Jonathan. Never forget that."

"I won't. I promise."

Stan wagged a finger. "Careful what you promise!"

"I promise anyway!" said Jonathan, his chin raised proudly.

Stan nodded and started toward the stairs.

"Uh . . . Stan?" asked Jonathan tentatively.

Stan turned. "Yes?"

"I was just wondering . . . where are you going?"

"Traveling. I go everywhere, see everything, but mostly I go where I'm needed," said Stan. "And I'll tell you one thing . . . it's never boring! I love just being alive!" He waved, turned, and disappeared down the stairs.

Jonathan watched him go, then straightened his jacket and crossed to the knot of people. "Charles Blankenship?" he said, taking Chuck's hand firmly in his.

"I'm Jonathan, your spirit guide. Welcome *home*."

ORDER FORM

I enjoyed *I Hated Heaven* and would like to order more copies.

Order: _____ books at $12.00 each $ _____

Sales Tax: Utah residents add 6.35% $ _____

Shipping: $ 3.00 for the first book,
$ 1.00 for each additional book $ _____

                                    TOTAL $ _____

Please mail my order to:

Name _____

Address _____

City, State, Zip _____

Send your check payable to ALTA FILMS to:

ALTA FILMS PRESS
Box 71395
Salt Lake City, Utah 84171

Please allow three weeks for delivery.

We'd love to hear your reactions to *I Hated Heaven!*
Call us at (801) 943-0321 or e-mail to: nekpmek@aros.net